JESSICA WATKINS PRESENTS

The Other SIDE OF A THUG

SHE WAS A THUG'S WEAKNESS 2

by SANTANA

PROLOGUE

Five weeks earlier…

"Listen fellas, I called you all here because we all got a common enemy: Isabella DeMichael," Tre announced.

"How the fuck is she my enemy?" Chase asked.

"Glad you said that. You killed her father, she wants you dead," Tre told him matter-of-factly.

"How the fuck is she yo' enemy?" Marcus asked.

"Cuz she want my muhfuckin' brothers dead. Are you niggas not listening?" Tre yelled.

"Why is he here?" Chase pointed to Tony.

"Because he has proof of her infidelity and that will make her forfeit the money. Anymore questions?" Tre asked.

"Why are we here?" Chase asked, becoming frustrated.

"Because, my family, we are going to pull off quite possibly the funniest prank of the year. She wants y'all dead, I'll kill Y'all." They all looked at him crazy. "Fake kill y'all and make her think everything good. Then I'll convince her I love her and shit, then it'll all be revealed when she go try to get that money. I want us all there so we can watch her fall apart, as a family."

"How you gone convince her you love her? How, all of a sudden, y'all get so close and shit? You was supposed to be findin' her for me! Did you even try to tell her I was lookin' for her when I first asked?" Marcus questioned.

"No," Tre stated.

"Why the fuck not? Y'all fuckin?" Marcus was becoming more and more agitated.

"Yes. If I woulda told her about you, she wouldn't have let me fuck, genius."

"Nigga, what the fuck is yo' problem?" Marcus hopped up from his seat ready to fight.

Chase jumped between them. *"Come on, y'all. We not gone fight over no bitch. Let's just do the shit and laugh about it later."*

"You need to listen to him. He's the one that got rid of the problem yo' black ass was supposed to handle." Tre nudged Marcus.

"And what problem was that? Huh?" Marcus was visibly irritated.

"Giovanni. Thank Chase. He did the job. Clean job too." Tre smiled.

Tony looked like he was about to say something, but decided against it. He just listened intently.

"Anyway, I fake kill you three, tape it and that's it. Here is your bulletproof vest. Marky, you'll be the first, Tony, you'll be second, and Chase you'll be the third since she really mushy over you."

"Man, this the dumbest shit I ever heard. And don't fuckin call me Marky!" Marcus yelled.

"You wanna make the bitch pay? I got a recording of her ass agreeing to this shit. She'll go to prison for conspiracy to commit, plus she won't get the money. She tried to get my brothers knocked off and y'all really on some bullshit right now." He paced back and forth. "Y'all niggas in love or some shit?" Tre laughed heartily.

"Nah, nigga. Since when the fuck do we snitch, though?" Chase asked.

"We not. She gone snitch on herself. I know she was tapin' me when I offered to kill y'all. For that, I don't trust the bitch. You see, she tried to get down on all of us. Y'all wit' it or not?" Tre was getting pissed off.

"I'm down." Tony put his hand up.

Marcus and Chase looked at each other. "We in," they said simultaneously.

After Tre finished giving Isabella the rundown, she just stood there. She couldn't believe he had betrayed her. She thought for a moment he loved her but that all went out of the window as he explained in detail how he'd set her up for failure.

Isabella locked eyes with Chase who gave her a nod. Just then, the attorneys assembled in the room and took their seats. Isabella pulled herself together, wiped her face, and took a seat.

"Gone tell her, Mr. Buckley. Inheritance denied!" Tre laughed as he slammed his fist on the table.

Marcus and Tony both laughed with him.

"Before we go any further, I'd like to submit evidence of infidelity on behalf of Antonio Ricci." Isabella went into her purse and grabbed the manila envelope.

Tony's eyes got big.

"What the fuck?" he asked Tre.

"Doggg, I don't know how she got those." Tre shrugged.

"Thought I was dumb enough to only have two sets?" She turned to them and smiled.

The lawyers and board members reviewed the lewd photos.

"In light of this evidence, we have no choice but to deny you, Mr. Ricci, your portion of the inheritance. Now, if anyone else has anything else they'd like to submit please do it now."

Tony looked as though he was about to have a heart attack. He couldn't believe his eyes and they stamped the documents addressed to him "DENIED" and "NULL AND VOID". His check was immediately sent to the shredder. He dropped to his knees, pulling at his own hair, holding back tears.

"Bailiff, remove Mr. Ricci please." They did as they were told and escorted Tony out.

A few minutes later, the bailiff returned with another envelope that he handed to Mr. Buckley. Inside were some rather compromising photos of Isabella.

"Where'd he get these?" she asked.

"Doesn't matter. As of June 12th, all of Mr. DeMichael's assets, estate, and monies are awarded to Isabella DeMichael, his only successor. It was written that in the event of his death before she turns age twenty-five, the marriage contract becomes null and void and everything becomes her property."

Everyone except Isabella and Chase had a shocked expression on their faces. Isabella sat there smiling as she signed off on the paperwork. Not only did she get the three million she was promised, but she got an additional twenty-five million from her father's accounts, his estate in Florida, all of his cars and anything else that was of value. They gave her a list of his assets and it was extensive. Isabella was now a very rich woman. As she collected her paperwork, she filed it into her briefcase and headed toward the door.

"It was a pleasure fucking you all, gentlemen." She gestured, tipping her hat, and calmly exited with security closely behind her.

Tony was in the hallway downstairs as Isabella sashayed past.

"You got denied, huh, you whore?" He laughed maniacally.

"No, Tony. I got everything!" She returned his evil laugh and skipped off to her G-wagon.

The Last Laugh

Isabella lay on the beach sipping Mimosa's with Nakita. After that horrific meeting, she left town immediately. She hired a lawyer to dissolve her marriage and ultimately left Tony the house and everything in it. She gave her father's estate in Florida to her mom, along with all the cars he'd owned.

She took out restraining orders on everyone and vacationed out of the country in Barnes Bay in Anguilla until things died down. They had videotaped the whole proceeding and had evidence on everyone there, including Isabella, but she paid them to hush up about it and they took the money.

Everything was going great. She was thankful that things had worked out for her in the end. She had walked away the victor and got a chance to throw it in all their faces. Victory was sweet.

Later that night, Isabella and Nakita were drunk. They had convened inside the beach house and Isabella was naked and ready for some fun. She heard the patio door creak open.

"Come on, baby, and get this," she signaled to Nakita.

She heard footsteps approaching.

"Girl, you heavy footed when you drinkin'." Isabella laughed to herself.

When a dark figure stood in front of her she almost lost it. She knew it wasn't Nakita.

"Surprise," the masked man said to her.

"What the fuck! Nakita, I'll kill you!" She got up, looking for her.

"Sit yo ass down!" The barrel of his gun made Isabella sober up and follow instructions.

She recognized the voice, however.

"Chase?" she asked.

"Yeah," he responded, taking off his mask.

"What are you doing? You came to kill me?"

"Yeah." He cocked his gun and let off two bullets right into her.

She fell to the floor gasping for air and holding her stomach. She watched as the man she loved and who had ultimately saved her, walked over her dying body as if she meant nothing.

Isabella woke up in a cold sweat. That was the fifth nightmare she'd had this week about someone killing her. She stirred from her sleep and sat up, looking for her water on the nightstand.

"Another nightmare, baby?" Chase asked.

"Yeah." She sipped her water and lay back down.

The Other
SIDE OF A
THUG

SHE WAS A THUG'S WEAKNESS 2

by Santana

CHAPTER ONE

How It's Goin' Down?

CHASE

I was back at home with Aaliyah. She was cooking dinner and I was sitting on the couch in the living room, consumed with boredom because she had left "Love and hip-hop" on the television and hid the remote. Did I wanna be here? No. I wanted to be with Isabella. Despite the shit we'd been through, I still longed for her terribly. I'd be lying if I said I didn't miss her. We both did some treacherous shit to each other, but that's the danger of love. It'll heal the deepest of scars. It'll force you to forgive. I had forgiven her a million times already. Now, all I wanted was a chance to see her again.

It had been weeks since I heard her sweet voice, caressed her soft skin, tasted her lips, heard her moan my name, and it was eating me up. I wondered if she ever cared about a nigga for real. I remembered how innocent she was as a child. She didn't deserve any of the fucked-up shit that happened to her, even as an adult. She was a sweetheart but life had taken a toll on her. She was still innocent in my opinion. I missed her so bad. I wanted to call, to see what she was up to, but I knew she was livin' her life and had probably moved and changed her number.

1

by Santana

I sat clutching my phone tightly in my hand, with her contact info on the screen, trying desperately to hold back from shooting her a text and pouring my heart out. Then I heard the doorbell ring.

"Who the fuck could that be?" I wasn't in the mood for interactions of any sort so I let Liyah grab the door.

"Baby, umm your cousin, Camille is at the door!" Liyah hollered at me.

Cousin? What muhfuckin cousin? I thought to myself as I got up from the couch.

When I got to the door, I saw none other than Isabella standing there beautiful as ever. She had blonde hair now but sported a mean black eye that made me cringe after she removed her shades. There was blood dried around her nose. Somebody had beat her ass badly.

"Camille?" I played along as I approached the door where she was standing with a suitcase.

"Oh my God, Chase!" She grabbed and hugged me. I hugged her back tightly. Damn, it felt good.

Then Liyah stepped in front of me, turning her back to Isabella and cut in, "I never met this cousin before."

Isabella then flashed a gun she had tucked in her waist. She pulled it out and pointed it toward Liyah's back, urging me to continue with the charade.

by *Santana*

"Baby, this is my cousin Camille, on my mother's side. You know I didn't go around them much but she and I always kept in touch." Once I calmed Liyah a little, Isabella returned the .45 to her waist and closed her jacket.

"Well come in, Camille." She faked a smile and made way for her to enter.

"Thank you." Isabella sniffed and wiped the tears from her eyes as she grabbed her suitcase and wheeled it inside.

"So, what happened to you?" I questioned as she took a seat on the couch next to me.

Liyah stood posted against the wall with her arms folded and a mean scowl plastered on her face. I knew she had questions but they would have to wait.

"Brian. He hit me. He beat me up and put me out. I had nowhere else to go. I am so sorry for intruding but you know I don't even live here. He said he wanted me to come visit for a while, cuz he's tired of the long distance. After a couple of weeks, he started pressuring me to just give my life up and move here with him, but I told him I couldn't. That's when he got violent. He punched me in the eye and nose. He took my phone and money. He took everything." She sat there crying and lying through her teeth.

"Need me to handle that nigga li'l cuz?" I offered.

3

by *Santana*

"I don't want him dead Chase, but I need to go back to Tennessee. I need to get away from him." She put her face in her palms.

"I see."

"I just need a place to sleep tonight."

"You can stay here as long as you need," I offered and I was serious as fuck. I didn't want her to leave, ever.

"Excuse me, Chase, let me speak to you really quick," Liyah interjected.

I got up and followed her into the kitchen. When we were out of earshot, she went off.

"So, you're just gonna offer to let her live here? I know she's family but she said one night. Don't go adding extra shit. We got enough goin' on right now."

"Baby, this is my family and she's sitting here with a black eye and shit. I need her here safe until I figure out what to do wit' this Brian nigga. You know what the fuck happens after a man beats the shit out of a woman and she leaves. He usually kills her."

"She said he put *her* out," Liyah dryly added.

"Really? That's all you can say?"

"Babe, I'm just sayin'…"

"What you sayin'? You want my family on the fuckin' street when she got someone with a big ass house that can take

4

her in? You'd rather see her dead or something, right? This *my* shit! She not goin' no fuckin' where until I take care of that nigga. Got it?" I stepped close to her face so she knew I wasn't playin.

"Yep." She reluctantly gave in and followed me back into the living room.

"I'm so sorry I came here. I didn't mean to barge in. I-I should go." She grabbed her bag and proceeded toward the door.

"No, you're good. You can sleep in the guest room." I grabbed the bag from her and led her up the winding staircase, leaving Liyah standing there lookin' foolish.

Isabella waited until I closed the door behind us, then she walked up to me and planted the softest kiss on my mouth. I grabbed her by her tiny waist and engaged deeper, palming the back of her head as our tongues danced around each other's mouths.

"Chase, baby," she whined.

"Yeah." I broke the kiss so she could catch her breath.

"I missed you."

"Did you?"

"Why didn't you come for me?" She wiped a tear that fell from her right eye.

"Isabella, I didn't think—"

"You don't get paid to think Chase."

"Don't do this shit right now," I told her as I took the opportunity to stick my tongue back down her throat.

I was not about to argue with her right now. My dick was struggling to get out of my Polo boxers and my wife was a level below us, or probably listening outside the door.

"Clean up and get ready for dinner. We'll talk later," I said as I kissed her forehead.

If I stood there any longer, we would've been fuckin' and I wasn't ready to blow my cover that fast. I walked out after adjusting my massive hard-on and joined Liyah in the kitchen where she stood fixing our plates.

"So, what's going on? What y'all talk about?" She stood defiantly with her arms folded and nostrils flaring.

"Aaliyah, mind your business. She's going through enough. Why are you being like this?"

"Because I ain't never heard of this 'cousin' and all of a sudden she appears on your doorstep. Like seriously, Chase. Who is she?"

"She's my damn cousin! In a minute, you gone be on the same doorstep she was on," I warned before grabbing two plates and heading toward the dining room table.

Isabella had cleaned up and joined us at the dinner table. Liyah uncomfortably shifted in her seat when she emerged from the hallway in one of my t-shirts that I hadn't even given to her. I struggled to hide my smile and opted to keep my head down until the tension somewhat died.

"Camille, I'm sorry this happened to you and if it seemed like I was being rude earlier, I apologize for that too. I have been with Chase for some years and I have never heard him mention you. It kinda caught me by surprise, that's all," Liyah explained with a half-smile.

"Thank you. I know how it looks but you know our family has always been dysfunctional. I mean, Chase just found out he had other brothers so I get it. Chase and I were close growing up but after Carmen died, we lost touch for years. When we got older, we decided to stay in touch even though we had grown apart, and he told me he'd always be here if I needed him. He's always been protective over the women in his family." Isabella was a model, but with this stellar role she was playin' the muhfucka should've been an actress.

"Makes sense. Well listen, you're more than welcome here. Any family of my husband's is family of mine. Maybe when you're feeling better, we can hang out, go get our nails done or something."

"I'd like that." Isabella smiled and dug into her food.

We all sat there eating and making small talk. Isabella and I told lie after lie about our childhood and relatives. It was

7

terrible. I felt like shit because once again I was lying to my wife, the same woman I had put in the hospital and had made lose our child. The same wife to who I promised I was done with the shady shit. Now I was sitting there with my mistress, pretending to be my cousin, still lying and still heavily planning on fucking.

It was just something about Isabella. I mean, despite our history, I feel like even if we had just met, shit would still be the same. I would still be inclined to protect her, I would still want her with me, and I would still be as attracted to her as I am now. Even after all the shit we had been through, I couldn't forget about her. She made me hate myself for loving her. But I couldn't stop. This may have been the dumbest shit ever, but niggas make dumb decisions everyday, B. Isabella was the best and worst decision I had ever made and I was gone keep makin' that muhfucka too.

*****

Isabella had been staying with us for a few days now. She and Liyah had been bonding. They even went to get their nails and shit done together. Every time they returned from an outing, Isabella wore this cheesy-ass grin when we were all in the same room. It was like the Xscape song. Nobody knew our little secret but us, I hoped. By this time, I was kinda confused though. She had been in my house for days and ain't came up off no pussy. I was beginning to question her motive. Other than a few kisses here and there, we had no physical contact at all. It was just knowing stares, wicked smiles, and her grabbin' my dick when Liyah turned her head.

"Chase, I'll be gone 'til tomorrow. I got something to handle with my mom," Liyah said as she grabbed her overnight bag and left.

"Cool, see you..." Before I could finish, I heard the door slam.

Isabella was glued to the couch with a smirk on her face, playing in her hair when Liyah abruptly left. I didn't care though because I needed some alone time with her. Once I knew Liyah was gone, I took the spot next to her.

"Why you here, man?" I removed the strands of hair from her face and looked into her innocent eyes.

"I missed my Chase face. I've been having nightmares since that whole court shit happened. I just keep thinking someone's gonna come after me. And I needed you. I know you'll protect me." She smiled and returned my gaze.

"This stunt you pulled, though?"

"Desperate times call for desperate measures. You obviously weren't gonna come for me so I had to come for you. You know I have no problem finding you, baby." She playfully tapped my nose then straddled me.

"You know I'm back with Liyah." I sighed as I felt my dick rise.

"You don't mean that though, baby. You were cheating on her before I even came around," she reminded me.

"Well I was gonna try to make it work and…"

"And now you're not. You can't repair that shit. It's way too broken. Plus, you know you missed me. You can cut the tough shit now baby." She pushed her warm tongue in my mouth and it was over after that.

We fucked all over that house, from the kitchen to the bedroom that I shared with Liyah. I was just so happy to have her back that I really didn't care if Liyah walked in and caught her naked in our bed. I craved Isabella. Her warmth, her touch, her smell, it was all I needed right now. It brought back memories, both adult and childhood. It was like a rollercoaster ride with her. There were so many twists and turns, I couldn't seem to get enough.

By the time Liyah had gotten back, I had cleaned any traces of her and I sleeping together, so she still didn't know anything for sure, but her attitude was still stank.

"What did you do while I was gone? Did you find 'Brian'?" she quizzed as she unpacked her bag and plopped down on the bed.

"Nah, but I know where he lay his head. We took a ride over there but the nigga dipped," I lied.

"Okay, Chase. How long is she gonna be here then?"

"Just a few more days until she finds somewhere she can live when she goes back to Tennessee. I see you still upset about this, huh?" I laughed and sat next to her, trying to calm her ass down before she started some shit again.

"I just don't want her here. This shit is still not sitting well with me. I want the bitch to leave." She had blurted that shit out and I didn't get a chance to close the door to our room. Isabella walked by midsentence and had heard everything.

"Aaliyah, I understand how you feel about me being here but it's family over bitches. Get hip," she spat and marched to the guestroom.

Shit! I screamed in my head, preparing for World War IV. Yeah, four.

"You better get that bitch before I choke the fuck outta her." Liyah was crazy, and nobody really knew that but me.

"Choke who, bitch? I tried to be nice to you but I see hoes ain't appreciative of shit! This is *my* cousin's house, not yours hoe, married or not. Act like you got an education bitch!" Isabella had stormed back into my room.

I stood between the two ladies as their tempers flared. They squared up ready to fight and I kinda wanted to let them go at it.

"Chase, you better get this disrespectful bitch outta my sight!" Liyah screamed to me.

"And if he doesn't? I'll fuck you up all over this nice-ass house." Isabella lunged at Liyah and knocked her clean off her feet.

They tussled around, knocking over the lamp and vases that sat on our overly-expensive night stand. Isabella was hangin' tough with Liyah, though. I had witnessed her punch a bitch before but I had no idea she really had hands. Then I saw Liyah reaching for a shard of glass as Isabella held a handful of her hair, punching her repeatedly in the face.

I threw Liyah so fast, I didn't even realize how hard I had slung her until she crashed into the dresser and started screaming like someone had stabbed her. It was instinctual for me to protect Isabella, but I felt like shit as I watched Liyah glaring at me with disgust. If looks could kill…

"Are you fuckin' serious!?" She struggled to get up.

"Liyah baby, I'm so sorry, but you was finna stab her with—"

"I don't give a fuck!" she screamed as she got up from the floor and limped to the master bathroom.

by Santana

I looked down at Isabella and her nose was bleeding. I helped her up and carried her to the bathroom in the guestroom.

"I can't believe you let that bitch fight me," she said as she cleaned her leaking nose.

"You rushed *her!*"

"Cuz she was talkin' shit. Control yo hoes." She scowled at me.

"Isabella, you came up in here—"

"So? I came to get what was mine. You need to get rid of that bitch before I do."

"And if I don't?"

Pop! She slapped the shit outta my face.

"If you start that shit, you gone get fucked up for real," I warned as I grabbed her throat and choked the life outta her.

Then came that crybaby shit. She knew I hated that. I took the liberty of slamming her onto the cold sink and spreading her legs apart. I kissed her bloody nose-ass while releasing my dick from my boxers. I slid in slow, staring into her eyes that were wide open from feelin' this big muhfucka in her stomach.

"How you gone come in *my* house and beat up my wife?" I held her throat while I stroked her nice and slow like she liked.

"Fuck you, Chase." Tears seeped from the corners of her eyes.

"Fuck me, huh? You a li'l disrespectful bitch." I smirked as I increased my pace.

She tried to cover her face but I moved her hands. I wanted to see her tough ass crumble right in front of me. And she did, she always did. She was just like Liyah in a way, so hard 'til this hard-ass dick got in her.

"Chaseeee!" she cried out.

"Shhhh. Be quiet and take that dick. You tough. You a big girl." I taunted her, laughing as I flipped her around and entered her from the back.

Them backshots were lethal. I watched her struggle to hold back screams through the large mirror that hung over the sink. She was helpless, powerless against this dick, like any bitch I fucked wit'. Only thing was, I was powerless against that pussy too. Against her...period. Isabella had me sick, like the guy from Cadillac Records when his ass died after leavin' Beyonce. I felt like if I cut her off, I would die in the process.

I choked her and made her cum for me. She was ugly cryin' and all. I was so deep in her shit, I could feel her heart. I squeezed her small body in my arms and whispered in her ear.

"Gimme that pussy, baby. Give it to daddy."

by Santana

"Oh my Godddd, Chase!" She spilled heavy tears as her knees weakened and she almost lost her balance.

"Didn't I tell you to be quiet?" I whispered as I put my hand over mouth.

This bitch's pussy was so wet it was crazy. I bent her all the way over, grippin' a fistful of hair wit' her mouth still covered and fucked her 'til I bust a nut so hard I almost cried. I came inside her too. It was magical. Crazy how intense sex was when yo' wife was in the next room. That shit at the club ain't have shit on this.

*****

"Chase, it's been almost four weeks since she's been here. I think it's time."

"Aaliyah, we talked about this."

"And she's still here."

"And you still complaining. You and all this extra shit ain't gone help the situation. I told you I wanted her here until I handle this Brian dude. I don't know why you still trippin'."

"Cuz you haven't fucked me since she's been here." She folded her arms and turned over.

I really hadn't touched her since Isabella showed up that day. I hadn't even noticed until now. Even though I was hysterically in love with Isabella, I still loved and was very much attracted to my wife, and if she wanted some dick, she was damn sure about to get it. I was trippin' on how trash I was as I sucked on Liyah's clit. She was screaming at the top of lungs as I pleasured her. I know she wanted Isabella to hear.

I kept going despite the consequence, which was prolly gon' be Is goin' off the moment I exited my bedroom to grab a drink. I had successfully snatched her soul and she was trying desperately to recover. She lay there gasping for air as I slid in and reminded her who the fuck I was.

"Oh my God! Chase, I love you daddy!" She moaned loudly, shaking the walls with her shrill screams.

Isabella couldn't be mad, technically. This was my wife and she made it her business to barge into my home, so however she felt, I didn't care. All I cared about right now was makin' Liyah bust on this dick. I was drivin' her crazy as I pounded her from the back.

"Yup, give it here," I urged as she arched her back perfectly.

Fuck, her pussy was so good. After it was over, my heart sank into my chest. I don't know why I was scared to leave my room, but I was. I took a quick shower and crept into the kitchen to get me something to eat. Thank God Liyah took her ass to sleep cuz I knew what I had coming when I went downstairs.

by *Santana*

Just as I suspected, Isabella was in the kitchen, waiting for me. She wore this blank, unreadable expression. I ignored her. That was until she approached me, grabbed my hand and rubbed it on her pussy. Her shit was drippin'.

"I liked what I heard." She grinned and kissed me. "Mmm, she tastes good."

See? This is why I couldn't get enough. She did shit like that. What bitch you know does this type of shit? If we wouldn't have lied already, we could've gotten a bomb ass threesome poppin'.

"You are somethin' else." I chuckled at her craziness.

"But you knew that. Also, I missed my period. Congrats," she said as she put a positive pregnancy test in my hand and walked back to her room.

FUCKKKKKK!

LIYAH

That day I left, I went to Tre's house. I needed answers.

"Liyah, what you need man? You know we ain't on that tip no more. I'll be moving to Detroit soon, so you ain't gon' be able to just pop up when you and yo 'man' not getting along."

"Fuck all that. I need you to tell me who this is?" I pull my iPhone out and showed him the picture of Camille.

"I don't know her." He chuckled but I knew he was lying.

"Okay, but is this Chase's cousin? Have you ever heard of a 'Camille'? I mean I know y'all just found out you were related but has he ever mentioned her? Just tell the truth for once in yo' damn life."

"Nah, but we never discussed no cousins and shit. That could be true."

"She looks hella familiar. I know I've seen this bitch somewhere before." I sat and pondered this bitch's face.

She came to the door all beat up and shit but now that her face was normal, I was certain I had come across her ass before.

"Liyah, you just trippin'. Bro been faithful and he really wants to work shit out," Tre reassured me but he still had this ridiculous smirk plastered on his stupid-ass face. I knew he

18

knew something but of course he wasn't gonna tell me cuz he was "loyal" to his brother.

"Okay so if you don't give her up, how about I tell Marcus about you and Ava? Right now." I pulled up Marcus's number and threatened to dial.

"Bitch, get out my crib! I told yo ass I don't know her. It ain't about snitchin.' I really don't know this bitch."

"You always so extra." I took his word for it and left it alone.

I found my way to the kitchen and made myself a sandwich, still thinking about where I saw this Camille bitch at. I barely went anywhere other than work so I thought back on every instance I'd been out of the house. Then a bright idea popped in my head.

I grabbed my phone and called Nakita. She was the only person I had been around damn near the whole year and she was the only person who had brought company the time we hung out.

"Hey Kita!" I sang into the phone when she picked up.

"Hi boo. How are you?"

"Amazing. But I have a question. I'm about to send you a picture. Can you tell me who this girl is? She looks familiar as hell, like I know I've seen her before."

"Okay, send it."

by Santana

I sent her the picture and when she got it, my suspicions were confirmed. Her name wasn't no damned Camille.

"Yeah, that's my girl, Isabella. Remember the one that was at the mall that day?"

"Thanks girl, that's all I needed," I said and hung up.

"Bitch, that's Isabella," I yelled at Tre who was sitting there looking foolish.

"Okay and?" He shrugged.

"You think I don't know who that bitch is!"

"If you know then why you asking me?"

"Cuz you a fuckin' liar! I know Chase cheated on me wit' that bitch before. I never knew much about her except a few times when I checked his phone and saw their conversations. Now this nigga got her livin' in my house pretending like she's his cousin!" I pounded the coffee table.

I was irrationally angry. I wanted to kill the both of them. I mean, leave it up to Chase Greene to make a complete fool of me, *again*! After I took his lying ass back on multiple occasions, and he did all that bullshit to get me back after putting me in the hospital and making me lose our baby. I was done. It was no coming back after this. I was gonna make him pay.

THE OTHER SIDE OF A THUG
SHE WAS A THUG'S WEAKNESS 2

by Santana

When I got back home, I still pretended to be clueless as to what was going on but I knew everything. I was just plotting and planning.

CHASE

Liyah had stopped trippin' for a while and I was happy, but knowing I had a baby on the way by Isabella had thrown me for a loop. Hearing her throwing up every morning gave me constant panic attacks. I wanted her to be safe while she was carrying my seed. I went with her to doctor's appointments and all. I catered to her at home and Liyah even helped out. She cooked for her and ran to her side every time she was suffering from morning sickness. I didn't know what had sparked the change in her attitude but I felt bad. I had my wife assisting my mistress who was carrying my child. What a fuckboy.

I had money moves to make so I couldn't focus primarily on the situation at hand. I had to think about transporting this product to Detroit so my brother, Tre and his right-hand, Rico could get this shit off. It had just hit me that I hadn't heard from him in a few weeks. I chalked it up to him trying to get acquainted with his new living arrangement. That was far from the truth, but still close to it.

It was eight a.m. and my phone was ringing. I didn't know the number so I answered immediately.

"You have a collect call from Tre Carter at the Jackson Correctional facility."

The fuck? I thought to myself.

"Yes," I spoke into the receiver.

"Mannnn bro, they got me," he said as soon as the lines connected.

"The fuck for?"

"DT," he told me.

"Fuck! How?"

"Hell if I know. Call my lawyer. These niggas expeditin' round here."

"I'm on it, bro."

After that call, and the news, I wanted to disappear. Feds scooped bro for drugs, meaning they was gone be nosing around in everyone's business who was affiliated with him. Then, I got a baby on the way. Lord Jesus, I need you right now.

I called David Steinberg as soon as I got off the hook wit' Tre. I told him I had everything he needed to get this case expedited. I also asked him why the fuck he didn't alert Tre that someone was on his ass tryna open a DT case. He said no one consulted him at all. That meant some sneaky, underhanded shit was goin' on.

I paced the floor in my bedroom until it seemed like I had worn a hole in it. "Who the fuck snitchin'?" I yelled aloud to myself. Then I called Marcus.

"I already heard bro. He just called me."

"Damn, so what you thinkin'?" I quizzed.

"I'm thinkin' this shit gone have to dry up for a minute. We can't be out here on no hot shit. If they got bro, you know they lookin' at everybody around him."

"Fuck yeah. This shit hella bad for business." I put my head in hands as I sat on the edge of my bed contemplating how we could work around this shit.

"We gotta link soon. It's a way around this but we gone have to strategize. We gotta get this shit off. At least the shipments we got now, then after that, we gotta lay low 'til we get him out. You know they finna try to tie that nigga down for a year at least," Marcus told me, and I already knew.

They had gotten to him with no lawyer and I had no idea what they caught him wit,' but it had to be something for them to throw that nigga straight into Jackson without any other litigative processes. I bet he ain't even get to see a judge.

"Yeah I heard you. Hit me up when you ready," I told him and disconnected the call.

Then I heard Isabella screaming from the bathroom.

"What? What the fuck happened?" I rushed in to find her on the floor bleeding to death.

"I don't know, call an ambulance. Please." She held her stomach, wincing in pain.

I just knew it was the baby. I knew we had lost her. Liyah already had her phone out dialing 9-1-1 as I helped her

by Santana

up. But she fell back down as pain ripped through her abdomen and sent her crashing to the floor.

"Ohhhh my Godddddd!" she cried.

"The ambulance is almost here. Just hang on." Liyah panicked as she got an ice pack and applied it to her forehead.

We rushed her to the hospital where we found out she had indeed lost the baby. She had miscarried. I was cryin' inside. This was the second fuckin' time my seed had died. Even though I don't know what made her miscarry, I still felt like it was my fault.

"The doctors wanna keep me overnight," Isabella told me when Liyah left to go to the bathroom.

"Okay, I'll be here tomorrow to get you." I kissed her forehead and left.

I was in the car with Liyah trying not to crash that bitch. I was literally holding back tears. I wanted that baby so bad.

"What you so upset about?" Liyah rolled her eyes.

"Bitch, my fuckin' brother in jail and my cousin in the hospital! How you think I feel?" I almost didn't say cousin.

"Well, I'm sorry baby. We gone get through this though." She grabbed my hand as I weaved through traffic. I was driving all types of sporadic.

"Slow down before we crash."

"I really wouldn't give a fuck right now," I admitted.

CHAPTER TWO

The Re-Up

TRE

After all the bullshit in Cali ended, I left for Detroit about a month and a half later. I dipped after I tied up my loose ends. I had spent way too much time and energy on things that weren't gonna make me richer. After that attempt to take Isabella down failed miserably, I decided love wasn't my thing and I had to get back to business. I had my boy Rico in Detroit running shit so I was already good. However, I was smacked with a case as soon as I found myself getting comfy in my new city. The Feds had hit my ass with a drug trafficking charge. With all the connections I had, someone would've told me they were coming but no one knew. I knew right then that it was a setup. Someone had snitched and it was someone close to me.

Imagine my face when I got pulled over for a routine traffic stop, and ended up being hauled off to jail because these fuckin crackas wanted me so bad they planted drugs in my whip. All of this shit was so illegal. It was a wonder how they were able to pull this shit off. I had to wait until the morning to start makin' calls cuz them racist bastards had beat my ass to sleep. When I got out of here, I was suing the shit outta the State of Michigan.

My first night was my worst night. I didn't sleep even after I came to, and I had a pounding ass headache that made my eyes hurt. It was prolly one of the top three angriest times I had ever had in my life. I mean, fuck being arrested and framed for drugs, I could beat this, but the fact that someone had really told the pigs that I was involved in drugs is what killed me. I mean, most of the people close to me were involved right along wit' my ass so who the fuck was envious enough to put their own foot in their mouth? Who slept on me so hard that they didn't know what I was capable of?

I had beaten three murder charges. I had gotten caught red-handed wit' an 8-ball. I slept through two traphouse raids. Nigga, I was untouchable. So, who the fuck thought I wasn't? The stupid muhfucka didn't realize that I had the best lawyer money could buy. Did they not know who I supplied to? The muhfuckas that employ the muhfuckas that locked me up. I laughed to myself at that revelation. Somebody was *not* hip. My mind swirled with thoughts of betrayal every day I was locked up. I had an idea of who it could've been. Isabella. She was the one person who had means, motive, and opportunity. I was banking on her being the culprit so I had my brother, Chase grill her with questions about her involvement.

by Santana

According to him, she wasn't the one. But of course, he would think that. They were still heavily involved after that whole incident went down so I couldn't fully trust him to give her up. It was crazy. She literally tried to have me kill him and yet he still fucked with her. I couldn't understand their relationship for the life of me but if bro was layin' wit' a snake and tryna protect her slitherin' ass, I would surely find out. I mean, this ultimately affected him as well. Unless of course, he too was involved. I ain't wanna think he was cut like that but at this point, I didn't know what to believe. He told me she had been with him every day since and gave him no reason to think that she was in any way responsible. She was the woman that ruined many lives so I was sure she was behind me going to prison for the last year. Well, I wasn't *sure* sure but she had every reason.

I began to wonder if this was all a scheme, but after months had passed and they were still rockin', I knew he was really in love with this bitch. Shit, I was too. Part of me could see her treacherous ass reporting me to the Feds but part of me couldn't. She seemed to be happy after the situation ended. It seemed she had gotten all of her revenge when she walked away with that check. But who knows? The matter would be closely investigated.

by Santana

Whoever was behind this, I was surely gonna find out. That person would pay, with their life. Not only was I wrongly imprisoned, but the sanctity of my drug empire had been somewhat compromised and the Feds now knew more than what I had wanted them to know. I hadn't been on their radar prior to this but now, I knew I was being watched. And if I was being watched, then those closest to me were being watched too. That would now make *me* have to watch *them*.

*****

12 Months Later

My first move was to get out of the drug game as quickly as I entered. I knew when I got out the pen that my boy Rico would have work, and I wanted to get it off as fast as I could to get my money up for these bigger moves I had in mind. I was about to attempt to become a legitimate businessman but I needed the backing of my right-hand man to make it happen.

I couldn't wait to get out of this hell-hole and after today, I would be a free man. The day had come after being locked down like an animal. I was being released from the Jackson Correctional Facility. Before I was able to fully get my bearings, the guard was at my cell yelling that I was being released today. I rose from my uncomfortable cot and stretched, trying to ground myself while taking in the fact that my next

by *Santana*

move could possibly land me right back in here. I didn't expect to only do a year after the charges that were brought against me, but I guess when you got money and a good lawyer, shit just moved faster.

"Alright boss," I replied to the guard beckoning me to get up.

I had to correct some things in my life if I wanted to walk away a free man. My drug empire was never the problem. The problem was my dick. It had a mind of its own and if Isabella wasn't behind this then my dick was the reason I went to prison. I vowed that this time around would be different and I wouldn't allow my need to get pussy to land me in any more fucked up predicaments.

I had always been known to live life on the edge. Now, I never let sex stop my money flow—according to my brother Marcus I did—but I'll admit I got myself into some sticky situations because of it. No woman was off limits in my book and after I ended up fuckin' my own brother's wife, I knew I had to do better.

As I walked my last steps down the hallway and past all the inmates that would never see the light of day again, I silently made a vow to God to never come back. Strolling out, no cuffs with my belongings packed neatly into a bag, I spotted Rico waiting outside his black G-wagon, smiling that approving smile he always gave when he witnessed me making shit happen.

"My mans, how does it feel to be free?" Rico asked rhetorically.

"Mannnnn, it feels like I need some pussy," I said bluntly and we shared a hearty laugh.

I was serious though and Rico knew I wouldn't be able to talk about any business until I got what I needed. That was my first order of business.

"Same nigga man." He shook his head. "Big Bro, you betta lay low, boy. Carter niggas don't get Fed cases."

Marcus shook his head as he smacked hands with me.

"Then why Daddy in jail?" I chuckled at his remark.

"He don't count."

We decided to ride in silence so I could breathe, think, and take in the fact that I eluded prison and it was time to get back to business. Rico was my partner in crime and held the business down while I was wrapping things up in Cali. Marcus visited and made sure I was good on commissary. My stay was good thanks to these two niggas.

I was in deep thought, taking in the scenery as we drove for over an hour to my home he set up outside the city. My assets were frozen because while inside, they tried to throw a murder case on me. I had Rico take over everything since he was a resident of Michigan where I was arrested. I had a bit of a worried expression on my face and he noticed it immediately.

"Everything is everything, boy." Rico interrupted my thoughts. He wanted me to know that he held it down. He told me the money was in the safe, my cars were there, and the bricks were still moving.

"Nigga, don't read my mind," I joked but I was instantly relieved and that was all I needed.

We pulled up to a phat-ass crib in Eastpointe about an hour and a half later. I knew Rico was still moving weight but this home looked to cost nothing short of two million dollars, and had all four of my cars lined along the circular driveway with a new addition to the team. A Maserati Gran Turismo was now among my fleet and I couldn't hide how happy I was. That was the car I wanted for my birthday right before I went away.

"Yooooo! Dog, I swear you the realest nigga in the camp!" I dapped up Rico while admiring my new car.

"Aye man, you was talkin' about that car more than pussy," he joked.

"Good lookin,' bro. You know I got you soon as I get back on," I promised.

"Don't worry about all that. You the reason I'm alive and eatin' good. You ain't gotta pay me shit, ever." Rico felt he owed me his life.

THE OTHER SIDE OF A THUG
SHE WAS A THUG'S WEAKNESS 2
by Santana

I saved him from death's grip some years ago, put him on to the game, and helped made him the solid nigga he was today. Rico was a li'l nigga when he got introduced to the drug game, making runs for local dope boys, robbing and killin' niggas at the age of fifteen. He met me one day when a deal went bad and a shootout ensued after this older cat, Dro set Rico up.

I was there to do a job, and that was to take out everybody, get the drugs and money, and leave. But seeing a young nigga like myself about to be murdered was something I couldn't let happen. I quickly started taking niggas out, starting with Dro, the nigga with his gun on Rico. He quickly ducked and ran for cover. Once shots were fired, the two opposing teams started to kill each other and the work basically did itself. Rico ran for cover behind some crates until no more shots we fired. There were two men left standing from Dro's camp and I quickly put two bullets in each of them. Once the smoke cleared, Rico stayed put. He had no clue where those last shots came from and he was terrified to move.

"Yo, my mans?" I called out.

"Go head and kill me man." He reluctantly came out with his hands up awaiting his fate.

"Chill man, nobody gone kill you, unless you tryna kill me." I eyed Rico suspiciously and checked him for a gun.

"Why you kill everybody?" Rico needed answers. He was skeptical about why he was saved and everyone else had to die.

"Look you about what, sixteen? You my age man and I see you got heart but you caught up in some shit you ain't ready for. These niggas was setting you up. You the one that robbed that nigga, Dro didn't you?" I asked but he already knew.

"Yeah, I did but," I cut in.

"Them niggas was finna start a war with the man you making runs for. He ain't want it so in exchange he sold you out and told them you hit they trap on yo own. They some snakes man and I don't work for snakes, so I killed everybody." I added sounding gangsta.

"Bro, you raw my nigga!" Rico smiled widely and tried to give me play.

"Just help me get this shit outta here." I had wet some niggas before but seeing this many bodies had me feeling nauseous. We gathered the drugs and money and fled the scene to his getaway car he had parked in the alley. With his people now dead, Rico had nowhere to go, no way to eat and no money.

"You gon' be good man." Those words were just the beginning of a bond that would last a life time.

While reflecting on the day I had saved Rico's life, I picked up my new iPhone 7 that he replaced. All my contacts were there. I decided it was high time to fall up in some pussy. I wanted a night to just lay up in something because after this, business would resume as usual.

First, I thought about getting fresh and going to a strip club or bar and take somebody's baby mama home, but decided against it once the thought of Liyah crossed his mind. She was someone I never pictured myself with but after her and Chase divorced, she stayed around and we became quite close. She showed how loyal she was. She wrote me, accepted my calls, and sent money, even though I insisted it wasn't necessary. My brothers Marcus and Chase took care of everything in addition to my partners Rico, Quentin, and Kalief. Everything was good on the commissary end but she still sent money.

"Hello?" Liyah answered hesitantly.

"Well hello love, how are you?"

"Tre?" She recognized my voice but was confused at the regular cell number and not the prison intro.

"Yeah, it's me Ma. I was wondering if I could see you tonight?" I asked as if she knew I was out.

"How is that possible? It's way after visiting hours." She sounded disappointed.

by Santana

"I'll explain everything later. Right now, I need you to get sexy for me and send me your address. Can you do that?"

"Okay, baby." She still sounded unsure but texted me anyway. My baby.

Being out of prison came right on time. I don't know how much longer I could be around a bunch of angry ass niggas with no future. A nigga like me was going places, and now I had lost out on money cause I'm addicted to fuckin' other niggas' bitches. It's a shame. Yeah, I know, a talented, successful young man with money and a degree can't get a woman of his own? I can, but why do that when I can get everybody else's? Naw seriously, they threw the pussy at me. It would be rude not to catch it.

I showered and dabbed on some Armani Acqua. That was Liyah's favorite and it was sure to get my dick sucked extra thorough tonight. I threw on a red Nike jogging set and some red Retro Jordan 12's, nothing fancy. I made sure to finish my look off with a pair of Cartier glasses, white buffs. Yays were a Detroit thing but this New York nigga wore them well, and just like niggas say, they get the bitches' attention. I decided to pull out the new whip. I had been dying to fly down the freeway in it before I went to prison. I hopped in, put on the GPS with Liyah's address, and sped off. The ride was so smooth. It was nothing like freedom and a new car that cost well over a hundred-grand.

What would have normally been a twenty-five-minute drive took me only thirteen minutes. I was hittin 100 on 75-South to get to Liyah's loft in downtown Detroit. I pulled off the exit, hit a couple corners, and finally came to her place. It looked desolate and abandoned, but once you got inside, it was immaculate.

I pulled out my phone and called to let her know I had arrived. She snatched the door open so fast I would have thought she was setting me up if I didn't know what type of girl she was. She was lookin too right. She had some type of Mohawk bun thing goin' on. It was weird but it fit with her high cheekbones. It really didn't matter what the fuck her hair was like because it was finna be fucked up sooner than later.

Her heels clicked across the polished wood floors as she embraced me. She did exactly what daddy asked her when I said get sexy. Her ass was poking in the one-piece, red lace leotard. Her perky breasts sat up and her nipples hardened as soon as she got a whiff of her favorite cologne.

"Mmm, you smell good baby." She stared at me long and hard. I returned her lustful gaze, admiring her nearly perfect body.

"Come here." I motioned for her to come closer.

I hugged her tightly and started to kiss that spot on her neck that she loved. I wasn't tryna be rude but I was ready to handle business. I knew what I came for but I didn't wanna make her feel used. I hope she understood that I just got out of jail and out of all the bitches I could call, I chose her. She should feel honored.

I took my time and kissed all her hot spots. Once I got to her ear, it was over. That drove her crazy. That was a spot a lot of men overlooked, but not me. I knew all the places that made women lose it.

"*Babyyyy*. I wanna talk to you first," she panted, losing her breath.

"We can talk later. Right now, I'm tryna make you scream, okay?" I continued my assault on her neck and ears.

My hands found their way to her clit, and I massaged it until she was too gone to even try to press the issue anymore. I backed her up against the island in her kitchen and sat her on top. Unsnapping her lingerie, I got a view of her swollen clit and started to gently lick and suck it until she was clawing at my head and gasping for air. I inserted two fingers into her wetness. I rubbed her spot while sucking on her pearl and any minute now I knew she was gonna explode.

"Ahh! Oh my God, Tre. You gon' make me cum!" she screamed out.

THE OTHER SIDE OF A THUG
SHE WAS A THUG'S WEAKNESS 2

by Santana

That was what I came for. She tensed up then went into convulsions. I was slurping and sucking her clit the whole time and I didn't let up until I felt her body go limp. As I came up for air, we made eye contact. She was consumed with lust as she whimpered from the aftershock of the orgasm I just gave her. Sweat began to form around the edges of her hair. Her eyes were low and she could barely speak.

I picked her up, threw her over my shoulder and proceeded to her bedroom. I gently lay her down and began to release my dick from my pants. It was dying to get out. She took that as a sign and dropped to her knees, taking at least seven of my nine inches down her throat.

"Ooh shit, Liyah. You know I like that." I tried not to moan so much but she was suckin' the fuck out my dick.

I grabbed her head and pushed my shit to the back of her tonsils. She loved when I choked her on my dick. She gagged loudly as tears filled her eyes. Her mouth salivated as she attacked my dick like an animal. She spit all over my manhood and used both hands to massage it while she sucked the tip. It took everything in me not to bust all down her throat. I grabbed her by her hair and pulled her up to me.

"You must not be tryna get no dick." She was suckin' me so good, it was finna be over.   "Sorry daddy, I just missed it," she cooed seductively.

by Santana

"Bend it over for me, so I can show you how much I missed this pussy." That was my problem. I knew damn well I didn't miss her like that but I just had to put on. I made bitches feel too special, then came the love shit and next thing you know, a nigga in jail.

I helped her out of the rest of her clothes but kept those sexy ass heels on. She was already soakin' so I slid right in and went to work. She gasped like it was her first time or at least her first time in a long time.

"Shiiiiitttt babyyyyy." She moaned in my ear. I grabbed her throat, choked the shit outta her, and gave her rough dick 'til she peed on herself.

"You know that pussy mine right, Aaliyah?" Mistake number two, but oh well. I was in too deep and didn't give even the slightest fuck anymore. She was so wet I had to hold her hips to keep from slippin' out her pussy.
"Tre. Yesssss, it's yours daddy." I smacked her ass 'til she had a red mark and continued drilling her 'til I felt my nut coming.

"Shit Liyah, daddy finna cum. Where you want it baby?" I urged her.

I wanted to bust all in that pussy. I didn't give a fuck about consequences right then. Just hearing her yelling for help, tryna run from the pounding I was giving her, that pretty ass jiggling as I piped her from behind…*man*.

by Santana

"My mouth, Tre." She managed to get those three words out. The rest was cursing and her pleading for me to stop.

"Come catch it!" I commanded.

She immediately turned and dropped to her knees, mouth wide open as I exploded all over her lips and down her throat. She swallowed every drop and cleaned all her cum off my dick. If I wasn't such a hoe I would've known that Liyah was a good girl. The type you settle down with, but I wasn't ready for all that. Plus, it was a too much of a tainted story behind it all.

"Good girl." I loved when she cleaned up after herself.

She smiled and went to the bathroom to brush her teeth. I had to recuperate after that one so I lay down in her king-sized bed, and reached in my pants pocket to grab my blunt. I checked my phone and saw a message from Rico.

"I know you doin yo thang but hit me up in the morning. We got shit to handle nigga." *"Fasho."* I hit send and took another hit while waiting for Liyah to come to bed.

My mind quickly drifted off to how I was about to get back in the drug game, even though I wasn't sure I wanted to anymore. It was so much more I could be doing but moving drugs and getting fast money had more appeal right now. I knew I had to tread lightly cause even though my case was dropped, I knew shit wasn't over. Whatever happened, though, I was always prepared.

LIYAH

After finding out once again that my sack of shit husband was up to the same games, I left. I couldn't stay there any longer. I left for two reasons: hate and fear. I had done some shit behind his back that I knew he would kill me for. See, I was hip to what was going on under my nose after I discovered who "Camille" really was. Then when I realized she had gotten pregnant in my home, it took everything in me not to kill them. So, I acted like I was helping by cooking for her but I was secretly feeding her plan B. Made that sheisty hoe miscarry. Chase wouldn't be having no precious bundle of infidelity on my watch.

I filed for divorce as soon as I left and I wanted half of them assets he was sittin' on. I went to Detroit where I thought I would reunite with Tre, but he was already locked up when I got there. I was smart, though. I grabbed some money from the safe before I left just in case Chase froze my account, and he did. It would be months before the divorce was final and I would be able to get what was owed to me. I mean, I still had enough to sustain myself but as time went on, the money dwindled. I was sending so much to Tre attempting to prove my loyalty that I had gone into debt. I was behind on my rent and I needed a way out, and he came right on time. But let me tell you how we first met, back in Cali.

THE OTHER SIDE OF A THUG
She Was A Thug's Weakness 2
by Santana

I was screening clients during my first week working at Steinberg and Associates law firm and in walked this tall, chocolate specimen in a perfectly tailored dark blue Armani suit and Giuseppe Loafers. I was taken aback immediately.

"Hi, I'm Tre Carter, here to see David Steinberg please." His smile was friendly and endearing but wicked at the same time. I was visibly impressed but I had the pleasure of reading his file earlier that day and I would never have thought he was the man accused of murder. He legit looked like a business owner or GQ model. Looks were indeed deceiving.

"Sure, I'll go get him. You can have a seat if you'd like." Now I knew damn well I could have just called him on the office phone or buzzed him over the intercom, but I had to get up and strut by him so he could get a full view of this ass. I sashayed past him and into my boss's office to let him know Tre was here.

"Give me five minutes, Aaliyah. Did you read over his files? This should be an easy one," David said with a smile. He was known for getting his cases the lightest sentencing. He had major clout with judges in California.

"I did, sir." I kept it brief so I could get back to my desk. I wanted to get another look at Mr. Carter. I sat back down and read over his file again.

by *Santana*

"Will I be able to see David, Miss…I didn't get your name." His voice was so deep and he had the sexiest New York accent.

"Oh, I'm sorry. I'm Aaliyah and he says he'll be about 5 minutes, sir."

"Sir?" He wore a slight frown.

"Yes sir, it's just proper etiquette in a place of business, sir." I put more emphasis on it this time. I smiled at him and he gave me one in return.

"Well Miss Aaliyah, what's a beautiful girl like yourself doing working at a law office? You look like you should be in front of someone's camera." I was most certainly model material, not in height but in beauty.

"I'm way too short and I would rather use my brains than my body to get ahead in life," I responded.

"Smart choice, but I'm looking for a lady to do some photos for my new club I'm opening in LA. You think you'd be interested? The pay is great and you'd get a chance to be around me." He sat back with a smirk on his face.

"Excuse m—?"

He cut me off before I could finish. *"Come on, Liyah. I saw how you were lookin at me. And I noticed how instead of calling Mr. Steinberg, you opted to get up and switch yo' ass past me. I see you baby and I'm interested."* He licked his juicy

lips and just stared at me, reading my thoughts. He was like
Professor X or some shit. I knew I was married but I didn't
care. My husband didn't give a damn so, why should I?

"Tre, I don't see how you'll manage anything with all
this legal drama you got goin' on," I challenged him.

"It's called an alibi. It was over before it started. You
gone give me your number or I gotta take it?" His
aggressiveness was a huge turn-on. I wrote my name and
number down on a sticky note and handed it to him from my
seat.

"Naw, get up and hand it to me. You wanted me to see
that ass anyway." He was so demanding and I loved it. He was
a thug and a gentleman, just like my husband.

After that encounter, we hooked up and ended up
fuckin' the first night. At the time, I was hiding out from Chase
at a hotel. He was cheating again and I needed revenge. I was
tired of being treated like a toy, and I was weak and vulnerable.
I thought Tre would just toss me to the side since I had given it
up so easily, but he surprised me by sticking around. Our little
rendezvous had turned into a full-blown love affair.

My husband was a dictator and used sex to control me.
Tre was the total opposite. He let me do as I pleased and used
sex to bond with me. After we had been sneaking around for a
while, I finally told him I was married and he said he knew. He

could tell. It wasn't until Chase came over to handle business one day that not only was our affair uncovered, but I found out they were related.

The drama that ensued was tumultuous but we remained friends through it all. And now we were in a different state living a different life. To say the least, I was relieved that he was now home and back in my arms. Something told me shit was about to get crazy, but I had more than shown him I was the woman for him. It was up to him now to make it official, or shit would get ugly.

CHAPTER THREE

Fuckboy Mania

RICO

My boy was home and we could finally take over the streets properly. We kept the product moving but we were trying to be legitimate businessmen now especially since Tre had gotten knocked for trafficking. Thank God, he had a good lawyer and all these connects in the streets though. We still don't know how that charge was placed on him but we'd find out. A full-on investigation was being held since the incident.

I was ready to broaden my horizons. I wanted to open some businesses and clean more of my money. Not enough of it was being run through my cousin's and auntie's hair and nail salons for me. I wanted to have less of a hand in the drug trade. Don't get me wrong, flippin' birds was a part of me but the Feds played dirty.

After sending him the text setting up our meeting, I decided to call up my unofficial girlfriend, Kia and tell her about herself. Yeah, a grown ass man starting drama but only because I had a hard time trusting women. I had been hurt by every woman who ever entered my life, including my own

48

mother. What made Kia any different? Once a rumor hit the streets that she had fucked one of my homeboys, I was hot. That was until I realized who it was and knew instantly that she didn't do it.

However, I decided to take the info and run with it only because I felt Kia was getting too close to me. I wasn't ready to settle down yet. Close, but not yet. She was all in love and planning futures. She was the sweetest thing but when a man ain't ready, he just ain't ready. I didn't have the heart to tell her so I used this opportunity to put some distance between us. Not enough to make her stop fuckin' wit' me, but enough so that I could still hit that pussy when I wanted cuz she thought I was mad at her. Weird, but it works.

I used my phone to shoot her a text. *"Aye you home, I need to talk to you."*

"Yeah, I'm here baby," she responded almost immediately.

I was about to piss her off so bad but I needed to create some space. She was fuckin' my head up. Had me considering leaving the dope game, making babies and getting married. Rico don't do all that so I had to throw in a monkey wrench. I put on a gray sweatsuit, a pair of Jay's, and a White Sox fitted cap, casual but fresh for no reason. I grabbed the keys to my black Porsche and headed toward her house in Farmington Hills. It was a nice drive so I took the time to think about all the foul shit I was about to say to her. I had to laugh at myself. I'm a pitiful-ass nigga, man. I got the type of girl niggas would kill for but I'm really finna try to break her heart.

I pulled up in her driveway and got out. I contemplated calling her but I started bangin' on her door to let her know it was urgent.

"Who is it!?" she yelled from the hall.

"Open the fuckin' door, Kia. I just told you I was coming, now you askin' who it is. Who the fuck else you be having over here huh?" My fake mad could win an Oscar.

"Boy what is wrong with you? What happened?" She snatched open the door with a frown.

She was lookin fine as hell with her shoulder length hair hanging down, a pair of shorts that showed off her ridiculously curvy shape, and a sports bra. Kia was gorgeous. Her piercing gray eyes burned a hole through me.

"Damnnnn, Kia you ain't tell me you be smashin' homies." I leaned against the doorway with a wicked smile on my face.

"What!?" She frowned and crossed her arms.

"Yeah. Just know I know about you my baby. I asked you to be honest from the beginning about who you slept with. I know we not official but you could at least fuck somebody I don't know!" I got so loud she pulled me in the house before her nosy neighbors started to take wind of the fiasco I was causing.

"What? What the fuck are you talkin' about? I haven't fucked nobody but yo pathetic ass! Don't come over here with no bullshit, Rico. You the one been fuckin' other bitches. Don't try to pin that shit on me." She was furious. She hated being accused of things she didn't do.

"Kia, don't fuckin' play wit me man. I try to be lenient with you cuz you suck my dick so good but you pushin' it. You foul, man. My nigga, though?" I was hoping like hell she didn't ask who. If she did, it was gone be over for my little charade.

"I'm sorry, what the fuck is your problem? I understand you can't commit but if you wanna make up shit just to get out of being with me then fine, just leave. Don't fuckin' disrespect me cause *you're* having problems. I don't know why you do this." She was fed up with my antics. I could see the energy draining from her as I pressed the issue.

"Do what? Huh, Kia? Try to be a good nigga to you? I knew you was a hoe. From the fuckin' start I knew, only hoes can suck dick that good, that's exactly why I never wifed you. I try to take yo thot ass out the hood and show you a better life and you wanna fuck around on me, and with one of my homeboys on top of that? You foul, Ki!" I was laying it on thick. My disgust with her seemed so real even I was convinced.

"Rico, get the fuck out before I fuck you up!" She looked defeated. I could see tears forming in her eyes and she struggled not to break down.

"Bitch, I should put a hole in yo ass for lyin' to me!" I continued with my fuckery.

"Rico, you don't have to be with me. You don't think I've caught onto your routine by now? You start some bullshit every time you feeling like you wanna dip off on me for a while. It's old now. And so is this relationship. Just go, okay? You don't have to do this anymore." She massaged her temples then wiped her eyes. Damn man!

"Naw, I just don't want no pussy the team done smashed." I put the final nail in the coffin with that one.

She turned to leave and slammed the door in my face. I felt like shit. I didn't expect her to know what I was doing. I thought she'd cry and beg for forgiveness, not flip the shit on me. What the hell had I done? I was scared she may really leave this time.

"*Fuck!*" I yelled as I yanked my car door open. I lit the blunt I had rolled on the way there and had to laugh at myself. I was a foul muhfucka.

THE OTHER SIDE OF A THUG
SHE WAS A THUG'S WEAKNESS 2
by *Santana*

I decided to go to the strip club, "The Pantheon" for a few drinks alone to clear my head. When I arrived, I grabbed my pistol, walked past security and went to the same section I always go to.

"Sup Rico?" I heard the fine ass bartender, Alesia, ask me as I seated myself.

"Nothin' much. Just chillin' tonight. You good?" I asked.

"Yes, thank you. The usual?" she asked me with that pretty ass smile.

"You know it, Ma." She went to the bar and brought me back a bottle of Hennessy.

I needed it, especially when I had a lot on my mind. This relationship shit was a struggle. Hoes kept offering me lap dances and trying to make conversation but I wasn't interested tonight. My mind was on Kia, and also finding the bitch that would change that. It definitely wasn't none of the thirsty-ass broads in my face. I was in deep thought when I looked up and realized I had finished my bottle. I waved Alesia back over and she brought me a second round. I was sauced by this time, but I wasn't too drunk to notice the fine ass caramel-skinned goddess that just graced the stage. She was a nice height but you could tell she was short without heels. Body was complete perfection;

tatted, perky, full titties and an ass that made me reconsider becoming a father.

I kept my eyes fixed on the lovely specimen that was on the stage poppin her ass and doing the splits. The stage was littered with bills. She was obviously the main attraction. Once her set was done, she walked through the crowd and it seemed like everyone wanted a piece of her. I usually was never pressed for female attention but something about her was so captivating. She looked so innocent and yet so dangerous. Her cat-shaped eyes reeled me in. The way her hips swayed when she walked was mesmerizing. I was hot, horny and drunk, and also rich as fuck so I was prepared to buy this bitch if I had to. She got closer and I just stared at her. We made eye contact and I didn't let up. I kept staring until she stopped in her tracks with a slight frown.

"What are you lookin' at?" she asked as she stood right in front of me. She smiled a little, remembering she was here to make money.

"I'm lookin' at yo fine ass. Can't help it, Ma." Compliments always work.

She was so damn fine I forgot who the fuck I was for a minute. I'm Rico, a major drug boss. Although I am known, she obviously had no clue who I was so I decided to be a little less arrogant. I'd never seen her here before so I figured she must be new. By her accent I could tell she was raised in the south, just like Kia. She even kind of looked like Kia, but thicker, more tan and more naked. I invited her to sit down and have a drink. We ended up talking and laughing for two fuckin' hours.

Everything this girl did was enticing. I had to have her tonight. After I told her who I was she had no problem leaving with me. Finesse!

KIA

The nerve of this nigga to pop up at my house at this hour, not to fuck, but to accuse me of some shit he and I both knew wasn't true! This man never ceased to amaze me with his foolishness and fuckery. He was a drama queen. I was through with it though. If he didn't want to be with me anymore, he could politely tell me. Yes, I'd be hurt but lies hurt more. Him coming to me with complete bullshit was completely unnecessary and just showed me why I was better off single.

Rico had gotten enough of my energy these past couple years. It started off great, dates, trips out of the country, bomb ass sex and minimal drama. He was fucking my brains out every chance he got. He was still slow to initiate a relationship but after a while he did, and that's when things started to go downhill. His trust issues from him sleeping with so many women in relationships ultimately turned him into a man who couldn't trust his own girlfriend. I know I'm not perfect but I've been loyal, faithful and honest this whole time. Why the fuck can't a man see when he has a good woman who's there for him, that's one you don't fuck over? But I guess they gotta lose it to appreciate what they had. I really didn't want that to happen though.

I paced slowly across my bedroom floor thinking out loud about how done I was, you know, the "fallback" speech, when my phone rang. It was my best friend. Jas. I needed to dump on her so I answered on the first ring.

"Jasssssss, guess what the fuck just happened!" I was prepared to give her the full run down until I heard her sniffling.

"Can you come get me please, Ki?" She was barely audible so I knew something was wrong.

"Oh my God, are you at home?" I immediately began to think the worst. I was shaking and my heart rate was rapidly increasing.

"Yeah, just get here please." She sounded weak, like she was crying.

"I'm on my way!" I ended the call, dismissing my own situation to run to my friend's rescue.

I quickly got dressed in anything I could find which was a Pink jogging outfit and Ugg boots. It was spring but it was still chilly enough for boots and a sweater. I started my truck with the remote so it could at least start to warm up. My anemic ass hated being cold. I grabbed my coat, purse, and my .40 and headed to the door. I said a silent prayer that I wouldn't have to use it once I arrived.

I was speeding west on I-94 almost passing my exit. I hopped off the freeway and hit the corner. I drove until I came to her complex. She lived in a condo in the suburbs. Most of us who made pretty good money did. I pulled up and her door was half open. I retrieved my gun and crept through the hall and to her bedroom. I opened the door only to find her lying on the floor crying. I wasn't the dumb bitch in scary movies. I cocked my gun, checked behind me, in the closet and her bathroom.

"He's dead, Ki…" she whispered.

She was a bloody mess. Her body was badly bruised, her eye was black, lip busted and her hair was awful to say the least. She had cried so much her voice was barely audible. On the floor on the side of her bed lay her ex-boyfriend, Monty. He was abusive, controlling and obviously refused to let go after Jas left him. He always threatened her but we didn't take him seriously. He lay there, eyes wide open in a pool of his own blood. His lifeless body sprawled across the floor covered in ripped clothes and shards of glass.

"Take me to the hospital please. I think something's broken," she complained.

She held her side and I saw the trail of marks on her rib cage. He had stomped her terribly as shoe prints were visible so I was sure her ribs were broken. She moved her other hand and I saw a bullet wound in her side. I broke into tears. I frantically dialed Rico. Regardless of us arguing, I knew he'd come for Jas. I needed help. I was scared to move her. I was so weak just from seeing her helpless. Jas was a trooper though. Lying there still alive after being beaten, stomped and shot, she mustered up the strength to call me and wait until I came.

I had to think fast. Rico didn't answer so I sent him a text letting him know she'd been shot. I dialed 911 and explained the severity of the situation. Knowing them, they'd probably take all day so I said we were white.

She was in and out, holding on for dear life. I had lost plenty of friends but I prayed especially hard that God spared this one. I also learned from being around Rico how to nurse wounds. I grabbed some ace bandages and a t-shirt and wrapped up the wound to stop the profuse bleeding. I talked to her and reassured her she'd make it. Jas was not only my best friend, she was one of the only people I trusted. She was like a sister to me.

Police arrived shortly after. Jas was rushed to Beaumont and had to get surgery to get the bullet removed. We didn't stick around to see how they scraped Monty's dead body off that carpet, but hopefully they torched that bitch and threw his remains in one of the many bodies of water that surrounded Michigan.

Monty was trash wrapped in treasure. He was fine as hell with a big dick and money. How'd I know he had a big dick? She showed me pictures and even videos of them fucking.

His ego, however, was bigger than his dick and pockets combined so being rejected by Jas drove him to the edge. After she broke up with him he became obsessive and tried hard to win her back. When that didn't work, he started with threats and stalking. Luckily, she had taken out a personal protection order and had documented every time he was seen within 100 yards of her, phone calls, voicemails and texts. Her self-defense case was sure to be a win.

I kept myself busy in the waiting room while the doctors attempted to save her life. I shuddered every time a code blue was called. I was so scared I almost had to be rushed back myself. I called our other friend, Simone and told her the news via voicemail as she too, did not answer the phone. What the hell was everybody doing? Kalief and Quinton had returned my calls and were on the way.

I sat quietly remembering all the good times Jas and I had shared and I don't think I've ever prayed so hard in my life. My phone rang, jerking me from my thoughts. It was Simone.

"Hey girl, I just woke up. I got your message. What happened?"

See, shit like that pissed me the fuck off. I told her what was up and she calls me to ask what happened! I swear to God after Jas recovers this bitch gotta go. A real one gone be on her way to the hospital, not stopping to ask what the fuck happened to her friend!

"She's gone, girl. Jas gone!" I screamed through fake tears.

"What! Oh my Godddddd, nooooo!" Simone started crying a bucket load of tears. I laughed inside but I was so mad at her for being stupid.

"Girl, I'm so fucked up right now." I continued with my story.

I didn't care if it was a lie. I just wanted this hoe to understand the severity of the situation. This was always her problem; she was not a concerned enough friend. Simone was self-centered. If had been her ass laid up she would expect the whole world to be there praying for her. I was livid so I knew I was gone get physical with this bitch soon as she got here.

"You still at the hospital?"

My patience was wearing thin.

"Yeah I gotta go." I hung up on that bitch before she could respond.

Kalief and Quentin had just arrived and I had to update them on her condition, so I had to end the call to save the lie. If this bitch didn't show up, I was gonna kill her myself. One thing I don't play about is Jas. She had been there for all of us and for a fake ass bitch to act like it wasn't something to jump out of bed for, had me steaming.

"Well y'all, she's finally stabilized and they say she'll make it. Her ribs are broken and her eye socket is dislocated." I cringed inside just repeating it. I was deeply empathetic. I could feel her pain.

"Damn," Kalief and Quentin said in unison. The hustle and bustle of the hospital, the nurses running frantically and all the lights flashing had momentarily distracted me from the fact that we almost lost her.

Kalief hugged me tightly just as Rico walked his bitch-ass in. I quickly walked back to my seat and plopped down. Since he'd recently accused me of smashing homies, I didn't wanna give him anymore ideas.

"I knew we shoulda killed that nigga the first time he called her talkin' crazy." Rico sat down next to me and put his head in his hands. The tension was thicker than a southern chick.

I was relieved when the doctor came in announcing she was being moved from the recovery room and could have two visitors once she was situated. I had been there for hours so I was going first and staying the whole time. I was fully prepared to spaz on any doctor or nurse who tried me tonight. I spotted Simone's bitch-ass registering at the front desk. It took

by $Santana$

everything in me not to go beat her into a damn coma. She walked over and immediately burst into tears hugging me. I pushed her off.

"Sit yo dumb-ass down, bitch. She's alive but it's funny how long you took to get here. It's funny how I left a voicemail detailing what occurred and you call me and ask what happened? Bitch, are you stupid or what? Please make it make sense." I was trying to be patient.

"I just asked a fuckin' ques…" Before the bitch finished I had punched her in her mouth so hard she flew into Quentin.

"Bitch, wasn't no questions needed! What the fuck didn't you get? Jas is shot, she's at Beaumont Royal Oak, get here! Why the fuck you need to call and ask me shit?! Fake ass hoe!" I charged at her and began raining blows all over her rock-ass head.

The guys pulled us apart and I came out with a handful of her crochet braids. The bitch had to be taught a real-life lesson. You don't play friend around me. Real bitches do real things. We don't stop to ask no questions other than location.

"Bitch, are you crazy?" she managed through a mouth full of blood. Rico collared me and pushed me into the wall.

"Chill the fuck out in here, man! Matter of fact, Que call me when the doctor calls for visitors." Rico grabbed me by my arm and walked me to his car. He opened the door and sat me down like a damn toddler that had a grocery store tantrum.

"Yo, you gotta chill. Whatever happened, now ain't the time to be fightin,' man." He pulled out a blunt and lit it. He tried to pass it to me but I refused. This wasn't the time for weed. I wanted to be alert when I saw Jas. I might get high and fall asleep.

"So, you not gone hit this?" he said, taunting me. He blew smoke in my face knowing I was a lightweight and I'd get a contact high.

"Come on, you too tense, Ma. You need to loosen up." His smile was seductive and reeled me in instantly.

Those pearly white teeth glistened, and the way his eyes slanted when he laughed and those dimples made him look almost innocent, even though he was the damn devil. I still have no idea how I started fuckin' around with a high-yellow nigga. I usually go for dark men but something about that wicked look in Rico's eyes made me melt.

He had seemed like the perfect guy at first but that soon turned out to be a false flag once he started showing jealous traits and being accusatory. In the beginning, we never got into arguments and no women had ever threatened our relationship. The only drama came from him being bipolar and a damn shit starter. He kept some shit goin between us and I was truly fed up with it. Rico loved makeup sex and sitting here with him had me ready to forget the bullshit he just pulled earlier and make up.

"No, I'm good. I need to be sober when I see my girl." I rolled my eyes and looked out of the window.

"What's yo issue wit' Simone suddenly?" he asked like he didn't know.

"Really, Rico? Come on now. You know how we roll. She doesn't belong around us," I fumed.

"That's your friend though, Kia. You know you rare. Everybody ain't like you," he stressed while taking a pull from the blunt.

"Yeah, I just wish you believed that." If Rico thought I was so "rare" then why the fuck did he behave like I was replaceable?

"Don't do that, Kia. You know how I feel about you."

"Yeah, you certainly showed me that. I don't know why you do the shit you do but you and that bitch Simone are done in my book. After this, please don't attempt to contact me. Please Rico. I can't deal with this anymore. It's so much real shit occurring but you makin' up fictional stories."

"What the fuck you mean?" he asked playing the confused role. This nigga was a trip.

by $\mathcal{Santana}$

"Rico, you know damn well I ain't fucked nobody and especially not homies. That was pure bullshit." I grabbed the handle to leave.

"Man, where you goin'?" He grabbed my arm and pulled me back.

"Away from you."

"Nah, not 'til I say you can. You not finna go in there and fight again. I don't care how mad you are at me."

"I'm not mad. I'm done." I snatched away from him. This time I got out of the car and made my way back inside.

"They said anything yet?" I asked Quentin once I got inside the waiting area.

"Yeah, I just text Rico. Simone already rushed back so I'll let you go in before one of us does."

"Naw fuck that, we all goin' in," Kalief stated as he got up. He was a hothead and didn't give a fuck about no nurses or other hospital personnel.

We all walked back to find her room. When we entered, Simone was sitting in the chair crying her fake-ass crocodile tears. I wanted to continue beating the stupid out of her.

"Jas!" I squealed as I approached her bed.

I just stood and looked at her. She was broken up so I didn't want to touch her.

THE OTHER SIDE OF A THUG
SHE WAS A THUG'S WEAKNESS 2

by Santana

We all stood and waited for her to try and talk. She said she was okay but we knew she wasn't. Jas always had to seem strong no matter what. I mean, she was strong but damn girl. You fucked up right now and you smiling and sayin' you good. My girl was a soldier. I don't think I would've made it if I was her. I felt so bad for her, struggling for her life because of a fuck nigga and his feelings. She won, though. She made it and he didn't. Karma was truly a bitch.

Jas strained to speak. I knew it was hard for her but she just had to be strong. I could tell it hurt to even talk the way she grimaced as she tried to move a little.

"I love y'all..." she managed to get out.

"We love you too," we all stated in unison.

I rolled my eyes heavily when I saw Simone smiling. That bitch ain't love Jas and as soon as she got better, I was gonna tell her.

We sat with her for hours until she finally fell into a drug-induced sleep. Everyone left eventually but I stayed. I wanted to be there first thing in the morning when she woke up.

by Santana

TRE

I met up with Rico a few days later to discuss business. He told me about one of his friends being in the hospital because of some fuck nigga. It was tragic and I felt bad for shorty.

"Yeah, she was fucked-up man. But she a fighter. I never seen a woman so strong in my life," Rico told me.

"Yeah, we need her on the team too."

"She is. That's my bitch. She handles business. You can meet her when I put some shit together soon."

"Cool. So, what it's lookin like?"

"Everything smooth. We just gotta go over some contracts and sign for the club. I want the grand opening to be crazy."

"I'll get my lawyer on it," I said as I took the stack of legal papers Rico handed me.

"I think you gone like her too." He smirked at me.

"I'll have to pass on that. You know I'm wit' Liyah. She loyal so I fuck wit' her."

"Yo brother's wife?" He scowled.

"*Ex*-wife nigga."

"You so foul my guy." Rico burst out laughing.

"Says the nigga that just lied on his own girl. You a trip."

"Well anyway, you ain't gotta fuck her, but you gon' want to. Just watch. She bad as hell, like Kia."

"This nigga here, boy. I'm a faithful man now." I shrugged. Kia was a bad muhfucka though.

"Nigga, if you don't kill yoself." Rico laughed heartily. I was gon' show him though.

"A'ight, I'll show you better than I can tell you." My phone buzzed. It was Liyah.

"See, this bae now." I smirked and answered the call. "Hey baby."

"Hey boo, what you up to?" Liyah spoke with the sweetest voice.

"Nothin', just tellin my boy how much I fucked wit' you."

"Aww I fuck wit' you too. When am I seeing you again? I need to talk to you about something serious."

"I'll be there soon as I finish up here."

"Okay baby. Bye."

"See nigga? Real love," I told Rico when I hung up.

"You wanna make a bet?" He offered a little too confidently.

by Santana

"Hell naw!" I laughed hard as hell. I had no intention of cheating on Liyah but I sure as fuck wasn't gonna bet on it.

"Exactly fool. Go tend to wifey and we'll meet up again whenever nigga."

"Least I got a girl while you still cheatin' and makin' up shit."

"You know how Ric do." He shrugged.

"A'ight, I'm up. Aye, but you heard anything about who may have dropped my name wit' that case I caught?"

"Nope. If Isabella really ain't do it then we got our work cut out for us."

"I see. This shit is not needed right now. I'm tryna come up and somebody wanna see a nigga down. Everybody eatin' though."

"You sure it ain't Chase? I mean you did smash his wife and girlfriend."

"Nah, taking me down would incriminate him. He don't move like that."

"Well nigga, we just gon' have to keep lookin'."

"Right bro. Well I'm up." I dapped Rico and left.

My mind was getting the best of me as I made my way through traffic to Liyah's house.

"Hey babe." She opened the door lookin fine as always.

70

by Santana

"Hey." I grabbed and kissed her. "What's up? What did you wanna talk about?" I asked, making myself comfortable on her leather sectional.

"Well, I needed a favor. My rent is overdue and I need to pay it or I'll get evicted." She took a seat next to me, pouting.

"Well how much do you need?"

"$6,000."

"Damnnnn. I mean it's no problem but why so much?"

"Because I haven't been able to pay. I used all my money when you were in jail," she admitted, dropping her head in shame.

"See, that's why I told yo ass not to send it. I didn't need that shit, Liyah. I know you were tryna prove your loyalty and I love you for that but you know better. I got you. But why you don't just come stay wit' me? You won't have to pay nothin' at all," I offered. I wanted her close to me.

"Really, Tre? Sure, I'd love to."

"Cool. I'll pay your balance off and you can move when you ready."

"Thank you, daddy." She then went in my jogging pants and blew me off so good my toes curled.

Things with Liyah were going fine, I couldn't lie. I had been through enough with women to the point where I was ready for a real relationship. I was stable financially and Liyah had more than proved she was loyal. I couldn't lose. The only thing that weighed heavy on my mind was the fact that somebody close to me tried to jam me up. Once I got to the bottom of things, I could fully dedicate myself to Liyah. Even though the way we hooked up was foul, Chase ain't care. He let me know that shit once he found out Liyah came here. I still had my eye on him though.

KALIEF

In the hood, they call me black Jesus. I be savin'
everybody ass. I'm not yo self-proclaimed good-guy but my
loyalty is real. A nigga stay down like post-partum depression.
Nothin' gets past me and I'm always on the lookout. I'm the
eyes, ears and hell, the brains of this operation, but I'm quiet
and stay out the way. I'm in a sometimes-happy relationship
with my girl, Kema and she about the only problem that I can't
seem to fix.

I treat her like a queen, a goddess, an empress and
whatever other royal title you can think of and what do I get in
return? Bitchin', complaints and cold food. Kema and I have
been together for 4 years and after the first year, the perfect
year, the only good year, it's been a shit show. She feels like I
abandoned her when I left her ass to go to Cornell when I was
18. We had just graduated high school with her barely making
it. She was a 1.8 GPA, school-skippin' hot ass. I couldn't stay
in the hood and not do shit wit' my life, so I took my full-ride
and went where I got accepted, which meant leaving her ass
behind for four years.

I had a 4.0 GPA since I started school. My attendance
was perfect and my conduct had me on the honor roll since
Kindergarten. I attended private school in Michigan and New

York. My IQ is 127 and I have two degrees, one in Business
and the other in Law. So now you're wondering how I ended up
runnin' wit' thugs and gangstas right? Simple, I came up poor
and still lived in the hood. I was just a highly-intelligent ghetto
nigga. I went to private school off drug money from my father's
operation once he really got in the game but the niggas I grew
up wit' never lost touch.

They saw me as an asset to the team. I'm prolly the main
reason we never failed thus far. Aside from Tre havin'
government officials on his payroll, Marcus being an expert at
that murder shit and Rico knowing numbers, I knew business
plans, how to wash money, and how to run an undetectable drug
empire. Aside from me being all-around astute, I just had this
sixth sense when it came to danger. I could always feel some
shit coming. They needed my keen eye.

When I got done with college and came back to Detroit
to visit, Kema was still here but now she was a successful
hairstylist. I was happy she had done something with herself so
I wifed her and invested into her business. She had a fly-ass hair
salon and even booked celebrity clients. Even after my large
investment, she still was sour about me leaving. It was like she
ain't want a nigga to do shit wit' his life.

What did make her happy was when I joined the drug
game. I shook my head at how wet it made her that I was on this

gangsta shit in the streets. Yeah, I had a Tasha from Power, only she ain't know how shit about accounting. Sometimes I regretted being with her but when she ended up pregnant with my daughter, I committed myself to her fully. I wanted Jayla to have a family. These days I was wishing I hadn't. My eye had been on someone else for a while and it was eating at me every time I saw her crying over some hoe-ass nigga that had done her wrong.

Simone and I had been friends for years but out of respect for Kema and her, I never made a move, but I made it my business to always make her feel better anytime she was going through shit. I was there for Jas and Kia too. They were like my sisters.

I was on my way to Kema's shop to bring her flowers one afternoon. I did little shit like that to let her know she was special. When I got there, I noticed her and some guy having a heated conversation. He seemed to be harassing her so I came in ready to blast the nigga. When I walked up on him, he just smirked. Then the comment he made almost took the wind out my chest.

"You sure that baby is yours?"

Then he smiled and excused himself.

"Kema, what the fuck is he talkin' about?" I was trying not to make a scene in front of her clients but that shit had me hot.

I've killed niggas for less but if this nigga thought I wasn't Jayla's father, I knew it was because Kema had cheated on me. Hell, it would certainly confirm suspicions that I already had about her. All the times I was away on business, she never even acted like she missed me. Probably cuz she was laid up with the nigga who just walked out of here. I trashed the roses and abruptly left before she could even open her mouth to explain.

I immediately went to a hotel. If she came home and even looked at me, Jayla wouldn't have a mom anymore. When I was done getting checked in, I immediately went to grab Jayla from preschool. I took her to do a mouth swab, however, I didn't mail it off just then. I didn't know how I would handle it if it came back and she wasn't mine. I would for sure kill Kema. Whether she was mine or not, I still wanted her to have her mother, so I kept the packet for a while until I calmed down.

Why did the good niggas always get the worse women and vice-versa? I know I did some fucked-up shit in life but I was always faithful in my relationships. Now my daughter may not even be mine. I made a note to keep this to myself cuz if she wasn't mine, I didn't want my friends to hate Kema. I didn't want to taint her image in any way so I decided to stay quiet.

But if she wasn't mine, I had no idea what would happen.

RICO

I hadn't seen Kia since the hospital. She blocked me and wouldn't answer the door when I came to her house. A nigga was goin' through it. I guess she really was done, but guess what, I wasn't. I was gone have her when I felt ready. In the meantime, I had been kickin' it wit' the li'l chick from the club. She turned out to be cooler than I thought. She was fun as hell and down to earth and not to mention, absolutely gorgeous.

We had a date scheduled for the night. We were going bowling and to a movie. Oddly, we hadn't fucked yet. Even that night I picked her up from the strip club. She left with me but we ate and talked instead.

"You ready?" I asked when she answered the phone.

"Yeah Rico, I am." Mercedes said with an attitude.

"You a'ight? You sound a li'l snappy."

"You were supposed to be here an hour ago." Her arms were folded as she stood outside my car.

"But I'm here now."

"But I don't care now." She hopped in my car, frowning.

I could tell she was a total fuckin brat. All the pouting and nose flaring was cute.

78

by Santana

"So, what, you wanna stay here? Fuck the date? It's waste my time Wednesday huh?" I asked her. She wasn't gone cut up on me.

"If that's what you want." She poked out her bottom lip like a small child.

I watched her behavior and couldn't help but laugh. She had a high-pitched, squeaky voice when she got upset. It was adorable.

"Well I don't so now what?"

"Well pull off then." She rolled her eyes.

"You are being a brat. It's so cute though," I said and reversed the car.

We went to Emagine Royal Oak where we bowled for about an hour, got some food then caught a movie. I can't say I didn't enjoy myself. Mercedes was fine as hell and all the men were jealous. I pulled her close as we walked from the bowling alley into the movies.

"Don't be all up on me cause these niggas lookin,'" she playfully teased me.

"Shid, they lookin' too hard. I'ma pull my 9 and air this bitch out," I joked back making gun gestures.

"You're sad." She shook her head at me as we entered the dark corridor to the movie theatre.

"And you fine as fuck. What that mean?"

THE OTHER SIDE OF A THUG

SHE WAS A THUG'S WEAKNESS 2

by *Santana*

In all honesty, I wasn't in a rush for sex with Mercedes but I can't lie and say I'm not interested. This girl had my eye from the moment I saw her on the stage that night and believe it or not, I don't judge strippers. As you can see, a lot of "hoes" turn out to be cool people.

We continued to watch the movie, laughing occasionally while she laid her head on my shoulder. I was feelin' this girl already but it would take more than a date for her to make headway with me. After we left, I drove toward her house. She was gonna go her way and I was gonna go mine. I had things to do so I didn't press the issue of coming inside. Some things could wait. I wanted her to understand that just cuz she was bad it didn't mean I was pressed to fuck her.

I got out and opened her door. We hugged and I watched her disappear inside. I cranked my car back up and headed in for the night. I had business at home and contracts to be signed. I also had parties and grand openings to plan. Me and the team were not only gonna be richer but we were gonna be legit. I wasn't about to keep playin' in drugs. After this last shipment, I was out and whoever wanted to stay in, that was their choice. It was too many niggas dyin' and getting knocked and I wanted a family at some point and a chance at life.

The way I was feeling though, shit with Mercedes could be promising. I could handle her. Maybe it was because she was

80

new to me and I hadn't done anything fucked up to her yet. With Kia, there had been so much drama, all caused by me. It had me feeling like we were done and there was no coming back from it.

JASMINE

Life had been a horror scene since the day my fuck ass ex-boyfriend tried to kill me. As if it wasn't already bad. Monty was the biggest and worst mistake I've ever made in my 27 years. I honestly don't even know what I saw in him. He started off sweet but my intuition told me something was off about him.

I mean I am a strong person and I can handle damn near anything but I certainly don't want someone who's going to try to take my life. At first, Monty was everything I wanted and needed in a man. He was kind, attentive, funny, showed me off, protective, and I never had to pull out my wallet with him. We dated even after the relationship was "old." We were the perfect couple. He hid his jealousy and craziness well.

After I was released from the hospital, I was on heavy medication not only for pain, but for anxiety, depression and post-traumatic stress disorder. I knew something wasn't right so I accepted the doctor's referral for therapy when I got out. I was paranoid and experienced recurring nightmares so I decided to stay with Kia for a few days. When that didn't work, I went to a "hospital" for mental and behavioral therapy and stayed for a couple weeks. I was heavily medicated and had daily sessions with the therapist. I was almost back to normal by the end of the two weeks although the paranoia followed long after I was released. I lost my job and my home shortly after so now I had completely moved in with my best friend.

"You need anything, boo?" Kia asked me as I sat on her couch flipping through channels.

"No thanks. The only thing I need is Monty's death certificate." I scoffed at the mention of his name.

I was still having a hard time believing what he'd done, but the stabbing pains from the broken rib I acquired quickly brought me to reality. My eye socket was still very bruised and tender but the swelling was going down.

Kia had been doing an excellent job nursing me. It felt good to have someone who truly cared. Kalief and Quentin dropped by every few days, bringing flowers, cards and gifts. My friends were so freakin' sweet. I couldn't ask for better ones. The only two I hadn't seen were Simone and Rico. That shit was odd.

"Why haven't I seen Rico or Simone?" I asked Kia. I knew it had to be something going on cuz he would've been here by now.

"Girl, fuck him. You know he came over here one day and accused me of fuckin' some nameless homeboy of his? I just let him talk cuz I know if he didn't say a name, it's cuz he didn't have one." She rolled her eyes as she recanted the story.

by Santana

"Well, just cuz y'all into it don't mean he can't come see me."

"Yes, it does." She smiled, knowing she was super petty.

"You are a kidddd." I laughed back. My girl could be terribly vengeful at times. "What about Simone?"

"Jas, really? That bitch doesn't care about nobody but herself. It was like pullin' teeth to get her to the hospital. And besides, I beat her ass at that hospital too. She knows not to come here."

"Straight?" I laughed so hard it hurt. I grabbed my side and grimaced in pain.

"Don't hurt yourself, Jas. But seriously, we need to get rid of her. She has never been what I consider a real friend. Ain't no way I would need an explanation after the voicemail I left. She's flat out a fake ass bitch." Kia shrugged as she finally ended her rant.

Simone had never really done anything fake to me per se, but I could honestly agree she wasn't the best friend in the world. But that's what I had Kia for. Kia was there whenever I needed her. No matter what she was doing, if I needed her, she came. Anybody else was just for decoration. Kia was my *best* friend and that's all that needed to be said.

by $\mathcal{S}antana$

Over the next month or so, Kia showed me why I didn't need any other friends at all. She waited on me hand and foot until my ribs were better and my eye was back to normal. I was almost back to the gorgeous "Jas" I had lost for two months. My light skin had healed exceptionally well from the bruising that riddled my body. Now everything was better, including my mental state. The only thing still plaguing me was the fact that I had a court case and was harassed by the investigators during the process. They couldn't seem to accept the fact that this was truly self-defense.

I had a lawyer and he went digging deeper into the case and had discovered information on Monty that cleared me completely and allowed me to file a lawsuit. The craziest part was that Monty was mentally-ill and was supposed to be supervised, medicated, and wasn't supposed to have access to any weapons. I had a strong chance of walking away with some good money. I thanked God every day I left a meeting with my lawyer. I was closer to having the financial relief I desperately needed.

SIMONE

Since that day at the hospital I wanted desperately to beat the shit out of Kia. I don't understand why she was so mad at me. Like damn, I can't even ask a question without her flippin' out. I hadn't seen or talked to Jas yet because of her, and every time I called it went straight to voicemail. I felt so bad that shit happened. Out of all the people in the world, it had to be her.

Nobody understood how I felt in this. I know Rico, Quentin and Kalief had listened to her lies and probably all turned against me. And now clearly Jas had too. If she only knew what was going through my mind. I had my own shit going on and I only called and talked to her so my abusive ass nigga could hear that I had a real emergency.

Keith was an older man; 41 but looked all of 30. Medium height, had a nice body for his age and has lots of money, which makes his average looks go from a 6 to a 10. He says he's never had a woman as fine as me and it makes me blush. I am fine though. Not even a mirror could tell me I wasn't. From my shoulder length, thick hair and honey brown skin to my full pouty lips, thick thighs, hips and ass. Nobody could tell me shit. Keith adored me and the pussy was good so I understood his possessiveness.

86

I was gonna tell my girls what was going on eventually but Kia beat me to the punch, literally. I felt bad about the distance between us but I never felt it would come to blows. Right now though, I had no choice but to tell her.

I stood at Kia's door trying to work up the nerve to ring the doorbell. My heart sank. I hated this feeling. What if she wanted to fight again? What if she said I couldn't stay? I eventually said "fuck it" cuz it was chilly outside and I wasn't sleeping in the car.

DING-DONG! The loud sound could be heard from the porch. It was after 12 at night and I knew she was gonna be pissed that I showed up but hopefully she would have a heart.

"May I help you?" she answered the door smugly.

"Kia can I talk to you please? This is serious," I told her. I guess the worried look on my face prompted her to let me in, cuz she stepped aside and let me pass.

"What's poppin'? What the fuck?! What happened?" she screamed once she saw me in the light. I was covered in blood.

I saw Jas sitting on the couch, covered from head to toe watching cartoons on Nickelodeon. She hadn't lost her spirit. We locked eyes and I almost cried. I ran to her.

"Jasssss I'm so happy to see you!" I was on my knees hugging her. She hugged me back and I started to cry.

THE OTHER SIDE OF A THUG
SHE WAS A THUG'S WEAKNESS 2
by Santana

Kia's ill feelings hadn't spilled over onto Jas after all and it made me feel better. Looking at her after surviving a horror movie, it was crazy. After seeing how Monty did her, it made me look at Keith differently. Before that, he had never done anything even mildly disrespectful to Jas, and seeing how he just flipped, it was scary to say the least.

"Simone, what the fuck happened?!" Kia screamed snapping me out of my genuine moment I was sharing with my friend.

"Can we talk please?" I hesitated.

"*Talk bitch*! Why are you covered in blood?" She was getting angrier by the moment.

"Listen Kia, I know I haven't been the best friend in the world but I've been going through some shit myself."

"Aww shit, this bitch came to play victim. You slit your wrists? What did you do?" She rolled her eyes and threw her head back.

"Y'all know Keith. Well lately, he's been acting crazy. Like he hasn't hit me but his words and threats were getting worse. He was emotionally abusive and took things from me and put me out of the house with no money. That's kinda why I'm here." I put my head down as a few tears trailed down my face. I was tired. "The reason I even called you asking about Jas that night is cuz Keith was in the background badgering me

by Santana

about lying. I needed him to hear you say it, or it was gonna be a problem with me leaving. Then tonight, he actually hit me and I lost it. I stabbed him."

"Is he alive?" Kia asked.

"Nope." I finally broke down.

"Did you call anybody!? You just left him there?" She covered her mouth in utter shock.

"I called them. I'm not stupid, Kia." I rolled my eyes.

"Damn, both of y'all done murked a nigga. I feel left out." She would be the one making jokes right now.

We all found ourselves huddled together like some *Waiting To Exhale* shit. All the attention was on me and I was happy. I'm sorry; yes, I'm an attention whore who is the life of the pity party. But honestly, I was just happy my friends understood my pain. I went through a lot of shit no one knew about. Then Rico, Quentin, and Kalief came over and sat with us. They had handled the body and cleaned up the scene. They made it look like a home invasion. I sighed a sigh of relief.

*****

A week later, I got a phone call from my mom. She rarely ever called me so I knew it had to be important.

"Hey baby, I've got some news. Good news. I want you to come see me."

"Sure. When Mom? I need some good news in my life."

"Come now."

I quickly got dressed and sped off to my mom's house. I hope whatever news she had was something to benefit me.

"Hey Ma, nice to see you." My mom was still as beautiful as the last time I saw her.

We had a strained relationship and we rarely ever spent time together since I was grown. She felt like I could be doing something more with my life and while I agreed now, she and I just didn't see eye-to-eye. She was extremely judgmental. I hated that about her so I shied away from her as soon as I was old enough to. I never knew my father so I think that's the reason why I liked older men. They were like the dad I never had.

"Hey baby. Come in and have a seat."

Although my mom was a single mother, she always worked hard and maintained a cozy life. I never wanted for anything growing up because she managed to get through college and obtain a Master's Degree in psychiatry and opened a clinic where she set her own schedule and made her own prices.

Her house seemed to have recently gotten a makeover because her furniture was updated and more modern than the last time I had visited. My mother hadn't fallen off and it inspired me to go harder for what I wanted. In a weird way, I wanted to be like her although I hated her guts at times.

"What's the good news, Mother?" I said as I took my shoes off and plopped down on her comfy leather couch.

"Okay, as you know, your father walked out on me when you were born. The drug dealer life had him by the balls. Although I didn't approve, I let him. I don't chase men."

"Mom, I know that."

"Anyway," she chuckled "I just got word that his ass is dead now. And he had me in his will. That's the best thing he's ever done."

"Wow! So how much?"

"A couple million. Baby, we rich!" My mom shouted as she did the cabbage patch.

"Million?! Who the hell was my dad?"

"Nobody important, honey. But he was a notorious drug boss back in the day. Keith was known all around the city."

"Keith? Keith who?"

"Keith Sellers. He was in the group called…"

My mom's voice faded out. I felt ill. I wanted to puke.

The man that I just killed, the man that I'd been fucking for months, was my father.

CHAPTER FOUR

Lust Blossoms, Love Blooms

JASMINE

I had been feeling so much better. The medication I took helped me tremendously but the some of the side effects were awful. All in all, the mental anguish was disappearing day by day and my girls were making everything better. I honestly was ready to get out and have some damn fun, so we all decided that the grand opening of "Club Lit" was gonna be on our agenda this Saturday.

I was finna get fine as hell. Hair, nails, toes and makeup. I had my appointments set and my outfit ready. Kia, Simone and I had been together all day getting pampered for the party and we were so excited. Well Kia and I were excited, Simone had been sour as fuck since she went to visit her mom. We tried to talk to her about but she insisted that it was nothing that needed to be discussed. Dropping the situation, we proceeded to get our wigs snatched and after, we all met back up at her house because we had different hairstylists. Carmen the Hair Genie was mine and I didn't know why my girls hadn't converted to her. She slayedddd. Anyway, we had drinks flowing and the music blasting as we all got dressed in the living room. Kia had this big ass mirror which we used for being vain as fuck and snapping an unreasonable number of selfies.

Kia and Simone both gathered in front of me with huge smiles. It was apparent they were buzzed and I would be driving.

"Girl, you look so fuckin' pretty!" Kia beamed as she snapped several pictures of me posing on the chair she exclusively used for photo-ops.

I was killin,' though. I couldn't lie. My dark hair was big and curly, shiny and healthy and when the light hit it, it had a bluish tint. My makeup wasn't excessive but my eyelids were adorned with sparkly glitter, my light skin covered in a light foundation, pink blush and a nude pink lip. My lips were juicy as hell and the lipstick I wore made them look even plumper. My eyes were low and slanted and the full set of lashes I had made me look Oriental.

My outfit was a killer. I sported this body hugging pastel pink, knee length dress with gold bead accents. My slim-thick curves stood out because of my tiny waist and it left room for this ass to jiggle like Jell-O when I strutted. I finished the look with matching ankle stilettos and a small clutch. I had to give it to myself, the flawlessness was evident.

Kia was stunning in a sheer purple two-piece. Her thick ass filled those leggings out perfectly. I couldn't stop staring at her ass. The midriff, short-sleeved top left her arms and flat stomach exposed, and her creamy skin bore several eye-catching tattoos. Rico was gonna be here and he was gonna be *pissed* when he saw her. I couldn't wait to see the look on his face when she walked in with this tight-ass, camel-toe-showin', booty-huggin' outfit on.

Simone typically dressed in all black. She felt like it made her look slimmer but she was super thick in anything she put on. Her honey-kissed brown skin was exposed through cut-outs in the arms and chest of the top of her glittery black body contouring dress. It stopped just at the hips, which were wide and plump. She was murdering this number per usual.

I decided to drive since I wasn't nearly as lit as my friends. We all hopped in Simone's Porsche truck. The night air was cool but still a little muggy from the day's warmer than usual temperature for springtime. My birthday was technically tomorrow but tonight was an early celebration. I was slightly buzzed, horny as shit and ready to shake my ass.

We pulled up to the club in one piece and I was so impressed with the design. My bros had really outdone themselves. It was rather elegant and looked extremely expensive. Everyone who stood outside was dressed to impress. Tonight looked like it would turn out amazing. There were so many people waiting to get in. Shit was finna be lit, no pun intended.

I got the car valeted and we all walked to the front of the line and got our special guest VIP passes. Kia and Simone were drunk and slightly stumbling while my poised, half buzzed-ass strutted like a black panther. All eyes were on us as we entered. The club attendants escorted us to the section where Kalief, Quentin, their girlfriends, Rico, and some other guy sat drinking and having small talk while assessing the crowd which increased rapidly by the minute.

"There they go!" Kalief smiled and stood the minute he saw us approaching.

We all ran to him and exchanged hugs and cheek kisses. My eyes immediately got stuck on the unknown gentleman that sat amongst the crew. He was fine! He had this mysterious air about him. He sat back on the plush silver couches and his presence commanded your attention. His brown skin was riddled with tattoos and his piercing gaze was focused on the crowd that had convened on the dance floor. Everything from his attire to his haircut was crispy. Rico ended up introducing me to him because he wasn't paying me any mind.

"Jas, this is my nigga Tre. Tre, this is Jas. The one I told you about." He finally rose to his feet and his 6-foot 2 frame *by Santana*

towered over me. He smelled like lust as he walked closer and shook my hand.

"Nice to meet you," was all he said.

Now I'm no narcissist but I did not get the response I was looking for. That irritated me. Nigga should've been falling all over himself but instead he shook my hand and returned to his punk-ass seat. Shit had me on fire.

After getting acquainted, the drinks came non-stop and we were all completely toasted while the DJ had the best hits of the 90's and early 2000's bangin' through the speakers. Juvenile's "Back that ass up" was on and I couldn't help but feel it. But when Nas' "Oochie Wally" blared through the speakers, my good girl façade left the building and the party heaux replaced her.

I loudly rapped the words to every verse while seductively bending over and bouncing my ass to the beat. I just knew Tre was watching by now but when I turned around, he wasn't. I was devastated but kept my composure. How fuckin' dare he?

Then I noticed Rico's face. He had been looking extra salty since we arrived. Kia was giving him no attention and he just sat there giving her angry glares as she gyrated and wound her hips to the beat. I laughed so hard inside. I went and sat next to Rico with a petty smile plastered on my face.

"Don't start no shit, Jas," he warned, still staring a hole through Kia.

"I just wanted to know why you didn't come see me."

"Because you was at Kia's house and she ain't fuckin' wit' me. I called you though, several times and sent gifts."

"Called me? Didn't get any of those." I pulled out my phone and went through my missed call log and showed him.

He then went to my block list and found his name.

"See?"

"Oh my God, how?" I was floored. How the hell did he get blocked?

"Yo girl." He pointed his finger at Kia who was still showin' out a few feet away. I knew Rico was hurtin' cuz even I was turned on looking at Kia dancing like a li'l slut.

"Damn." I laughed. "I guess if you cut off to her, you cut off to all of us." I giggled as nudged him, signaling him to lighten up. It was his fault she left him.

"Jas, the shit not funny. I want that hoe back," Rico said seriously. I burst out laughing at his honesty.

"For real, Ric? That's how you feel huh?"

"Yup, but I got somethin' for her hoe-ass though."

"What you got for her?" I egged him on in his drunken, sexually driven rage.

"She gone see. Just know dat." He then got up, adjusting his obvious hard-on and sneaking up behind Kia.

I watched him wrap his hand around her throat, which got her attention. He then whispered something in her ear. I could tell it was a threat by the way her body language went from care-free to tense and irritated. She struggled to get away but he overpowered her with his strength until she stopped fighting. He finished his speech, let her go, then walked off and disappeared into the crowd. *Boss*! I recited inside my head. I'm sorry, but I love Kia and Rico's weird-ass interactions. I loved seeing men and their sexual jealousy play out.

I remained seated as the party roared. Everyone seemed to be enjoying themselves, except Tre. He sat there like a statue, only moving to throw back a shot or two every now and then. His eyes were glossy from the weed he had clearly been ingesting all night. He seemed to have loosened up a tiny bit from earlier but still, his disinterest bothered me.

After a while, Rico returned to the VIP section and summoned us all to come into the upstairs office they had built inside the club for business meetings. We all followed him, filed in and closed the door behind us.

"Well family, the club is a success," he said while popping open a bottle of Dom and pouring it into glasses.

We all toasted to Club Lit.

by Santana

"Yes, I am so happy for y'all," I told them.

Everyone nodded in agreement. Kia then sat her glass down and headed back out the door.

"What's wrong wit'cho girl. dog?" Tre asked Rico.

"I don't know, nigga. That bitch be trippin'." Rico sat down and lit a blunt.

"Don't call my girl no bitch, Rico." I rolled my eyes and took a seat on the edge of the wooden desk, prepared to argue.

"That's what she actin' like though," Tre added.

"And what is Rico actin' like? Goin' to her house and purposely upsetting her all the time? Not a bitch?" I retorted.

"I don't care, man. She know a nigga be playin'." Rico weakly defended his childish antics.

"Your behavior was trash, Rico and I'm happy she's treating you as such."

"Treat these bitches accordingly big dog," Tre told him.

"My friend ain't no bitch though, nigga. So, watch yo' fuckin' lips," I rudely interjected.

"Like I said, bro." Tre talked around me.

I was visibly irritated. "And like I muhfuckin said, my girl not no bitch."

"Is it gon' be a problem, Miss Jasmine? You seem awfully hostile." Tre finally addressed me directly.

"I don't know. Is it Mr. Tre?" I turned to look at his fine, black ass.

"Not if you don't want one." He still didn't back down.

"It's gon' be one if y'all keep disrespecting my best friend." I slid off the table and stood.

"Chill, Jas. You know it ain't even like that." Rico stood up. He knew exactly how the fuck I got down. I'll cut or tase one of they ass. I'd done it before. That's why Rico got that scar on his neck.

"Police yo nigga, not me. He the one being rude."

"Is niggas supposed to be scared of this girl or somethin'? I just need to know." Tre continued to challenge me.

"We just met and obviously yo' niggas ain't warned you yet, so I'll let you slide this time."

"Warned me? About what exactly? Just cuz you got these niggas scared don't mean I'm gon' kiss yo ass."

He really wants this, I thought to myself, so I decided to walk up on him, invade his space a little. Everyone watched with smirks and quiet mouths.

"Warned you that I'll slice yo muhfuckin ass, no lie nigga."

Tre chuckled then threw his hands up. "A'ight gangsta. How you feel about me puttin' a bullet in yo ass though? Huh?" He readjusted his standing position.

I was triggered.

"Do it bitch," I said as I pulled my blade out and walked up to him.

I was drunk and with my recent trauma, plus his triggering ass statement, and I was truly ready to cut his ass. Everybody cleared the room, walking out like people did in church wit that one finger up. Nobody was stopping anything and I was heated. Guess they knew better.

I held the knife to his neck and to my surprise he didn't flinch. I pressed it harder until it slightly dug into his skin. He smiled, chuckled even, as my sadistic ass was really about to slice him. He suddenly snatched my arm and squeezed it until I dropped the knife. He grabbed both my arms and lifted me onto the desk behind us.

"Let me tell you a little bit about me. I'm Tre and I don't know or give a fuck about who you are. However you got them niggas feelin', ain't got shit to do wit' me. Got it?" He was close to my face as he verbally disciplined me. I was so turned on.

"Nigga, fuck you!" I spat.

"That's what it is? You must wanna fuck me." A wicked grin appeared on his face.

My eyes told it all. I was sick with lust.

by *Santana*

"Nigga, you fuckin' stupid. Let me go." I wrestled to escape his grip.

"You been tryna get my attention all night, Jas. You got it. What you gone do wit' it?" He continued to challenge me while simultaneously holding my arms against my thighs and squeezing so I couldn't attack him.

"Let me go," I demanded.

He reluctantly released me from his grip. The sexual tension was evident as I slowly lowered myself from the desk. I fixed my dress and exited the office with Tre close behind. He even held the door open for me and said, "after you" with a smirk on his face. My pussy was wetter than fresh rainfall. Who the fuck was this nigga and why did I wanna fuck him so badly? This was not the plan.

"Wear some panties next time. I can see straight through yo dress," he said from behind me, still taunting me.

As we both made our way back to the VIP section with our friends, the looks on their faces let me know that we were the topic of conversation. I didn't wanna hear shit. Rico looked like he had so much to say, so I sat next to him so he could go ahead and get it off his chest and maybe I could learn a little more about this Tre character.

"Met ya match huh?" he teased.

by Santana

"Nah, that ignorant ass nigga ain't my match," I stated with my nose in the air.

"Jas, you an ignorant ass nigga yoself."

"Oh?"

"Oh?" He mocked me with this stupid ass face.

"That nigga gone learn just like anybody else. I'm not the one or the two."

"Aye but honestly, I'm so glad y'all met. I think y'all would make excellent friends." He flashed a huge and annoying smile.

"Why would you want that?" I furrowed my eyebrows to show my disdain, but I was really pissed because he'd been around for a while and I was just now encountering his fine ass. I shoulda been hittin' that.

"Cuz that's the nigga that's gone tame you." He was so confident.

I let out a hearty laugh, so loud it drew the attention of everyone else.

"What's funny? That nigga really not for no games though." He went on about his weak-ass friend.

"What's funny is you know me personally and you were still dumb enough to suggest I can be tamed. You've really outdone yourself this time, Rico." I continued to cackle at his foolishness.

THE OTHER SIDE OF A THUG
SHE WAS A THUG'S WEAKNESS 2
by *Santana*

We kept on drinking and dancing until the party ended at 2 a.m. I was tired and slightly drunk but I had truly enjoyed myself. I was proud of them for what they had accomplished tonight and that their business venture was a huge success. I found Kia and Simone and we all walked to our car with Tre and Rico following closely behind.

"Y'all ladies be careful," Rico told us as he and Tre opened our doors. You know Tre was at my door still silently challenging me with his eyes. I wanted everyone to just leave and let me show this nigga why I wasn't the one to fuck with.

"Thank you," we all said in unison.

Rico walked around to my door as I let the window down.

"You sure y'all gone be good? Can you drive, Jas?"

"Yeah, I got it. Thanks though," I said and started the car. I cranked the heat cuz it had gotten chilly and the liquor had worn off.

"Man, look at them two. They sleep already. Let me follow y'all to the house."

He was right so I agreed and pulled off with him following me. Once we arrived, Tre and Rico helped to get Kia and Simone from the car and I wish it was me who was sloppy drunk and unable to walk so Tre could've carried me in.

TRE

All I been thinkin' is "that Jas girl is lucky I ain't the nigga I used to be." She violated. Pulling a knife on me in front of my people but I ain't even sweat it. Rico told me about her li'l sadistic ass way before we met. He also told me about how she killed her ex-boyfriend after he had beat and shot her, so I had to respect her gangsta but shorty was crazy. In a good way, though. In a "bend her over a table and fuck her 'til she cry" type of way.

After we dropped them off I took Rico to his car. He wore this cheesy grin waiting for me to speak.

"You wanna hit that shit don't you? Don't lie either nigga."

"Correction. I'm *gonna* hit that shit. Where the hell you find her at?"

"I've been knowin' Jas for a minute. I met Kia through her. We been friends for a few years but you wasn't around. You was in Cali then you got knocked."

"Damn man, I wish I woulda met her before all this. I need that."

"I told you, nigga." Rico sat back in his seat with a smug look on his face.

"You did. Why you ain't tell me she was strapped like that? And she crazy. Nigga, you know it's over for her."

"My nigga." He chuckled while slappin' hands with me.

After dropping Rico off to his car, I headed home. Liyah was sleep but I had to get this nut off. It was too much sexual tension that had built up between me and Jas, and unfortunately Liyah was gone get this werk. I slid into bed behind her and removed her panties. I kissed her back softly cuz I didn't wanna startle her. I wanted my dick in her and she coulda stayed sleep.

Once I got in, Liyah started to wake up. I noticed the pill bottle on the dresser and knew she must have taken a sleeping pill cuz usually she woke up when I entered the house. I grabbed her throat lightly and then covered her mouth with my hand.

"Shhhh, let daddy get this nut," I whispered in her ear before she could protest.

She did as I instructed and just lay there while I pounded her 'til she came. And I was right behind her. We both rolled over and went back to sleep.

The next morning, I got up and had to go meet up with the crew to discuss last night with a sober mind. We were fuckin' businessmen now and I was so glad to have these niggas. It was like my other two brothers kinda disowned me after that one situation with this fine ass she-devil bitch named

THE OTHER SIDE OF A THUG
SHE WAS A THUG'S WEAKNESS 2
by *Santana*

Isabella blew over. My brother, Chase was still fuckin' wit' her and tryna protect her. That's why I helped myself to Liyah.

That whole ordeal was crazy. I found out I had a brother I knew nothing about, hit his wife, and ended up slidin' up in the hoe both him and my brother, Marcus were in love with. When I met Chase, I was already fuckin' his wife. Chase and I still kept in touch. Matter of fact, he was comin' out here next weekend to see the club and talk about some more avenues of revenue. I was open to anything. With the proceeds of the club, plus the old money we were already sittin' on, I was free to invest in whatever. This club idea was already wielding a nice return. We rented it out for day parties, fashion shows, and just a hangout spot for lunch and dinner on the weekdays. Money was comin' in every day.

I had gotten dressed and pulled up to the club. As I headed toward the office, I thought about calling Marcus but decided against it. I opened the door to find Rico, Quentin and Kalief respectively, sitting around dressed like street niggas.

"Boyyyy, what the hell you doin'?" Quentin asked referring to my choice of attire.

"Niggas, what is y'all doin'? We businessmen now and you niggas still in sweats and jays. Grow the fuck up. We supposed to be out here takin' this shit seriously and you niggas

107

by Santana

in here lookin' like the typical drug dealin' black niggas." I had to set these niggas straight, as always.

"Calm down, Hill Harper." Rico burst out laughing.

"Naw, y'all swore y'all wanted to be different and you wanna clown a nigga for wearin' dress clothes to a business meeting? I don't give a fuck if it's just us, dress reflects the attitude. Y'all still street-minded. Y'all ain't ready to give that shit up." I took a seat.

"He right, though," Kalief admitted.

"Chill nigga, I know he is but shit this our first real meeting. Damn," Quentin argued.

"Right. This nigga come up in here lookin' like Malcolm X in his prime and shit. Caught niggas off guard." Rico sat back smugly.

"And y'all need to do the same or not be taken seriously. Chase comin' next weekend and we finna discuss some more business. If you niggas wanna keep up with the bullshit, I can just handle everything myself from now on."

"Man chill, we got it big dog," Rico said tryna hide his irritation. I didn't care who was mad. It was the truth.

"Now who wants to go first? Any news?" I asked everybody.

"Well since I'm the only qualified accountant and shit, I'll go," Rico volunteered. Rico had a degree in business and accounting so I trusted him.

"Nigga, I got a whole business degree," Kalief chimed in.

"But not accounting. A'ight so, the club brought in nearly 500% more than our goal. Attendance was a little over capacity. Of course, all of the licensing went through but they'll be doing another inspection so we need to frame these." He pointed to a box with the certificates and licenses for liquor and maximum capacity.

"I also wanted to add another wing or expand later on down the line, that way the Fire marshal will raise the capacity limit. We have two new investors and a long-ass list of people looking to rent the club out for social events. We need a receptionist cuz even thinkin' about how to schedule all this shit is makin' my head hurt." Rico massaged his temples.

"Damn, that's good. I am impressed fellas. Keep up the good work." I shook all their hands, grabbed a few things and dipped. I had other things to do before the day was over, like try to find Liyah a new crib.

With Chase coming into town, I didn't want him comin' to my shit and seeing I was still with his wife. I mean he said he ain't care, but it would've been too awkward for my tastes.

by Santana

They filed for divorce but it wasn't final and the last thing I wanted to do was stir up any old feelings. I also prayed he wasn't bringing his bitch, Isabella either. I can't say I hated her, but just cuz my brother vouched for her didn't mean she was off the hook.

I had a meeting with a realtor in an hour so I drove around a little then arrived at our meeting place with twenty minutes to spare. I sat at the table at Bistro 1, fake reading a newspaper and even sported some reading glasses for added affect. A nigga had a pocket watch too. I wanted to come off as one of those nerdy black men that were non-threatening and totally not knee-deep in drugs and murder.

"Tre?" I heard a voice say to me as I had actually become engrossed in one of the articles.

"Daniel, nice to meet you." I stood up and shook his hand.

"Nice to meet you as well." The frail white guy took a seat. He was tailored though but his well-fitting suit showed that he rarely hit the gym, and needed to.

"Alrighty, let's get down to business. I have my girlfriend living with me and we aren't at the stage where we are looking to be married. We have so many business ventures that are causing us to be apart. Our parents are both Christian families and they highly disapprove of us living together, although it was an emergency situation," I lied.

"Yeah, I know how that can be. So where are you looking to move her?"

"Southfield is actually a nice location. Pretty safe neighborhood."

"That's kinda far from Eastpointe, isn't it?"

"Yeah, but she works in Beverly Hills."

"Ahh. Ok, so here's the Southfield listing. It has pictures but it also has a website with videos of the homes." He handed me a stack of papers. "Give me a call once you've picked something and we can set up a viewing and go from there."

I had already spotted the perfect place.

"What about this? I like this one. It looks exactly like she said she wanted." It was a 2 story, 3-bedroom, 2-bathroom, ranch style.

"That's pretty fast. Umm, how will you be paying?"

"I have cash. I no longer bank. There was some racial stereotyping I ran into at a couple banks and I just can't have that when I need access to money I've worked hard to make." I lied again.

"Totally understood, Mr. Carter. Well I'll need a few days to go over everything and draw up the paperwork. How's Thursday to close?"

THE OTHER SIDE OF A THUG
by *Santana*

"That'll be fine Daniel." I stood up and shook his hand. A nigga could lie his ass off, I needed to be an actor. See these realtors don't fuck with the drug lords and shit but money talks.

I left the meeting feeling accomplished. The shit a nice suit and some lies could do. I went home to break the news to Liyah that she'd be moving this weekend. But first I grabbed food and dessert. I mean I really ain't give a fuck if she got mad, she still had to go but a nigga ain't want her to be tryna flip out and do some crazy shit. Liyah ain't have it all sometimes.

I walked in and found her sitting on the couch with a throw blanket reading some law books. I loved seeing a woman educate herself.

"I brought you some food baby." I sat the food in front of her.

"Thank you." She smiled and tore into the chic-fil-a bag.

"When you get done, we need to talk." I said in a more serious tone.

"Sure." She looked at me oddly.

Once she finished she turned to me and said, "So what's up?" With an attitude.

"Nothin too much. I found you a house that's closer to your job."

112

"Oh okay. But why? I thought you wanted me with you."

"Nothin' changed but I mean we ain't really official and we don't necessarily have to live together. I was just doin' this cuz I ain't have the money at first to just buy you a house or I would have," I explained calmly and lied again. I had hella money.

"So, you never really wanted me here? You just felt sorry for me and wanted some in-house pussy for a few months, right?" She was getting angrier by the minute and I had to think fast cuz I was not tryna argue. She was leaving and that was final.

"Listen Liyah, it is what it is. You getting a free fuckin' house. Don't sit in my face and act ungrateful!" I barked.

"Wow Tre. You're being a piece of shit." She got up and left. I ain't care as long as she knew she would be gone by Friday. Maybe even Thursday.

I would deal with her later though. Right now, I was finna sit back and plot on this money, and how to get Jas alone without coming off as interested. A nigga needed that but I was not finna be chasin' her li'l crazy ass. I was gone play it cool.

CHAPTER FIVE

Molly and Mishaps

JASMINE

Today was about to be eventful. The fellas were hosting a strip party at Club Lit and guess who the main attraction was? Me. It gave me the opportunity to not only make some good money but to strut half-naked around Tre. I was delighted to accept when Rico asked me to come through. I wanted to see if they had any more room for dancers because Kia also wanted to shake her ass that night, but I knew running that by Rico would be an automatic no. So, I found the next in command which was Tre.

I wore a rhinestone covered leotard with six-inch stilettos that were also covered in crystals. A diamond choker and matching bracelet adorned my neck and arms. My hair was bone straight and hung to the middle of my back with a side part and swept over bang. I ain't even look like the same bitch. I was Holly tonight, my party-girl persona. As I strutted into the office where Tre sat, pretending to be busy, I decided to play nice this time. Kia needed me to make this happen. She had revenge on her mind.

"Excuse me," I said as I walked into his office confident as fuck.

By the way he looked up at me I could tell he was pleasantly surprised. He tried to hide the lustful grin that threatened his calm demeanor.

"May I help you?" He stared a hole through me as his tough exterior managed to win.

"Umm, I had a question."

"No, I don't fuck strippers," he told me rudely. See this was the shit that pissed me off. How did he know I wanted to fuck him?

"That's absolutely not what I wanted. I was just trying to see if the roster for dancers was full. I had a couple girls that—"

"We got enough hoes in here." He grinned while letting me know he was referring to me.

"I didn't say hoes. though, I said dancers. What the fuck is your issue by the way? How the hell you hiring dancers but calling them hoes in the same breath?" I was already in attack mode cuz I had been drinking since earlier that day.

"Well ask Rico. He hired y'all."

"Rico not here, dumbass or I would have. Shit, I would've asked anybody but you, but you the only nigga here." I rolled my eyes as I inched closer to the desk. I had had enough of his mouth.

"Why the fuck you in my office? You ain't come in here to ask about no fuckin' dancers. You came in here to show off. You look just like the slut you was aiming for when you got dressed."

"Bitch!" I lunged toward him but he quickly got up and even in my heels he towered over me.

"We ain't doin this shit, tonight. A'ight?" He grabbed my arms cuz I was ready to swing.

"Nigga, I am sick of yo fuckin' mouth and attitude." I fought against him.

"Are you? Cuz you made it a point to bring yo ass in here to get my attention, once again. You wore dat' shit fa' me, Ma." He chuckled and let my arm go.

Pop! I slapped him hard as I could the moment he released me. He grabbed me by my throat and choked the shit outta me, just like I liked. When he caught my smile he quickly let go.

"Freak-ass bitch, you get off on being choked."

"You get off on bein a fuckin' asshole."

"Get yo slut ass out my office," he demanded.

"Make me, bitch!" I challenged him once again jumping in his face. This bitch had me hot. I wanted to fight his ass.

"Listen, I ain't that nigga!" he barked at me. His whole expression changed. I had him seeing red. Li'l bitch.

"You damn right you not. You a pussy." Bingo. As soon as I uttered those words, Tre had yanked me so fast then threw me against the wall. His hands wrapped tightly around my neck.

"Just say it, Jas. Say you want this dick." He smiled while taunting me with his words. I did want it.

A small moan escaped my lips. *Fuck*!

"Sick-ass freak!" He let me go. But this time I swung full force, raining blows to his face, to which he immediately started to take cover from.

"Man, what the fuck goin on in here!?" I heard Rico yell as he entered the office. He quickly got in between Tre and me.

"Dog, this bitch crazy," Tre exclaimed as he held his face.

"Go clean up. She got you bleedin'." Rico laughed as Tre walked to the mirror to survey the damage. That juicy ass bottom lip was indeed busted.

"Jas, what the fuck goin' on in here?"

"I came in here to ask this bitch a question and he just flips and starts being disrespectful as hell, callin' everybody hoes. I wanted to bring a couple girls to dance here tonight so I came to get permission," I explained to Rico in my best victim act.

"Girl, you know you ain't gotta ask for no permission." He smiled.

THE OTHER SIDE OF A THUG
SHE WAS A THUG'S WEAKNESS 2
by Santana

"Thank you, Rico." I grinned and walked out.

I went and immediately called Kia and told her to get here. I had to be sneaky cuz I didn't want Rico seeing her until it was too late.

I walked around scanning the crowd that was quickly filling the club. Niggas was in here hella thick on a Thursday night and the building smelled like money. I was the main attraction and I fully intended to make bank.

Just then, I caught Kia entering. I rushed to the front to greet her. I had thrown on a robe to disguise how fine I was in my outfit so I wouldn't spoil it. I secured the tie on my red, satin robe as I quickly whisked her away to safety in the dressing room.

"Yassss hoe, you made it." I beamed as we finally could talk.

"Girl, it's real tonight," she told me as she pulled out her outfit.

It was badddd. It was a Dodger-blue-colored two-piece that was all sheer. Her lace up, knee-high, gladiator heels matched and everything was clearly custom made. My bitch was finna cut up in here tonight.

"Well damn!" I exclaimed as she walked out after getting dressed. Her hair and makeup were slayed and flawless.

118

by Santana

She had gotten a blonde, frontal unit installed and she, just like me, looked like a whole new bitch.

"Girl, niggas gotta die tonight." She burst out laughing and so did I. She was most definitely dressed to kill.

Once we both finished dolling up, we waited. We would go on first, turn that shit out and leave.

"Sexy Santana!" was all I heard through the rowdiness and small talk that echoed throughout the locker room.

"Aww shit, bitch come on." I grabbed Kia and led her out. We were drunk and ready.

We both filed out of the locker room and headed toward the stage.

"She's got company! Double trouble! Y'all ready!?" the DJ announced over French Montana and Swae Lee's "Unforgettable." That was my song and I wanted to come out to it.

I dropped my robe to reveal my sculpted body and outfit that was so stoned out, it was blinding even me. The area around the stage was flooded with men anxious to make it rain the moment they saw my exotic lookin' ass approach the pole.

"It's not good enough for me, since I been with you

It's not gonna work for you, nobody can equal me

I'm gonna sip on this drink, when I'm fucked up"

As the song played I wound my hips like a Caribbean girl which instantly enticed the crowd who started raining money. I made eye contact with all the mesmerized-ass niggas that were looking on with lustful stares. I flipped upside down and landed in a split. I was on fire and heavily feelin' myself. I danced to two more songs and the stage was littered with money. The bouncers swept it up and I fit it all in my bag.

Then "Yeah I said it," by Rihanna came on and it was time for Kia to join me.

Our routine was erotic and sensual. It was like we were damn near fuckin'. Everybody was watching, including Tre and Rico. He knew who it was, I know he knew that body. I knew he was fuming inside as he stood there, chewing the inside of his jaw. I was kissing and touching and grinding all up on her and it was turning *me* on. Even more now that Tre was there. I really threw my ass into it, just for him. Once our set was done, the whole club was lit, no pun intended again. We took our money and walked right past Tre and Rico. Rico was side-eyeing the fuck outta Kia and I was trying to keep a straight face.

We walked back into the dressing room and prepared to leave. We got what we came for, a reaction. But then Kia spotted somebody familiar…

KIA

I looked over my shoulder and saw none other than my sister, Mercedes. She quickly made her way to me.

"Sis! Damn, I ain't know you dance now! You killed it. All these hoes was mad," Mercedes told me in her usual loud voice, immediately pissing the other dancers off.

"What are you doin here though?" I asked her. The last time I saw her she was in Tennessee kissing my mom and dad's ass tryna be the favorite. Now she was here in Detroit, shakin' ass in my man's club.

"This guy I'm dating told me to come dance here. He owns the club."

"Who, what's his name?" But then the DJ called her and she quickly ran off in a half-drunken stupor toward the exit. Mercedes was always money hungry so this didn't surprise me. Part of me wanted to stick around and find out who she was dating but I had to go. My message to Rico had been made.

Jas and I dressed and left the club. When we got outside something told me to look around. And I spotted it, the same pink ass car that was at Rico's house that night I had crept by. The night I conveniently kept to myself out of embarrassment. This could not be happening. My whole mood changed. I just had to find out who was driving this car but something told me who it was already. I grabbed Jas by the arm but she was already talking to some dude. I ear hustled a little while her and some musty-lookin' nigga made small talk. My ears perked all the way up when I heard him mention Rico.

"Oh yeah? Them niggas in there now?" he asked Jas.

"Listen fool, I don't know if you got a death wish tonight but if you go in that club on some stupid shit, you not gone make it out alive."

"I got this. I just wanted to make sure he was here," the drunk nigga said confidently.

Dude was obviously peeled and high off something because from what I overheard, he was planning on coming for Rico at his own club. He looked to be pissy drunk cuz he was staggering and was heavily drenched in sweat. He didn't even look sober enough to aim a gun but was standing here revealing his plans to rob Rico. Although I knew Rico could hold his own, plus he had back up, I still wanted to warn him that some crazy nigga was outside plotting on him.

Just then, the drunk guy's friends walked up.

"Nigga, what the hell is yo problem?" his homeboy asked him. He looked familiar.

"Nigga chill. I'm just vibin' wit the lady."

"What this nigga say to you?" Homeboy asked Jas.

by $Santana$

"That he plans on startin' some shit wit' Rico tonight. I told him it wouldn't turn out well." She smiled.

"Look, I don't know what he talkin' about but he off some shit. Pay this nigga no mind," the homeboy reassured her, grabbing dude by his collar and walking him off to the line.

"I don't know what that's about but I'm about to go tell Rico. You never know what niggas be up to. I'll be right back." She disappeared inside the club.

The guy that ushered his friend off had crept his way back over to me. He was fine, I couldn't lie.

"Sorry about that. That nigga be trippin' off that Molly. He think he Future."

"Oh, it's cool. I hope he'll be okay." I struggled to make small talk but this fine-ass specimen that stood before me was making my damn nipples hard.

"I'm Dro. And you are?"

"I'm Kia. Nice to meet you." I beamed.

"A'ight, I'll get to the point though. I like what I see. And I would love to take you out sometime if you're interested. I see the way you lookin' at a nigga." He flashed a set of teeth that were perfect. He already looked good but when he smiled, it made me gush.

Dro was about 6'2" and statuesque. He had a suave demeanor, very cool and calm but I could tell he had a super

aggressive side. He had that thuggish edge. I almost melted
talking to him. I know I had seen him somewhere before and the
name Dro rang bells. I knew he was in the drug game.

"What way am I lookin at you. Dro?" I rolled my eyes
as my hands found a piece of my hair to twirl around my finger.
I was nervous so I had to do something with my hands or else I
was gonna say something hella stupid.

"Like you wanna devour me," he said as his eyes bore
into me.

"That's funny. But yeah, I guess we can go out or
something." I finally caved in and agreed.

"A'ight what's your number, Kia?" He grabbed his
phone. I gave him my number and proceeded to my car. Just as
I walked away, I felt him touch my shoulder as he jogged
behind me.

"Who said we were done?" He grabbed my arm and
turned me back to him.

"Umm, I did. Goodnight, Dro."

"Nah I wanna talk to you some more. Go wit' me to
IHOP or something," he suggested.

"IHOP?" I frowned. Bitches like me didn't do IHOP for
dates.

by Santana

"This ain't hardly what I got planned for a date but I really wanna talk to you. You got me. Unless you want me textin' you all night, you'd come talk to me over pancakes."

"Okay Dro, but I gotta wait on my girl."

"Call her and tell her you leavin'."

I pulled out my phone and shot her a text then hopped in my car and followed Dro to the IHOP. It wasn't packed yet because it was only 12:30 and the clubs hadn't ended. We walked in and waited to be seated. I couldn't believe I had left with this man that I just met, but he was insanely attractive and had piqued my interest. He also took my mind off Rico for the moment and that was a blessing. I hated being submerged in thoughts of him all day when he was clearly fuckin' wit a whole new bitch.

I told myself I was done with that situation. Sometimes relationships just run their course and this was the perfect example. I love Rico, but dealing with him was draining. Fuck tryna figure out why a nigga wanted to play games. I used to want to understand exactly why he did the shit he did but now, I just didn't care. Whatever his reason was, I'm sure it was stupid and immature so I didn't need an explanation. He could play games with the bitch with the pink Benz.

125

by Santana

Dro and I were seated rather quickly and had our menus, scanning over them to place our order. I had the splashberry lemonade to start off and Dro ordered a coffee.

"So, Miss Kia, how old are you?" He leaned in and waited for me to speak.

"I'm 26. How old are you?"

"32."

"Oh okay. And when is your birthday?"

"December 26th. When yours?"

"May 30th," I replied.

"Oh, a Gemini? What have I gotten myself into?" He laughed as he poured sugar into the cup of coffee the waitress had set in front of him.

"Some shit," I admitted to him.

"I see. You definitely some shit. Some shit I like. So, you single or what?" He looked at both my hands, probably searching for a ring.

"Yes actually. I had someone I dealt with but he wanted to play games so I had to eradicate that situation." I laughed at myself. I knew I still wanted Rico but in an attempt to look unbothered, I told a whole-ass lie.

"Eradicate huh? Well I hope so. Cuz I want you," he blatantly stated while staring straight into my soul.

"Is that so?"

"Yeah. I like your style. This ain't my first time seeing you, to be perfectly honest. I've had my eyes on you for a minute now."

"Where have you seen me before?" I quizzed.

"Well for starters, I just saw you in the club fuckin' yo homegirl on the stage." He clasped his hands and sat back.

I blushed so hard. I was kind of embarrassed but a little turned on.

"Oh Jesus, you saw that?" I smiled so hard it felt like my face would break.

"Yup. That shit was hella sexy though. I knew I had to have you after that. I saw you come outside so I left too."

"And where else have you seen me?"

"At parties, clubs, and in the hood sometimes. We got a lot of places in common. I be watchin' you Kia, and now I'm makin' my move. So, you wit' it or not?"

Before I could respond, the waitress was there to take our food orders. I was happy that I had some time to process his question. Dro was moving in on me fast and I was a little scared. Now, I was a little more familiar with who he was. I remember anytime I was at clubs or parties, it was a rich nigga event, meaning Dro was that nigga. I remembered going to a few events hosted in his honor. I wondered if Dro knew Rico. That would be something I would have to find out later though.

by Santana

I was feeling him and didn't wanna ruin the moment with any questions about another nigga.

After ordering our food, the conversation had resumed and I was back in the hotseat.

"So, about what I said."

"What about it Dro? What you want from me?"

"I can think of a couple things, but we can start off with getting to know each other. If that's okay with you."

"Yeah, that's fine."

"Good. I'm gonna take you on a date tomorrow. I hope you're available"

"I should be," I told him while playing with the strawberries in my lemonade. He kept giving me all this seductive-ass eye contact and I tried so hard not to look at him.

He grabbed my chin. "You're *gonna* be," he told me, coaxing me to agree with him.

"Do I have a choice?"

"Nope. Just be ready at 7."

"Okay Dro, I'll be ready."

"Make sure you lookin' good too. I wanna take you somewhere nice, then have you to myself for the night."

"Excuse me?" I eyed him suspiciously.

"Not like that. But I wanna spend time talkin'. I like how you look when you nervous."

by *Santana*

This nigga was reading me like a 2nd grade textbook.

"I'm not nervous." I frowned. I removed my hand from his before he noticed how clammy it was. I truly was nervous simply by the way he had my girl throbbing. I wanted him, and *NOW*. But I was gonna play it cool.

"Yes, you are. You're fidgeting, playin in yo hair and can't keep eye contact for shit. What you goin through, baby?" He smirked, pleased with himself.

"Damn, you all in. Stop watching me so hard."

"Can't help it. I always pay attention to my surroundings."

by *Santana*

JASMINE

I had gone back inside the club and looked all over for Rico but they had disappeared somewhere. I went to the office after I couldn't locate him on the first floor.

"Rico!" I called out as I barged into his office. He sat there drinking with Tre, Quentin and Kalief.

"What's up, sis? That was real cute that shit you and Kia pulled."

I smiled hard as fuck.

"Later for that, nigga. Some dude named Silas was outside the club talkin' about getting at you. I was comin' here to warn you."

"Wait who?" Rico said with a shocked look on his face.

"Silas. I don't know this nigga but he was asking me if I had seen you and where you be at. Just a bunch of crazy questions. He was drunk as hell and told a little too much."

"Damn, that nigga must be off that shit again."

"You know him?" I quizzed.

"Yeah, I know that bitch nigga. He roll wit Dro," he said more so to Tre than to me cuz I had no idea who Dro was.

"What the fuck you tell that nigga, Jasmine?" Tre interjected in an accusatory tone.

by *Santana*

"The fuck you mean what I tell him? I ain't tell him nothin' important."

"Well why the fuck that nigga walkin' around this bitch lookin sus as fuck then?" He pointed to the security camera that Silas had just walked past.

"I don't fuckin' know, nigga!" I became irritated with the way he was tryna incriminate me in some bullshit I had nothin to do with.

"Well why was he so comfortable talkin' to you? Huh? Why he just gone walk up to some random girl and start tellin' her plans of robbin' some niggas, huh?" He got up from his seat like he was finna check me.

"Oh, I think the fuck not! You not hardly about to try to implicate me in none of y'all shit. I've met that nigga before. He was tryna get on. Other than that, I don't fuck wit' him. Rico, you kno…" And before I could finish, gunshots rang out. We watched on the camera as people scattered everywhere.

"Shit!" Rico yelled as everyone armed themselves and went to go handle whatever had popped off. Tre couldn't assist cuz he was on parole and couldn't have a firearm yet or be caught up in any drama.

"Where the fuck you think you goin'?" Tre asked as I headed back toward the party to leave.

"I'm getting the fuck from outta here," I told him.

"Nah, come wit' me. Why the fuck would you go that way and that's where they shootin' at genius?" He grabbed my arm and led me out the back exit. I could hear sirens in the faint distance as we scurried toward his car that was parked out back.

We hopped in his black G-wagon and pulled off.

"Okay, just drop me off at my car. It's in valet."

"Valet gone! It's been a shooting. You gone have to get that shit tomorrow. Besides, you comin' wit me. I got questions."

"Questions about? And going where?" I asked, folding my arms. I was highly irritated.

"Questions about this bullshit you into wit' this clown ass nigga, Silas."

"Nigga I ain't in no bullshit wit Silas."

"You can lie to that nigga Rico but you not gone lie to me. I'll bust yo shit."

"Yeah like I did yours earlier?" I smirked and turned toward the window so he wouldn't see me laughing.

"That's real cute but we gone see who laughin' by the end of the night. If my niggas ain't okay, guess who also won't be okay?" He threatened me like I cared.

"Y'all will be fine. Stupid-ass. Why don't you call Rico and ask him does he think I'm in on this?"

"I did, he ain't answer. Niggas prolly done got my boy."

by *Santana*

"Well if you think that then why the fuck you ain't back there helping?"

"Cuz I'll be in prison if I'm caught in some shit right now. I'm on parole."

"Typical black man." I rolled my eyes.

"Typical black woman settin' niggas up." He huffed as he sped toward the exit on 94 East.

We pulled up to a massive home in Eastpointe. It was beautiful. The driveway was a brick road that had several luxury cars lining the path. This hood nigga had taste. The house was immaculate. Even though it was against my will, I kinda wanted to go in just to see what the inside looked like.

"Hurry the fuck up!" Tre yelled at me. "And gimme this damn phone. I don't need you callin' no police or tryna have no niggas rob this spot."

He snatched my phone and purse from me.

"Gimme my shit," I screamed as he unlocked the front door and shoved me inside.

"Stop fuckin' playin' wit me man." I could tell he was angry because his whole demeanor had changed. He wasn't the non-threatening asshole. He looked menacing now. His eyes were fiery and his body language was aggressive.

"Fuck is yo' problem?" I asked him.

by *Santana*

"You thought shit was a game? You thought I was playin'?" He pulled his gun out and cocked it.

"I actually did. You a joke." I patted his arm and walked off to get a better view of his house. He might have thought that crazy shit scared me; it didn't. Tt just turned me on. I knew Rico could vouch for me that I wasn't on no setup shit so I brushed all his crazy antics off.

"I see you up under the impression that I'm some type of clown-ass nigga, right?" He grabbed me and shoved his gun under my chin.

"Call yo boy."

"I ain't callin' shit! So, what the fuck you tell that nigga Silas?"

"I didn't tell him shit. Why you can't just call and ask Rico?"

"Cuz Rico got a soft spot for you, but I don't. He prolly gone let you live even after you was clearly on some setup shit."

"He got a soft spot for me cuz I'm loyal."

"Haaaa!" He burst out laughing.

"Anyways, I'm hungry. What do you have to eat?" I walked into his kitchen. It was amazing. Everything was stainless steel and looked expensive, down to the marble countertops.

"Can you make me a sandwich with some chips and dip please? And I'll take one of those sodas too. Thank you." I pointed at the Dr. Pepper cans he had on the counter.

"Excuse me?" He stood there perplexed with his gun in his hand.

"*I'm hungry*," I said to him. Then I walked out and went to sit in his living room watching TV.

"Don't get fuckin' comfortable. This ain't for yo comfort."

"Well what's it for then, Tre? You got me here for a reason and it damn sure ain't shit to do with Rico cuz you would've called him already and cleared up the situation. If that's what you were really worried about," I said matter-of-factly.

"I'ma deal wit' yo ass the way I see fit! Don't fuckin' question me." He was trying so hard to be serious but I had already called his bluff. I'm not stupid.

"Right. Well, I'm hungry, Tre and I've been drinking so can you make me something to eat?"

"Make it yoself!" He yelled at me like I wasn't a guest and a princess.

I hopped up from his suede couch so fast. "Nigga, *you* make it! This is your house! I'm a guest who also didn't fuckin' ask to be here!"

"Aye calm down." He mushed me with his strong hand.

"And gimme my phone and purse." I held my hand out.

"No!" He walked back to the kitchen. After about five minutes of him pouting and clanking silverware around, I finally had my sandwich, chips and soda. He even gave it to me on a platter.

"Bring this to my room. I'm about to lay down 'til Rico calls me back and I don't want you tryna escape."

"Still holdin' on to your lie, huh?" I laughed as I followed him down the long hall to his bedroom.

Flicking on the lights, Tre took off his shoes and cleared a space on his bed, which had papers everywhere. He patted a spot on the right side for me to sit on. I followed his lead and sat there while he found a movie for us to watch.

After I finished my food, I needed to shower. I couldn't even get comfortable without one, and it looked like I would be here for a while. I saw Tre put his phone on Do Not Disturb, so I knew he wasn't waiting on a call from Rico to clear my name. This nigga did all this extra shit to get me alone.

"Well since it looks like I'll be here a while, may I take a shower?"

"Yeah, lemme get you some stuff. I need to take one too," he added as he got up and went to the linen closet. He returned with a black towel and two washcloths, Dove body wash, and a toothbrush and toothpaste.

I was impressed cuz most people didn't even have an extra face towel, alone toothbrushes. I went into the bathroom that was connected to his bedroom and I was surprised by how clean it was. No hair shavings left in the sink, no toothpaste on the mirror, and no pee stains on the toilet. Tre was either very clean or his ass rarely came here.

I brushed my teeth before stepping into the shower. The water was scalding hot, just the way I liked it. It quickly steamed up the mirrors. I washed my body thoroughly while fighting off thoughts of Tre burying his dick deep inside me. I had gotten so lost in my sinful mind that I didn't hear the shower door opening up until it was too late, and there stood Tre naked as the day he was born. Dick hanging like a nigga on a Saturday night. I almost melted at the sight of his chocolate, ripped body. He looked like a statue.

"What are you doing?" I frowned but kept washing. I wasn't about to show this nigga the slightest sign of fear.

"Takin' a shower." He stepped past me and turned his back. There was another showerhead behind me that I'd conveniently missed. He turned it on and lathered his cloth, washing his glistening body with a scent of axe soap that instantly made me wetter. He stood there teasing me with the way he was payin' me no attention.

"Wash my back for me," he instructed me, handing me his cloth.

"No," I said.

He then grabbed and pinned me against the wall. "Do what I fuckin' asked! Damn, you so difficult." He scowled, returning the cloth to my unwilling hand.

"You basically kidnap me then you want me to play nice?" I asked, washing his broad shoulders, while scanning over the artwork on his back.

"Hell yeah, and you gone do what I say while you here."

"Oh no." I dropped the cloth and turned back around.

POP! He had picked up the cloth and slapped the hell outta my ass cheek with it.

"Ahhhhh!" I yelled and jumped outta my skin.

He stood there laughing as I rubbed my red cheek.

"Next time do what I say and we'll get along fine." He stood in front of me, staring down with a look of sick satisfaction on his face. He had me so uncomfortable. The fact that I was butt naked in front of him, we had showered together, and he still hadn't made even the slightest move was honestly killing me.

THE OTHER SIDE OF A THUG
SHE WAS A THUG'S WEAKNESS 2

by *Santana*

He exited the shower and put his towel on while I unknowingly stared at him.

"Quit lookin' at my dick," he said before walking back into his room.

I snapped out of my trance and my face flushed in embarrassment. I turned the water off and grabbed my towel.

"I need something to put on." I pouted when I reentered his room.

"Take that towel off and lay down," he instructed.

"What? No."

"Muhfucka, do what I said. Ain't nobody gone do nothin' to you. If I was, I woulda took it in the shower."

I reluctantly removed my towel and lay down on my stomach. This nigga had turned the lights down and had candles burning and some music on in the background. I knew it. He was tryna seduce me, not kill me.

When I felt the warm oil pour on my back, I let out a soft moan. He started to massage it into my damp skin. His hands were massive and strong as he prodded my back, up to my shoulders and the nape of neck. I tried so hard not to moan but it had been months since I'd been touched and it felt damn good.

"I hear you tryna hold back. Let it out," he told me.

"It's nothin' to hold back."

"What's yo issue, Jas? Why you so tough?" He chuckled as he continued to make me feel too good.

"You. I shouldn't be here. But here I am."

"You don't wanna be here?" he asked seriously.

"Hell no," I snapped.

"Too fuckin' bad," he responded then poured oil onto my ass and massaged it. I was having fits tryin not to give in and start moaning like a weak bitch.

"Sssss ooh," I hissed like a snake.

"There it go," he said, smacking my ass a little.

"Nigga, chill," I warned.

"Shut up before I spank you," he threatened.

"Just do yo job."

He finished up the massage then got me a t-shirt from his drawer to put on.

"So, when you taking me to my car?"

"It's a little late and the club is shutdown. You ain't gone see that car 'til Monday."

"It's your fault." I folded my arms.

"Naw, it's yours. For conspiring wit' the enemy."

"Whatever, Tre. Lose the tough guy act. I conspired with the enemy but you giving me back rubs and shit. Boy bye."

"Couldn't help it. I had to see if that muhfucka was as soft as it looked."

"Well, was it?" I smiled coyly.

"Hell yeah. I wanna spank that fat muhfucka," he admitted.

"Why?"

"Cuz a hard head makes a soft ass, and yo mouth reckless. You need it. Matter-of-fact, come here." He reached over snatched me up, bent me over, and lifted my t-shirt.

"Tre stop!" I yelled as he slapped my ass with his big hand.

"Nope. Why you act so bad?"

"I don'ttttt. Stop!"

"Yeah you do." He held me over his knees and he slapped my ass every time he asked a question.

"Say sorry, Jas."

"Sorry for what?" I tried to shield my butt with my hands but he had pinned them down with one of his.

"For bein' a bitch, for bustin' my lip today." He stung my cheek again with another slap.

"Ahhhh!" I partly moaned.

"Apologize!"

"Shit!" I screamed as he hit me again. My pussy was so wet I was scared that he might notice.

"Say you sorry!" He yelled again but I was so damn stubborn, I just wouldn't say it.

141

"Owww, Tre. Please stop!" But he didn't listen.

"You not gone say sorry, huh? You must like that shit."

"No."

"You actin like you like it. That pussy wet?" he questioned.

God noooo. I was praying he didn't touch my shit cuz the muhfucka was dripping.

"No! Tre please." I begged as his hand inched toward my soaked pussy.

"Gahhhhdamn, you soakin'," he exclaimed as he played in my juices.

"Treeee stop!" I called out as he massaged my swollen clit. I swear I would cum if he didn't let up.

"Shit. Why you so wet?" This nigga had the nerve to taste his fingers.

"I don't know Tre but let me go. I'm sorry," I finally told him and just like that, he let me up.

He reached on his nightstand and lit a blunt. After a few pulls he handed it to me. I needed it. Maybe I'd fall asleep and this nightmare would be over.

"So, what's yo problem wit' me Jas? You been a straight bitch since we met." He sat up and looked directly at me.

by *Santana*

"You've been an asshole since we met, or did you forget?"

"I guess we got something in common then."

After we finished the blunt, I was finally sleepy. I turned over and drifted off before the paranoia I get when I'm high kicked in.

An hour into pass out and chill I started having a nightmare.

"Nooo, pleaseee!" I cried. "Stoppppp!"

"Jas baby, you okay?" Tre shook me, snapping me out of my horrible dream.

"Shit." I sat up, wiping tears from my eyes.

"Are you okay?" He seemed worried.

"Uhh, yeah. I was having a bad dream." I tried to steady my breathing.

"What about?"

"The day I got shot."

"Word? What happened?"

"My ex came over, beat the shit outta me, and shot me."

"Damn."

"Yeah, I take medication at night but you took my purse so I didn't get a chance."

"Shit Jas, I'm sorry." He got up and handed me my purse that he'd hidden.

"Thank you. But I'm not gonna take it tonight."

"Why not?"

"Because." I rolled my eyes.

"Because what? Talk."

"Because it makes me act strange."

"Strange like what? What type of medicine is it? I know about pills," he told me.

"It's MDMA."

"Molly?" he asked, perplexed.

"Technically, but it's for anxiety and shit. And it makes me act out sexually and I do not want to take it around a man that's been playin' in my pussy."

"Take that shit, Jas. I promise I won't do shit." He smirked and threw his hands up.

"But, I will."

"Jasmine, take yo fuckin' pill so you can sleep." He snatched my purse and got the bottle out.

"If you insist. Just please, whatever I do, tell me no."

"I promise."

"Pinky promise?" I held out my pinky for him as it is a legitimate foundation for trust as an adult.

"Dog, pinky promise." He chuckled.

As I swallowed the pill, Tre had turned on a music playlist. He cuddled close to me and held me, trying to put me back to sleep. We ended up talking for a couple hours about our exes and about life and goals and shit. Then Tre turned over. About 10 minutes later, the pill had kicked in and I was on a cloud of euphoria. I was so relaxed that I started to giggle for absolutely no reason. My pussy was completely soaked now and I had to have something inside.

"Tre? You sleep?" I cooed in his ear.

"Nope, I'm tryna make sure you okay."

"You wanna help me be okay?" I asked suggestively.

"Yeah, I told you that. Why you lookin' like that?"

I had a devilish grin on my face and my eyes were low and seductive.

"Like what, baby?"

"Like you tryna get something started."

"Cuz I am." I reached down and grabbed a handful of his hard dick. It was so big I was almost scared.

"Nope, Jas stop it." He popped my hand and removed it.

"Why? You know you want me to touch it."

"Aww shit, that pill done kicked in huh?"

"Yeah, now feel on my pussy like you was doin' earlier." I giggled coyly.

"No, you told me not to."

"Now I want you to. You wanna make me feel better, right?" I grabbed his hand and put it on my clit, and he snatched it away quickly.

"Yeah, but no."

"Please, Tre? Just make me cum one time. I swear that's it. I'll go to sleep. Please, I just need one."

"Man what?! No!"

"Tre please, I need it," I begged him as I started to touch myself.

I threw my head back as I circled my throbbing clit with my pointer finger. Then I slid my middle finger into my slick opening.

"Jas, please stop. Don't make me do this."

I took my finger and put it in his mouth so he could taste it.

"Tre please, just one. I promise I'll leave you alone."

"Man no!" He hushed me. He then wrapped his arms around me and held me. My body was hot but I was shivering cuz I needed to get off.

"Massage my nipples. Please."

"You actin so nice now. You weird." He started cupping my breasts and tweakin' my hard nipples.

"Ohhh yessssss," I called out as he pleasured me.

I guided his mouth toward my right nipple and he went to work while still massaging the left.

"Please Tre, please, let me suck it."

"What?" His eyes lit up when I said that.

"Let me suck it, Tre."

"Jassss, you gotta stop now. I can't help you wit you talkin' to me like that."

"Let me choke on that big ass dick, Tre." I grabbed and massaged his pole and he let me.

"Mannnnn for real, nah."

I had the dick out in seconds and down my throat.

"Oh shit!" He called out as I took his shit down as far as it could go. I gagged on his thick ass dick and my mouth watered.

I spit all over the tip and massaged his massive pole with my small hands before I went down on it again.

"*Sssssssss fuck!*" He hissed as I made his dick disappear. I cupped his balls and made loud slurping noises and I sucked it fast then slow, making him quiver like the li'l bitch he was.

"You like that?" I asked him as I tightened my wet mouth around his girth.

"Fuck yeah." He grabbed my head and pumped into my mouth, moaning like a coward the whole time.

147

by Santana

"Ahhhh shit, baby. Goddamn, you suckin' the fuck out this dick."

I sucked him so good my eyes were watering and my nose was running.

"Can I have some dick now, Tre? Please?"

"Come here." He snatched me up and laid me down.

"Give to me, Tre. I need it."

"Beg," he instructed. I had been begging the whole time.

"Pleaseeee." I clasped my hands together.

"Please what? You want this big dick?" He said jackin' his pole while lookin in my eyes. I was ready to die if he didn't give it to me.

"Yessss. Please daddy."

"Mannnnn." He roughly spread my legs apart and wasted no time entering me.

His dick felt like everything I had been missing. As he went deeper, pounding my spot, I started to cry. Dick had never felt so good. I came so fast, it scared me.

"Shit, Tre. Stop, I'm finna cum!" I screamed.

"Nope, you wanted it. Fuck you cryin' fo'?" He continued to pump inside me until I exploded.

"Cuz it feels so good," I admitted as tears streamed down my face. I was pathetic and I hated that he got to see me

by Santana

in such a vulnerable state. I woulda played tough forever if I could.

He turned me over and entered me from the back. He felt even bigger now. I couldn't take it but I wanted it so bad.

"Uh huh, take that shit. You been wanted this dick, didn't you?" he asked as he gave me rough, hard strokes.

"Shit Treeeee, yes, yes I wanted it!" I moaned loudly.

"Then why you playin games?"

"Cuz you were," I whimpered.

"You like that big dick in that li'l ass pussy?" He smacked my ass and grabbed me by my hair.

"Yessssss."

"Yes what?"

"Yes daddy," I cooed. This nigga wasn't snatchin' my soul. He was tearin' it out.

Loud smacking noises filled the room and he fucked me rough and hard, stopping every so often so he wouldn't cum so fast.

"Shit, this pussyyy." He moaned, reaching down to grab my throat.

"Yeah, gimme dat shit." I don't know why I said that. I already couldn't handle it. Then I heard the noise that told me I was finna wet this man's bed the fuck up.

by *Santana*

"I'ma cum, Tre!" I called out as my juices poured from me. He had successfully made me squirt all over his bed.

"Damn, baby. Look what you did," he said as he moved me from the wet spot.

He dog fucked me for the rest of the night. We went at it several times before we both collapsed and fell asleep.

*****

The next morning, I woke up groggy and confused. I instantly wondered why I was naked and in bed with Tre but before I could panic, he turned over smiling like the damn Cheshire cat.

"Umm, I hope not," I said as my nostrils flared with anger.

"Jas, calm down shorty," he said as he threw his hands up.

"I know the fuck you did not!" I yelled.

"Yo chill! Chill!"

"So, you really brought me here to fuck me? You fuckin' liar!" I pounced on him throwing blows as he tried to shield his face.

"Man, what the fuck? Get off me!" he yelled as he restrained me.

"I can't fuckin' believe you!" I screamed near tears. I was so mad I didn't even understand.

THE OTHER SIDE OF A THUG
SHE WAS A THUG'S WEAKNESS 2
by *Santana*

"You came onto *me*! The fuck is you sayin'?!"

"Oh, fuckin' really, Tre?" I cocked my head to the side, knowing the shit could be partway true.

"Yes, you did. So, don't come tryna attack me over some dick you begged for," he scorned me. I was fuckin embarrassed and was over this whole scenario.

"Take me home please and thank you." I sulked and got up to find my clothes.

"You gone chill the fuck out first though," he warned.

I ignored him and went toward the bathroom to shower. I smiled to myself as I turned the shower on cuz I had played that victim role so muthafuckin' well. I knew exactly what I was doing. When I was finished, I got dressed and went back into his room where he was smoking a blunt and looking stupid as hell.

"I'm ready to go."

"Can we talk for just a minute? I don't want you to leave here mad and not wanna be my friend no more."

"Friend? Bitch, I ain't yo friend!" I huffed as I grabbed my things and stuffed them into my purse.

"Whoa. That ain't what you was sayin last night. You know we had a long-ass talk for like two hours and you said we could be friends. *Best* friends. I felt like we got somewhere. You told me ya favorite color." He smirked.

"Nigga, what is it then?"

"Aquamarine." He smiled that irresistible smile revealing those perfect white teeth.

"Oh, hell naw." I gawked.

"Yep. We got to know a lot about each other. It wasn't just sex. If you would calm down just a little, you would understand. I really didn't mean for that shit to go down but you just could not be told no. I felt like you really liked me for a minute the way you was beggin' me for it. The way you opened up to me. But maybe not." He shrugged.

"Boy, whatever." I frowned, still resisting his attempts to coddle me.

"I mean, what's yo issue wit me? We had a beautiful night. All jokes aside. I got to see you in a vulnerable moment. I helped you get through it. I held when you woke up cryin' and shit and put you to sleep wit this good-ass dick. What's the fuckin' problem, man?"

"I didn't mean for that to happen." I sat down on the bed and dropped my head.

"I honestly don't think so. I think you wanted me but was too evil and stubborn to admit it so you let the drugs talk for you. Jas, it's ok. I enjoyed the fuck out of it. You somethin' else."

"I don't even wanna know what happened." I sighed.

"It's ok. I won't say shit, that's my word. Pinky promise." He stuck out his pinky.

"I went completely too far with you." I rested my hands on my big-ass forehead after locking pinkies with him.

Like, we really fuckin' bonded last night. Some things I honestly didn't remember too clearly, like this conversation we had that supposedly lasted two hours, but I even pinky promised wit this nigga? Lord Jesus, what have I done?

"Jasmine, I enjoyed it. I ain't even gon' lie, I been feelin' you since I met you but I had to play it cool. But I didn't bring you here just to fuck. I really wanted to talk to you. I wanted to understand you better and I think I do." He looked like he had an epiphany.

"And what exactly do you understand?" I quizzed.

"You was feelin' me too. You play that tough shit cuz you want a nigga to show he really want you. You try to scare weak niggas off wit that crazy-ass attitude, but that shit doesn't work on me cuz I love crazy women. You are strong but you also want somebody you can be vulnerable with. You obviously got that wit' me cuz as soon as I showed you I cared about you, you melted in my arms. And I know you mad as fuck about that shit right now, but I wanted to show you I got you. I ain't as bad as you think, a'ight?" He cupped my chin and stared deep into my eyes.

by *Santana*

I just couldn't let him in. I was burning inside at how mushy he was making me. This shit right here *was not me*. I really wanted to jump into his arms and kiss him and cry on his shoulder, but later for that soft shit.

"Yeah, ok nigga," I spat.

"Come here." He grabbed me and engaged me in a long, passionate kiss. "Stop bein' like that. I promise I ain't gone hurt you. I just wanna be yo friend."

"Friends don't fuck and especially not like we did. We went too far," I whined.

"I understand that, but I just said friend cuz I feel like we more than that or have potential to be. But you on yo tough shit right now. I'll let you cook though, baby."

"I'm not on tough shit. It's just the way shit went down, it's like you plotted on me."

"I ain't gon' lie, I just wanted to get you alone. But it wasn't just to fuck, I promise. I wanted to get to know you, and I did. And I like you, when you open." He puffed his blunt then handed it to me.

"Yeah right, Tre. This was just so wrong."

"But it felt so right. So, you gone be my friend or do I gotta beg you?" he said to me seriously.

"Why you wanna be my friend?" I huffed.

by Santana

"Cuz I told you, I like yo crazy ass. I don't think I've ever ran into a woman like you."

"You barely know me."

"Baby, the way you act during sex is mind-blowing compared to the way you act outside of it."

"Really?" I sighed.

"Yes, really. You evil as hell but when that dick in you, you submissive as fuck." He leaned in further.

"I'm done with this. Take me home." I laughed.

"Not until you answer my question," he challenged me.

"Yes, Tre."

"Yes what?"

"I'll be your friend but we not fuckin' no more. Now pinky promise that. And we will never speak of this." I held out my finger.

"A'ight cool then. We gone act like this never happened." He obliged but I could tell he was hoping I wasn't serious. I was though.

He stopped to get me lunch then dropped me off. We officially exchanged numbers and he promised to call me. When I walked in I spotted Kia and Simone sitting on the couch with grins on their faces.

"Well what the fuck was that?" Kia blurted out.

155

by **Santana**

"Can I get in the door, bitch? Damn!" I burst into laughter. I couldn't wait to tell my heaux story. I knew it would top all heaux stories.

"Bitch, spill the damn tea. What the hell is goin' on?" Kia hawkeyed me.

"Yeah, bitch I thought y'all ain't like each other?" Simone's nosy ass added.

"Yeah, it looks like y'all liked each other a lot just now." Kia egged it on.

"Girl, so let me tell y'all. This nigga damn near kidnaps me cuz I went to tell Rico about Silas lookin' for him and a shootout happened. He thought I had something to do with it so he made me go to his house and threatened me if I was involved, girl. He knew damn well I wasn't. So, we get to his house and I wasn't hardly fallin' for his bullshit. So, we argue back and forth and he kept makin' excuses for not callin' Rico to clear it up, and that's when I realized he was just tryna get me close to him." I rolled my eyes like I wasn't impressed.

"Then what happened?"

"Girl, I popped one of my pills." I blushed.

"Bitch, them sex pills?" Kia's eyes bugged out.

"Girl, they not sex pills." I burst out laughing. "They're anxiety pills and yes I did."

156

"So, what the fuck did you do?" Simone chimed in. I could tell these thirsty bitches wanted hot tea and I was finna fill their cups to the brim.

"Girl, I fucked him," I admitted boldly.

"*What*!?" they both exclaimed in unison.

"And sucked his dick." I smiled widely.

"Whatttt!?" they both asked again.

"Yes heauxs," I gloated.

"But you never suck no dick on the first night," Simone told me like I didn't know.

"Blame it on Molly." I shrugged.

"So, how was it?" Kia asked.

"Bitch, the best dick I done had in forever. That nigga fucked me all night!"

"Damnnnnn, I'm like hella happy for you." Kia hugged me and we all laughed out loud.

"Y'all are crazy, but I can't believe I let that shit go down. I wanted to disappear so bad but I had to play that role. Couldn't let no nigga see me sweat."

"So what, y'all cool now?" Simone asked.

"Yeah, we just friends and I told him we not fuckin' no more cuz friends don't fuck." I stuck my tongue out and shifted my eyes cuz I knew I was lying, but I wanted to test Tre and see if he was obedient and scared of m,e or if he was the aggressive nigga I hoped he was.

"This bitch too gangsta for me." Kia punched me in the arm lightly.

"Gotta play these heauxs right. Or get played." I shrugged.

CHAPTER SIX

Old Habits Never Die

TRE

I fucked up. Bigly. Jas may not have remembered all of what went down last night but I did, and the shit had my head gone and nose wide open. I wanted to text her as soon as she disappeared inside Kia's apartment and make sure her pussy was okay. I wanted to turn around and pick her up, get all her shit, and move her and her good pussy in with me. She was already on my mind heavy before we even had sex but now that I got it, man! She had a problem on her hands now.

I generally don't become this infatuated with no female and especially not over pussy, but this muhfucka here got me ready to do the most. I mean she's beautiful, gorgeous body, attitude stank, and she know how to fuck and suck dick. Liyah ain't got shit on Jas and even though I knew I was finna be on some foul shit by cutting her off, I had to. At least she got a house out of the deal. Now I just had to find a way to let her know we done. This shit could get very messy but it was for the best.

My phone ringing took me out of my lustful thoughts of Jas. It was Chase. He ended up having to reschedule our meeting this weekend and I was glad because I got a chance to hook up with my love.

"What's up, bro?" I answered.

"What's up. I'm in yo city, tryna meet up."

"Cool. Let me text you my address."

"A'ight." He hung up and I texted him my address as I pulled into the driveway.

He arrived in the next 20-minutes and rang my loud-ass doorbell. I made a mental note to rip that bitch out the socket later.

When I opened the door, I wanted to jump out of my fuckin' skin and dissolve into ashes. Lo and behold, my brother had brought the devil herself along for the trip. Something I hoped and prayed he wouldn't even think of doing. But there she was, as beautiful as I remembered, on my doorstep with a scowl. Miss Isabella Demichael.

"Well hello." I greeted them with a fake smile.

"Sup bro, long time." Chase dapped me.

"Tre," Isabella said with much attitude.

I stepped aside to let them enter. I immediately wished Liyah was here. I felt so embarrassed seeing her again. My surefire plan had failed. I lost the woman I wanted and she was

by Santana

finer than ever. I silently cursed myself as the feelings I thought were gone had resurfaced. My heart beat faster as she switched past me in her skintight one-piece shorts and huarache sneakers. They were holding hands and it made me sick.

They both took a seat on my couch and looked so happy and comfortable together.

"Y'all thirsty or hungry?" I asked them, trying to be hospitable instead of jealous.

"I'll take some water," Isabella said.

"Beer for me," Chase told me.

I went into my kitchen to grab them a drink and returned smiling, tryna play it off.

"So, what's up? I didn't know you were bringing trouble along." I laughed, teasing Isabella.

"Aye man, I didn't wanna come alone and she didn't wanna be left alone. So, it all worked out."

"How are you and Liyah doing?" Isabella asked being petty and ignorant as fuck, as usual.

"Very funny. I'm actually seeing someone else now," I countered.

"Good for you. Make sure she isn't with Marcus." Straight for the jugular.

"It's cool, Is. Chill out, a'ight?" Chase said to her. She was way outta line.

by Santana

"Damn, you just go for the kill huh?" I asked her. I didn't wanna get disrespectful and remind her that she had fucked three blood brothers so I just let it be.

"Man listen, I got some shit comin' in and I need you to take a third and move it."

"Cool. Who's the other third goin to?" I quizzed.

"Marcus."

"You think that's a good idea?"

"Yeah, bro good now. I got him together. He been workin' wit' me for a good minute and never came up short or been on bullshit," he reassured me. I ain't trust Marcus since I found out he was dippin' his nose in product.

"If you say so. You want it upfront or what?" I asked, referring to the money.

"Hell naw, you fam. I trust you. I'll have the shit tomorrow."

"Good shit."

We talked for a good thirty minutes before Chase had to take an emergency call. He went outside and closed the door, obviously not wanting us to hear.

It was awkward as hell sitting there with Isabella. She nervously looked around my living room.

"So how you been?" I broke the silence.

THE OTHER SIDE OF A THUG
SHE WAS A THUG'S WEAKNESS 2

by Santana

"I've been amazing, Tre. You know that. After you tried to ruin my life and it backfired. Remember?"

"Yeah but it was in your best interest. You ruined people's lives. You ain't need that money."

"I need anything good that's comin' to me. You have any idea what would've happened had I forfeited? My family is good thanks to me. My future family is good. How dare you try to fuck me over like that?" She was angry but I truly wanted to help her, and look who she wit'. My damn brother still. The nigga that murdered her pops.

"Yeah, well I'm happy for you. It's crazy how you lay with the man that killed your father though," I added hoping it would bother her.

"Shit happens and it was a misunderstanding. He was trying to help."

"So was I."

"No, you weren't. You wanted to see me lose so bad, but I won." She smirked.

"Lemme ask you something. You got anything to do wit' me getting' hit wit' a Fed case?"

"Do I look like I had something to do with that? I left all the bullshit at that damn meeting you tried to embarrass me at." I searched her eyes and body movements for any signs of lying but I didn't find anything. She was telling the truth.

"I find out anything, my brother gone have to bury you, baby," I warned her in all seriousness. Me being investigated was detrimental to everybody close to me.

"Have I ever lied to you?" Her seductive eyes connected with mine.

"Nah but..."

"So why are you still threatening me? You need to look elsewhere. I got all my revenge when I made you look stupid and kept fucking your brother." She squinted, looking at her freshly polished nails.

"Yeah? I know you miss this dick though. Now tell me I'm lyin' about that." I stepped close to her face.

Before she could lie, I grabbed her face and pressed my lips against hers. I knew it was wrong but damn, I couldn't help it.

Then Chase came back in and our little convo came to a halt.

"Aye I gotta go, niggas trippin'," he told me. Isabella stood to leave and I honestly didn't want her to.

"A'ight bro, catch you later." I let them out then locked my door.

Damn that was crazy but it was good to see her. The shit I had been through before I went to jail was mad wild. Isabella truly flipped a nigga life upside down but she wasn't responsible for the shit I was dealing with now. There was still no word on the investigation so I would just have to bide my time. Drew and Marcus had been working on this and if those two couldn't find anything, then I had an even bigger problem on my hands. This was a real case.

"Marky," I called when my brother picked up.

"Dog, what I keep tellin' you about that shit?"

"My bad. You found anything yet?" I quizzed.

"Nah. Daddy said this shit might be real. I mean we ran everybody down. It's not none of them. We about to start lookin' into agents and shit cuz I swear it ain't lookin' like it's nobody close."

I was happy to hear that it wasn't anyone in my camp. I would hate to have to off one of these niggas.

"Cool li'l bro. Then what I need to be doin' is getting' my lawyer on this police officer that planted the drugs. That shit just hella foul. I ain't know   they did shit like that in the D."

"Dirty cops gone be dirty, big fella."

"True. A'ight nigga, you stay low," I said and hung up.

Thank God. Now all I had to do was get this crooked cop handled and I was good. Or so I thought.

by Santana

KIA

I was getting dolled up for my date with Dro tonight. Simone flat-ironed my hair while Jas made snapchat videos and took pics. They both were so happy that I was dating someone now cuz I had been a complete wreck ever since me and Rico split from each other. Even though I tried to hide it, I was depressed. This date was exactly what I needed to de-stress.

I looked damn good in my teal sequined mini-skirt and matching half-top. I knew this was past the level of sexy Dro required of me but I wanted to give him more than what he asked for. I was feeling myself and couldn't wait for him to feel me too.

"Bitch you badddd!" Simone exclaimed when she finished fluffing my hair. I was pleased. I looked perfect.

I had on this 28-inch, jet black unit. I wanted to fuck myself, that's how fine I was.

"Goddamn!" I said as I applied my dark purple lipstick.

"Listen bitch, you gone have that man ready to give you that werk!" Jas yelled.

My phone then rang and it was Dro letting me know he was outside.

I had Simone open the door and let him in. He was lookin' drop dead fine in all white. He was too fuckin' crispy in

166

fitted Balmain jeans and a logo tee. He had flowers too. When I approached him for a hug, his scent made me weak. I didn't wanna let go.

"You a'ight?" he asked, noticing the hug was a little too long.

"Yes." I laughed. "These are my besties Jas and Simone."

"I met Jas. Nice to meet you again, and nice to meet you Simone." He shook both their hands.

"Nice to meet you too," they both said.

"Bring my friend back in one piece. I see you lookin' at that ass," Jas joked.

"Hell yeah, how you know?" he played along.

"Don't be tryna do it to her either," Simone added.

"Simoneeeee!" I burst out laughing. None of us had a filter but Simone was being wild right now.

"Don't worry, if I do, she'll love it," he reassured her.

I went to put the flowers in a vase. When I returned, he grabbed my hand, escorted me to his car and opened my door, like a gentleman.

We ended up everywhere. First, we went to an art exhibit. It was amazing. I couldn't believe how vast his knowledge was of art and artists. Especially the period pieces that were displayed. We went to eat, had too many drinks and talked for what seemed like an eternity. We capped off the night by taking a walk somewhere. I had no idea where we were cuz I was so drunk. All I knew was that the night air was warm and had me feeling so free.

"How you feelin' so far?" he asked as we stopped at a bench in the park.

"As far as?"

"Us, nigga. What you think?" He chuckled.

"I feel good. I mean you seem like a cool person."

"That's it? I just seem cool?" He smiled, knowing I was too drunk to really give him a good answer.

"I mean, I gotta get to know you more." I smiled shyly.

"So, you do wanna get to know a nigga huh?"

"Yes, Dro. I would like that. So far, you treat me good."

"And I always will. Soon as you let a nigga in."

"That's gonna take time though," I admitted.

"I know, baby. But I want you to be open to this. I really see us bein' the shit together. That is, if you allow it. I like you a lot. And I ain't gon' lie, I been wanting to snatch yo' ass up for a while."

"I like you too." And then he went there. He kissed me. And kissed the shit outta me too.

We sat there, lip locking for what seemed like hours. I wanted him to take me right there on the bench but he stopped and just looked into my eyes.

"You had yo eyes open, didn't you?"

"Yeah." I looked down.

"Means you ain't trust shit I said." He looked disappointed.

"It's gonna take time," I told him again. I could tell he was a bit impatient.

He could tell me a hundred times how good he was and how great he'd treat me but I had to see for myself, over time. Not after two dates.

"I see. But just promise me when I show you, you'll admit it and be grateful."

"No problem, babe."

He took my hand and helped my staggerin' ass back to the car. He dropped me back off in one piece and I was surprised he didn't try to fuck. I was pleased. We shared one more kiss before I went inside. It was late and Simone and Jas were sleep, so I would have to wait until the morning to give them the lowdown on this beautiful date I had. I plugged my phone up and went to shower.

After I finished my hour-long bath, I noticed I had a text. It was from Dro.

by *Santana*

*I had a great time with you. I hope I can see you again
soon. For some reason, I can't shake you.*

I was feeling the exact same way. Which was why most
of my time in the shower was spent masturbating to thoughts of
him. How I wished he had just taken it on that park bench, or
pulled over while driving and got it poppin'. Man, I couldn't
wait to tell my girls about this shit.

I enjoyed myself too, babe. Hope to see you again soon,
I responded then turned my phone on Do Not Disturb. I knew if
he texted me back I would be talking to him all night, furthering
the feelings I didn't want that were slowly creeping in.

The next morning, I smelled breakfast cooking. The
smell of bacon woke me right up. I went in the kitchen to find
Jas and Simone making a big spread for no reason.

"Morning sunshine!" Simone greeted me with a huge
smile.

"Good morning. What's the occasion?" I sat down.

"Nothin', we hungry." Jas laughed.

These bitches had eggs, bacon, bagels, oatmeal,
pancakes, ham and a fruit tray set out.

"You want coffee or juice?" Simone asked.

"Coffee."

"So, spill about this date. Were you a heaux like Jas?"

"Excuse me, bitch." Jas popped Simone on the arm as they both laughed.

"Well y'all, it was beautiful. We went to an art museum and shit. We ate and had drinks then we went for a walk in some park. He kissed me y'all. Like some movie type shit." I smiled widely remembering the sweet kiss we shared that made my night so wonderful.

"Aww shit." Simone squealed.

"That was it though. He noticed I had my eyes open when we kissed. He told me how right he was gonna treat me and I could tell he was disappointed that I didn't believe him."

"He can't expect you to just trust him though. Y'all just met," Jas added.

"Right. I told him to give me time. He has to consistently treat me right before I trust him. But he said he would and then he dropped me off. I had fun. I really like him so far." As much as I didn't want to get involved with another drug dealer, I was.

"Yeah take your time. You fall too fast, Ki," said Jas.

"I know and that's why I said that. I'm taking my time with this. I don't wanna be depressed again, I wish I was like you when it came to feelings."

"Girl!" Jas laughed. "I have feelings, I just control them instead of letting them control me." She shrugged.

by Santana

"I know and you so solid. Like girl, I was crying and throwing up when I found out Rico had another bitch." I snickered a little trying to not be so embarrassed.

"Girl, fuck Rico. He's gonna regret it sooner than later. Y'all going to his party in a few weeks?" Simone asked us.

"You know I'm in there." Jas danced around.

"Nope," I said, sipping my coffee.

"You jokin'?" Simone asked.

"*Nope*! I don't care no more. I'm over him," I lied.

"If you didn't care, you'd go," Jas added.

RICO

I was out on yet another shopping date with Mercedes and we still hadn't had sex. Something about this girl had me invested. That night I took her home with me from the strip club, we didn't even fuck. We ate and talked until we fell asleep. I mean, I been wanted to hit but something always came up to where one of us had to go. For her, it was family emergencies or work and for me, it was drug shit. Today was gonna be the day though. I had taken her ass shopping, got her hair and nails done, and rented out a suite. I even had that shit decorated with flowers and shit and had champagne waiting for us after we finished riding around Birmingham and Royal Oak.

"Am I making you happy spoiled-ass princess?" I asked her as I put her thousand bags in the hatch of my truck.

"Yesss." She purred as she slid her thick ass into the passenger seat.

"I got a surprise for you but I wanna make sure you available and not gone dip off on me today."

"I'm here, aren't I?" She rolled her big eyes at me.

"Well yeah, for now. But you know how you are. Do me a favor and turn yo phone off or something. I want you to myself."

"Fine." She did as I asked.

by Santana

After driving for almost 5 hours, she had fallen asleep and we had arrived at our destination. I decided to take her to Sybaris. Now usually I would book a trip somewhere we had to fly but I hadn't had the time to plan and Chicago was close enough to drive on a whim. I loved driving so I had no problem randomly going.

"Wake up, sleepyhead." I tapped her after coming from the front desk check-in to get our key.

"Where are we?" She was groggy and confused.

"We here. Now come on." I went to the back and grabbed our bags, then I let us inside our suite.

It was the shit. The rose petals were there, the champagne was set out, lights were dimmed and it was about to be a lovely night.

"Aww baby, this is so sweet of you!" She smiled and jumped into my arms.

"It was the least I could do last minute. Since I can never have you for more than a few hours, I decided that I should think small."

"Nigga, don't think small with me." She rolled her eyes and went to sit down on the plush, king-sized bed.

"Just get ready for this lit-ass night we finna have. We got dinner reservations in two hours. Get dressed," I told her and sat her bags down.

by Santana

"Sí papí." she purred before rummaging through the bags I bought her to find something to wear.

An hour later, Mercedes emerged from the bathroom lookin heavenly. She wore a light-pink romper and some sexy ass strappy heels. Her hair hung down to her waist and whatever makeup she had put on was flawless. I was ready to say fuck that dinner cuz she was what I wanted to eat right now.

"Shit you look good, baby." I admired her lickin' my lips while she pranced around.

"Thank you. I love this outfit on me."

"I'm gon' love it when it's off later too," I reminded her.

We left the hotel and made it to our destination with thirty minutes to spare so we smoked a blunt before goin' in. She was so high I had to help her walk. The whole night she laughed at everything and I realized I was feelin' the fuck outta shorty. I couldn't believe how well we got along and how much she reminded me of Kia. I hated it cuz it made me feel like shit for treating her so badly. But I also loved it cuz I truly had feelins' for that girl and felt like I had a piece of her when I was with Mercedes.

"So, Miss Mercedes, why'd you move to Detroit? People usually don't move here."

"I haven't moved yet, just trying it out. I wanted a change of scenery and I do have a sister that lives here. I thought I told you that. I don't really get to see her much though. I saw her once at the club you had me dance at. I don't even have her number."

"Oh word?"

"Yeah, I couldn't believe her ass was in there dancing like that. Li'l sis gave me a run for my money." She giggled.

"She danced that night?" I quizzed. I was hella interested in who her sister was and why I was just now finding out she had family here.

"Yeah my sister, Kia. Light-skinned wit the big butt. She kinda looks like me only lighter."

And my fuckin' heart dropped. I suddenly felt weak. I know I didn't just hear what I thought I heard.

"Kia is your sister?" I asked, still confused.

"Yeah, you know her?"

"Yeah we met before. I know her from my circle and of course cuz she danced at my club." I lied my ass off. I had no idea why I was lyin' to her, it just happened.

"Oh okay. You can't see the resemblance?" She smiled and cocked her head so I could get a better look at her.

"More than you know."

I didn't know how to feel at that point. Everything was a drag from that moment on. My high was blown and my night was over. I felt bad but for some reason, I still wanted to fuck

Mercedes. I didn't know what would come of this but I wondered how I was supposed to ever get Kia back after this.

After dinner, we went back to the room and went for a swim. I was quiet and aloof for most of the night because my thoughts of Kia flooded my mind heavy. I wanted my baby back at some point, and I honestly didn't know how she'd feel about me dealing with her sister and especially on this level. I also couldn't lie or keep them apart so she would find out eventually.

"You okay, Ric?" Mercedes snapped me outta my thoughts.

She was lookin' righteous in the little ass two-piece bikini she was wearing.

"Yeah, I'm good shorty, just thinkin'."

"About what, baby?" She threw her arms around me and looked in my eyes. She was so sexy and perfect.

"About all this shit I got comin' up when I get back. You know a nigga birthday party in a couple weeks."

"Cancer season!" she cheered.

We both were Cancers. I think that's why we got along so well. Mercedes was a great listener and she was down-to-earth and easy going. For some reason, I felt like I could trust her. Like she just wanted to be there for a nigga. And for everything I admired in Mercedes, I felt even worse cuz Kia was the same way. It was fucked up to be able to acknowledge all these good traits in a new chick that I took for granted in the one that had been there.

"Yeah, I gotta see how I'm gonna outdo myself from last year. We was too lit." I thought back on how we went to Dubai, had a fuckin' orgy, and almost got locked up.

After the swim, we both laid down, drunk as hell, sprawled across the huge bed. I didn't even know how to initiate sex with her. I was hoping she'd just fall asleep. So, I lay there pretending to be sleep, silently praying I'd hear snoring soon.

"Thought you was gone hit this?" She spoke softly into my ear. Damn man.

"Go to sleep, Cedes."

"Why?" She punched me in the back softly.

"Cuz we both drunk and tired."

"Wait, you drive five hours and get this honeymoon-ass suite and we not gone fuck? Okay, cool Rico." Then she turned over and left me alone.

The next morning, she didn't even look at me. She was up, dressed and ready to go. I followed suit. The car ride was unnecessarily silent. I wanted to say something so bad but I couldn't. I would have to either lie some more or tell the fucked-up truth so I decided to leave it alone.

When I pulled up to her house, she jumped out so fast it irritated me. She didn't even take the things I bought her. She left that shit and damn near ran into her house. *Shit!* I silently cursed myself. It was over between us. It was apparent the next week when I tried calling and texting her. I was blocked, blizzocked! She was done wit' my ass.

I had other things that I focused my attention on, though. I had a party to plan so I looked into renting a mansion with a pool and jacuzzi. The one I found was massive and I booked it immediately. I called my event planner and caterer to get it crackin' cuz I was bringing 27 in wit' a bang. Once everything was set, I sent out invites. The hardest thing would be getting Kia to show up but I knew my girl Jas would somehow convince her to come.

"Jazzyyyy," I spoke into the phone when she picked up.

"Yes, brother."

"You know my birthday comin' up and I know you'll be there, but are you bringing Kia?" I cut straight to the chase.

"Yeah I'm in that thang but you know Kia is not comin' nowhere near you." She laughed like some shit was funny. My feelings were lowkey hurt.

"I mean, I know but that's why I need you to convince her to come. I can handle the rest from there."

by *Santana*

"Ricooo, no. I'm not setting my best friend up for failure wit' yo' ass again. You know she onto you and yo new bitch you been fuckin' wit'."

"I ain't fuckin' wit' nobody so I don't know where she got that shit from. Look, I'm ready to act right. Just get her here and I promise we gone be good."

"Yeah, ok. We'll see. What do I get out of the deal?"

"I would invite you to a threesome but Tre wouldn't approve of that shit." I burst into laughter.

"What the fuck you mean?"

"Nothin, baby. I just know boy feelin' the fuck outta you. That's all."

"Well, I'll see what I can do. I want some money. I need some new swimsuits and shit."

"Sis, you know I got you. I got a couple stacks for you."

"Good. Send that shit through PayPal. I gotta go," she said and hung up.

I knew fasho' Kia was gone be at party now. Jas always got her way with Kia, and so did I.

by Santana

CHAPTER SEVEN

Party, Party, Party, Let's All Get Wasted

JASMINE

I was amped about Rico's party but I knew I was gonna have to do some serious begging to get Kia there. She was so wrapped up into this Dro nigga that she, for once, wasn't thinkin about Rico at all. Somehow, I had to convince her to go so I threw on my pouty face as I entered the living room where she sat flicking through television channels.

"Kiaaaaa," I sang as I approached her.

"Yes, Jasmine." She smiled back.

"So, you decided if you were going to Rico's party or not?"

"No, I'm not going, you know that." She rolled her big eyes.

"Why?"

"Why should I? Rico got a bitch, fuck I look like showin' up somewhere and he got some hoe on his arm?"

"Well he wants you to come, Ki. He misses you. And he said he's not dealing with anyone." I buttered her up, hoping she would cave soon cuz I couldn't defend Rico's triflin' ass too much longer.

"Well he gon' have to miss me."

"Go for me then. I don't wanna go by myself. Pleaseeeeee?" I begged her.

"Jas, please don't."

"Kiiiii, please do. I need you. I'll make sure Rico is on his best behavior. You owe me anyway. Several favors."

"Bitchhhhh." She pouted. She knew she owed me.

"Yes bitch, so you comin' and that's that." I smiled, feeling victorious.

"Why you don't just go with Simone?"

"You know Simone been on that weird shit lately. And you know I need my other baddie wit' me." I hyped her up. She loved it.

"Girl, gone." She laughed.

"Yasssss bitch, you know we gone be fine. Finer than all them raggedy hoes there. I can't stunt without light-skin twin."

"Okay bitch, but keep that nigga the fuck from 'round me."

"I promise."

After our little conversation, Kia sashayed her ass to the back and emerged a couple hours later looking like a Balmain model. I didn't know where she was going but by the looks of it, it was probably somewhere with Dro. He had been on her heavy lately and I barely saw her because of him. I was starting to get jealous. I loved hanging with my girl and he kept stealing her away every chance he got.

Tre and I had been talking and texting a lot but he was out of town and wouldn't be back 'til Rico's party. I couldn't lie, a piece of me missed him. I replayed that night we got a little too intimate over and over in my head and it made me want him in the worst way. I knew it was wrong and it also wasn't happening again. We both made a promise. I was on a mission and so far, I was the one losing.

"Have fun, boo." I waved Kia off as she waltzed out of the door with Dro. I was happy for her, but mad still.

KIA

Dro was taking me out again and I had no idea where we were going. He said it was a surprise. He was impulsive and liked to spend. I liked that shit a whole lot. He took me shopping and always had some type of expensive gift and flowers every time. Not once did he ask me to "chill" or for me to "pull up on him." With Dro, we were always somewhere with some live entertainment, food, or some hands-on activity I was usually overdressed for. I couldn't lose with him. He was such an upgrade from Rico, although they both were paid. Over the two months we had been dating, there had been no drama at all.

We ended up everywhere once again. I loved his spontaneity. It kept me interested. We had just left Ruth Chris and I was stuffed. We hit up "Painting with a twist" next and it was damn near erotic to watch Dro use his artistic side to create a picture of me. He had told me it was a hobby, but from the precision of his brush strokes and his knowledge of art, it had me thinking it was his dream before he became a dope dealer. Everything about him was sexy, the way he focused on his work but still stole glances at me every so often. His smile was infectious. He was funny. I mean, how could a girl not like him?

"You never told me why you were single, Dro." I looked at him inquisitively.

by Santana

"I never told you I was." He smirked.

"So, are you, or aren't you?" My brow was now raised.

"No Kia, but soon."

"No? What the fuck you mean no? Why are we dating and all this and you got a girl?" I stepped back. I was offended as hell right now.

"Cuz man, I needed you in my life. I had to have you but I'm workin' on ending my current situation." He tried to calm me.

"But you got a bitch?" I scratched my head and dropped my paintbrush. I was ready to go.

"I don't care. I want you," he insisted.

"Why, so you can drop me when you find the next bitch you wanna pursue?"

"Listen, it's not like that. I swear, Ki."

"Then what's it like? Enlighten me."

"It's over between me and her but she just don't know it yet. Bitch been stealing from me so she gotta go. Simple as that." He shrugged.

"And that's supposed to make it better? Dro, take me home!"

"Ki, baby listen…"

"*NOW!*"

by *Santana*

I walked off toward the exit and to his car. He followed close behind mumbling something under his breath as he opened my door, still being the gentleman he had always been.

The car ride was quiet. So quiet I dosed off for a second and when I woke up, we weren't at my house. We were at some nice-ass condo in Utica.

"Where are we? I wanted to go home." He ignored me and go out to open my door.

He grabbed my things from the backseat. He told me he wanted me to spend the night so I brought my overnight bag, but it was over for that. I wanted to go home now.

I reluctantly followed him to the door.

"You didn't hear me, I said I wanted to go home." I tapped his shoulder but he still ignored me.

"*DRO!*" I called as he opened the locks and stepped aside to let me in.

Still nothing. So, I stood there and didn't move. I heard him huff. Then he grabbed me from the back and physically carried me inside.

"Are you deaf now? I said I wanna go. I don't wanna be here with yo lyin' ass!" I raised my voice.

He slipped off his shoes like I wasn't talkin' at all. I was getting so upset. I got sick of it so I went and mushed his ass. That would get his attention.

THE OTHER SIDE OF A THUG
SHE WAS A THUG'S WEAKNESS 2
by Santana

"Take me the fuck home!" I yelled as I struck him in the
side of his face.

"Don't put yo hands on me," he warned me. I took heed.
he had the look of death in his eyes.

"Well, take me home then." I folded my arms, and
plopped down next to him.

He continued watching TV like I wasn't talking to him.
I really could not stand the sight of him right then so I excused
myself to the bathroom and called an Uber. I used location on
my phone to get the address here and stayed put 'til my ride
came. Once my Uber driver notified me of his arrival, I exited
the bathroom, grabbed my bag and walked right the hell out of
his front door.

In an effort not to look pressed, Dro finally came to the
door but it was too late. I was out and blocking his number
simultaneously. How dare he barge into my life, treat me like I
meant something to him and then pull some shit like this? I
wasn't one of these thirsty-for-a-man-ass bitches. I didn't want
no nigga that already had a bitch, no matter what the
circumstance.

I arrived home about thirty-minutes later and I was
exhausted but happy that I hadn't let myself fall for Dro. All
that sweet talk, nice dates, and gifts he bought didn't mean shit.

I was keeping them though. I let myself in and found Jas and Simone watching Love and Hip-Hop reruns.

"What's wrong, boo?" Jas asked once she saw me in a fret.

"Girl. You will not believe this shit. Why this bitch-ass nigga got a girlfriend?" Their mouths hung open when I spilled that tea.

"Noooo, what the hell is his problem?" Simone guffawed.

"Girl I don't know, but he swears he leaving her cuz she steals from him. I don't give a fuck what's goin on, you will *NOT* have a bitch and have me on the side. I wasn't raised like that." I was ready to cry.

Dro was like a fuckin' dream come true. He was attentive, he cared, he took me out, spoiled me, and didn't pressure me for sex or anything. Why the nigga have to have a girlfriend? That shit burned me! I wanted to scream. I trudged to my room and closed the door. I was over this whole night.

JASMINE

I had taken the girls with me on an impromptu shopping trip. We were getting new swimsuits and heels for Rico's party. I wanted us to be *thee* baddest bitches there so I took them to a boutique to get some custom-made swimwear. We were about to shut shit down later at the party.

"Y'all like or y'all love?" I swooned as we walked into the boutique I liked to call the Candy Shop because everything was covered in stones and glitter.

"Bitch I am head over!" Kia squealed as she laid eyes on the pieces on display.

"Why have I never heard of this place?" Simone questioned.

"It's new, now hurry up and pick out something cuz we have appointments with Genie." I referred to my stylist Carmen. She had made us some new frontal wigs and I was excited for my girls to see what I had for them. Carmen the Hair Genie was *thee* best stylist in Detroit.

"Okay, I see you spoiling us today." Kia smiled.

"It was the least I could do. Aren't you happy you decided to come, you would've missed out."

We picked out our pieces and the cashier rang us up. After we left we went straight to the Genie and she had our units ready. She quickly braided us up, sewed the wigs on and we were off to makeup. We looked like an unknown clique of bad bitches. I had this wavy, long black hair that was down to my ass. Kia had blonde and black, Indian silky that stopped at the small of her back and Simone had this bright red frontal wig which she wore in a high ponytail. She looked amazing in it too. Our makeup was on fleek as usual.

We had gone to sit down for lunch until it was time to get ready for the party. After lunch we went home, showered and got into our swimsuits. I had on this sheer silver number that was encrusted with Swarovski crystals all over. I was a walking diamond. My nails and toes matched. I also wore a pair on simple crystal studded heels with a thick ankle strap. Simone had on her signature black but with all the spikes and rhinestone embellishments, she looked like a thick-ass Rockstar. Kia wore this aqua one-piece that was sure to turn heads. It was cut low and stoned out with multicolored, iridescent rhinestones. I couldn't help but stare at my girls. They looked like something out of a magazine called "over-the-top". I snapped so many pics I just knew my phone would tell me I was out of memory.

We jumped into Simone's Porsche and hit the road to the address Rico gave me for his party. When we arrived, our mouths fell open. The mansion was huge. It was one of the most beautiful places I'd ever seen. Exotic cars lined the streets so I

by $\mathcal{S}antana$

knew niggas with money were there. We pulled into the driveway because we were special guests and were not about to walk like the rest of these birds. We found a spot and hopped out. We were looking so fine we didn't need the once over.

When we stepped into the back where the party was taking place, all eyes fell on us. We were fashionably late and demanded the attention of everyone in attendance. We spotted Rico and Tre talking by the pool and walked over to interrupt.

"Happy birthdayyyyy!" Simone and I said in unison. Kia just stood there with an attitude.

"Oh shit, thanks ladies." He gave us a big hug. He was nothing but smiles. "Thank you. I love you so much," Rico whispered in my ear.

"You're welcome," I mouthed back as we parted.

Tre was standing there with a smirk, lookin' fine as fuck. He didn't speak though, he just stared.

"Can't speak?" I frowned at him.

"Hello, Jasmine." He waved then looked down at his phone. I walked off. I could feel him tryna act funny and I wasn't in the mood. Kia and Simone followed.

"What's yo' problem?" Kia asked.

"Did you see how Tre spoke to me? Like he barely knew me."

"Well he does barely know you," Simone added.

"That's so not the point. No hug or nothin'. Exactly why I knew I should have kept my legs closed." I found the bar and ordered a few rounds of drinks. I needed something to calm my nerves.

After copious amounts of liquor, I was lit and had dropped my cover-up to my swimsuit. I turned around and like clockwork, niggas were gawking. I strolled around the party and grabbed a couple baddies and started dancing. They had Migos' Culture album bangin' and my favorite cut "Deadz" came on. "*You niggas in trouble, you niggas in trouble!*" I yelled and I hit the dab as the chorus came in." *Uhh ooh, fresh out da bed, uhh ooh, count up da deadz*!" Niggas were lined up tryna push up on this ass.

I had the party turnt as usual. My drunk ass had finally forgotten about Tre and the shady ass, "Hello Jasmine" he hit me with earlier. I was in my own little world as I bounced my ass up on this other dude who was paying me the attention I wanted. I caught Tre's eye and he didn't look happy. He chewed on the inside of his jaw as he gave me the death stare. Finally, my feet had gotten tired and I went to have a seat with Kia and Simone. Rico sauntered his way over with Tre and that's when all hell broke loose.

"You can't tell a nigga happy birthday, Kia? Damn." He smiled, tryna play the victim role. "That muhfucka know she evil." Rico chuckled, turning to me.

"Can you blame her, Ric?" I asked him like he didn't know how shady he was.

"Hush it, Jas." He put a blunt to his lips and lit it.

"Let up on my man's, Jas. Damn, let 'eem live," Tre interjected as he took the blunt from Rico.

"Nigga, I was not addressing you, stay over there." I cut into him. *Now* he could talk.

"Your friend got a nasty mouth," Tre said to the girls.

They laughed like two ditzy school girls instead of defending me. I couldn't wait to get them in the car and give them a piece of my mind. I was trying so hard not to show my other side but he was pushing it. I was irritated with him and his nonchalant demeanor as if I hadn't put this golden pussy on him so viciously a few weeks ago.

"Bitch please," I mumbled under my breath.

"Baby *too* disrespectful." Tre chuckled.

Rico interjected and suggested we all calm down and try to enjoy the evening. I really wasn't trying to ruin his party but the tension was thick between Tre and I, and not to mention Rico and Kia. Rico sat next to her and her smile instantly turned to a frown. He went as far as to put his arm around her. It was about to be lights out for him because I could tell Kia was about to rip him apart.

"Nigga, don't let your birthday excitement get you fucked up," Kia spat harshly.

"Yo, let me talk to you in private please?" he said calmly. Rico had a nasty temper and it was about to flare. It was finna be fireworks in this bitch!

"Anything you have to say to me, you can keep that shit to yourself." She eyed me and I pretended not to see her. She told me to keep him away from her but it was over.

Rico abruptly got up from the table and stood next to Kia.

"Are you gon' get up yourself or do I have to *get* you up?"

"Nigga, beat it!" She blew him off and before she could turn her head, he snatched her up and put her over his shoulder.

Halfway into the house, he put her down and she fought to get away. Rico overpowered her and successfully got her inside. No one was there to stop anything so he was about to have his way with her. I was happy for my girl. She needed some dick anyway. She was always so uptight. I sank deeper into my chair and smirked at the thought of her getting fucked by Rico. That was certainly not what she came for. But she came.

RICO

"Nigga, don't let your birthday excitement get you fucked up," was all I heard before I snapped.

After that, my aggression took over as I picked her up and carried her into the house. She tried to fight but deep down I knew she didn't want to leave. I saw the look in her eyes. She was hurt but I knew she still had love for a nigga. I pushed her against the wall and looked into her eyes.

"You can't even talk to me, Ki?" I pleaded with her.

"Rico, get off me. I don't have nothin' to say," she said still puttin' on a show. Quite frankly, I was over the theatrics.

I kissed her passionately and ran my hands through her hair. I grabbed her face and looked her in the eyes. It was still there. She still wanted me.

"You don't love me no more, Kia?"

"Rico, please don't do this," she said trying to hide the emotions that still made their way out.

"You don't love a nigga no more? Who got you feelin like that? Who you been fuckin huh?" I asked angrily, my nostrils flaring for added effect.

I slipped my fingers in her already wet pussy and started to pound her spot until she was too gone to stop me. I looked into her eyes and tried to stay calm but her tight, drippin' wet pussy was gettin' a nigga riled up.

"Nobody. Please stop, Rico," she whimpered.

"I said, do you still love me?"

I pulled her bikini top off and sucked on her nipples like I used to and it drove her crazy. She moaned loudly and bit her lip as I licked and sucked on each nipple. I teased her with my tongue and fingers and I loved how her body was responding.

I lay her down on my bed and slipped out of my Polo swimming trunks. I positioned myself on top of her and rubbed my meat all over her clit, which always drove her freak-ass crazy. I entered her slowly and gently. I wanted her to feel every inch of me. I wanted her to remember how I put it down. I could tell she was overwhelmed by the tears that were forming in her eyes. You know how that "I miss you" sex be. All these feelings come rushing back. Shit be all sentimental and what not. I was tryin to be the tough guy though but boy I tell you, that pussy was wetter and tighter than I remember. If I tried anything too slick, I was gone bust so fast.

Kia's emotional ass didn't know if she was comin' or goin'. I had her smiling and frowning and trying to hide her face. I threw the pillows off the bed. I wanted to see everything, her whole range of emotions. I put her legs over my shoulders so I could really hit that spot.

THE OTHER SIDE OF A THUG
SHE WAS A THUG'S WEAKNESS 2

by Santana

"It feel good don't it? You miss that?" I asked as I punished her pussy.

"Oooh God yes Rico!" she cried out unable to hold back anymore.

Once I started strokin' her long and slow, it was a wrap. Shorty held me so tight, it felt like we never left. I had her pinned down givin' her all of me. She moaned loudly and dug her nails into my back. She was fuckin' me like she hated me, which she had every reason to.

"Ricooooo!" she yelled as she orgasmed again.

I always had her cummin' back to back. She loved my pound game. I fucked her so hard I felt all her wetness dripping down my legs. I pulled her hair as I fucked her doggy style. I talked all types of shit in her ear as I was poundin' her guts.

"This my pussy, bitch. You better know that," I drilled her.

"Ohhh God, baby yessss!" I fucked her like a dog.

"Tell me this my pussy. I wanna hear it".

"Ricooo!" she begged. She wasn't ready to give in.

"Tell me what I wanna hear!" I demanded, smackin' her ass with all my strength.

"Ohhhh Goddddd!" she screamed. I went harder to show her I wasn't playin.

"It's yours, Rico, it's yours. I swear," she cried.

"That's my bitch, you still my bitch, Kia," I reassured her.

She was grippin' the sheets and bitin' the pillow while I was tearin' that ass up. Kia knew she couldn't resist me. That's why she tried to stay away. I guess it was the charm.

"Now I'll ask you again, you still love me, Ki?" I started to pound her harder to get the truth. I could feel her pussy start to contract and I knew she was about to cum again.

"I hate you," she moaned, trying to hold back tears. I knew what that usually meant but she sounded so sincere.

"Say you love me!" I demanded. I slowed down so I could control her next orgasm.

"Rico please, I'm finna cum!" she screamed.

I stopped stroking her completely.

"What you doin'?" she asked puzzled and frustrated.

"I said tell me you love me."

"Rico, please don't do this."

"Say it before I pull out!" I threatened. I started to fuck her again and as soon as her orgasm started to build, I asked her did she love me.

"You wanna cum don't you?"

"Yes Rico! Please don't stop!" she pleaded.

"Well tell me what I wanna hear. Tell me you love me, Ki!" I barked as I fucked her so hard she was crying.

by Santana

"I love you, Rico. I still love you!" she cried out as her orgasm ripped through her.

I exploded inside her so hard I saw stars. We collapsed on the bed and lay there until we could breathe again. I grabbed her face and gently kissed her. She lay her head on my chest and whimpered softly until she fell asleep. I knew she was disappointed in herself. She came here with every intention of ignoring me but she ended up getting fucked by the nigga she hated. *Way to go Kia, way to go.* I laughed in my head. Some things never change and she was one of them. I knew I could have her under my thumb, but as I got older I didn't even want to play her like that. I realized she really had love for me. *What to do, what to do?* I sparked an L and lay back with my baby. I was happy to have her in my grip again, even if just for the night...

TRE

I could tell Jas was fuming cuz of the way I was acting, but she had to learn that if she wanted to give a nigga some pussy like that, then wanna play that "this never happened" role, then that's exactly how I would play it. She ain't want nobody to know so cool, *nobody* would know. I couldn't help but feel awkward sitting there wit' her and her friend, Simone who I knew, knew. They kept making faces and smilin' and shit. I wasn't stupid. She had most definitely told her and Kia about this dick. I knew fasho' when Simone got up and left us alone.

Jas kept her head down, pretending to be in her phone, so I broke the silence.

"You still on that funny shit or you ready to act like you know me?"

"I'm not the one who couldn't speak a couple hours ago." She frowned.

"I'm talkin' about period, Jasmine. You ready to be my friend or you gone keep actin' stupid over some fuckin' dick that you know you needed?" I cut into her ass.

Every time we spoke and I mentioned that night, she abruptly ended the conversation. I was tired of her tryna act like this dick ain't have her in tears. Her tough ass was finna get cut into something serious.

by Santana

"Tre calm down, damn! Stop bein' so loud."

"Yo everybodyyyyy, I fucked Jas and she loved it!" I blurted out loudly and Kalief and Quentin's heads turned in our direction from the other table.

"Why the fuck!?" She stood up and walked off angrily.

"Jas, stop fuckin' playin wit' me!" I ran behind her and grabbed her before she got to wherever she was headed.

"Why would you say that out loud?" She gritted her teeth.

"You act like you embarrassed! Do you know who the fuck I am? You should be proud."

"I don't. And I don't care."

"You comin' wit' me. We need to talk somewhere where you not so scared. Where them pills at you be poppin'? You tense as fuck, Ma." I grabbed her arm as she continued to pull away.

"Let me at least give Simone these keys."

Once she came back, we walked to my truck and pulled off. I was going back to Kia's to get her some clothes cuz she was staying with me for a few days, whether she wanted to or not. Then my phone started ringing so I quickly answered it, not knowing who it was.

"What's up?"

It was Liyah.

"Tre, I need you, please." Her voice was low, almost a whisper.

"What's wrong?"

"I'm in the hospital. Receiving. Please come."

"Shit, a'ight. I'm on the way." I hung up the phone and dropped Jas back off at the party. A nigga was pissed but Liyah was in the hospital and I needed to see if she was alright. Even though we weren't on that tip no more, I still wanted to make sure she was good. It's no telling what was up with her.

I sped to Receiving hospital, signed in at the emergency desk and they let me walk back. She was laid up in the bed, eyes barely open, lookin' sick as hell.

"What happened to you Aaliyah? Did Chase do this?" I really hoped my brother wasn't the reason why Liyah was in this hospital bed again.

"Tre, why haven't you called me? Why haven't I seen you? It's been weeks." She mustered up some tears.

"I told you, I've been busy. Now tell me what happened."

"You really wanna know?"

"Liyah, stop playin' games." I was getting angry and she knew not to keep pushin' it.

"I-I tried to kill myself," she admitted, looking down foolishly at the armband on her wrist.

"What? Why?" I asked, perplexed. I had no clue she was suicidal.

"You."

"Me? What the fuck for?"

"You abandoned me, Tre. You all I got, all I wanted, and you just leave me all of a sudden? Who is she?"

"Mind yo business, Liyah." I warned.

"Who the fuck is she!?" she screamed at the top of her lungs.

"Listen to me, don't fuckin' worry about it. Nothin' I do got shit to do with Aaliyah Greene."

"Aaliyah Carter."

"What, girl?"

"I wanna be your wife, Tre."

"You buggin a'ight? I came here to see if you were good but you on some other shit. I ain't hardly tryna hear it."

"Why? Cuz you in love with some other bitch? Who the fuck is she?" She tried getting up from the bed but whatever she had done to herself had taken the strength that she needed to get up.

"Liyah chill, okay?" I couldn't lie, I felt like shit for doin' her so foul.

We were good before I met Jas. Liyah had never done anything wrong to me. I just up and left her for another woman.

THE OTHER SIDE OF A THUG
SHE WAS A THUG'S WEAKNESS 2
by Santana

A woman that couldn't even admit that we fucked and she loved it. See, Liyah wanted and needed me, and I loved to feel needed. Jas acted like she ain't give a fuck either way. She claimed she was into this friend shit but she ain't seem interested most of the time. It felt like I was chasing her, and I have no problem chasing but the bitch ain't wanna be caught. She just kept runnin' from a nigga. After she fronted on me at the party, I was pissed and the savage was gone show his head, but then Liyah called. I was gone fuck Jas and drop her off and ignore her. Now I think I'll just ignore her ass for a while for a bitch that actually acted like she wanted to fuck wit' me.

"Tre, stay with me please. I'm scared," She cried.

I did. I stayed with her all night. When Jas text me to ask what happened, I told that bitch I was with my girl. Checkmate.

*****

The next morning, I went home after telling Liyah we were gonna work things out. I pulled into my driveway, parked and hopped out. As I entered my crib, I noticed the door was unlocked. I grabbed my gun and proceeded inside. I looked in every room and nothing was out of place. After that, I went into my safe. That bitch had been cracked.

by Santana

"Fuck!!!" I yelled as I realized my money and drugs were missing.

"A fuckin' mill!" I shouted as I plopped down on my bed.

Whoever did this didn't know my code so they blew the bitch open instead. My closet smelled like a housefire.

I pulled out my phone and dialed Rico. He was the one that had the safe installed.

"Yo nigga, you got something you wanna get off yo chest?" I yelled into the receiver.

"What nigga?"

"You wanna tell me why I came home and my safe is blown to pieces?"

"Wait, you think I robbed you? First off, I had a whole-ass party last night. You forgot that?"

Shit, he was right.

"Cool nigga. My bad." I was still fuming though.

"So, somebody blew yo shit though? You ain't install cameras in that bitch yet?"

"Naw, I ain't had the chance."

"But you think I would be the nigga to steal from you though?"

"Nah, but you got me the house."

"So? You think I'm the nigga that got you the case too huh? Lay it all out now muhfucka."

"Nah Ric, but damn, who the fuck else would know about my safe? Ain't nobody been to this bitch."

"How you know? You forget what the fuck we do for a livin'? Niggas always watchin'."

"Look dog, I apologize. I been real shifty after that prison shit."

"Don't let it happen again, nigga. I'm on my way wit' the team."

"You got it." I ended the call.

I knew my nigga but shit, it was crazy that somebody broke my safe. He got me this house. Something inside me knew it wasn't him but I needed him to tell me. That money was about to get washed and now it was gone, a whole million and half-a-million in dope. I had to call Chase and tell him what had happened. I sat there for over twenty minutes before I finally dialed him.

"Bro, niggas done hit the safe."

"What!?"

"Hell yeah and they got the dope bro."

"*Fuck!* How much?"

"Half. The other half already got off." Thank God cuz that woulda been two million I had to recover.

"Shit, a'ight. Any idea who?"

"Man, hell nah but I'm tryna find out now. I'm finna ask these nosy-ass neighbors of mine. They were so interested when I first got here, I know they prolly been watchin' my house."

"Yeah do dat, we gotta find out who's doin' this shit cuz they fuckin' wit' the whole organization."

"Who you tellin'? Whoever it is don't wanna live long at all."

"Damn right."

After I ended the call with Chase, I sat there in a ball of anger, paralyzed with rage. Now I was down a million-five and would have to hit my personal stash to replace what was missing. First somebody tries to get me locked up, now somebody done violated and came to where I lay my head? I was about to do my own investigation into this shit, and everybody was a suspect now.

CHAPTER EIGHT

A Storm is Coming

CHASE

I sat there after disconnecting the call with Tre. I thought long and hard about who could've been behind this shit. Niggas done stole *my* work so now I was a part of this whether I wanted to be or not.

"Isabella, come here."

"Yes Chase?" She popped her head out from the kitchen.

"You sure you ain't got shit against my brother?"

"I know you not starting this again." She rolled her eyes to the ceiling.

"Can't hurt to ask."

"It can. You're hurting our relationship because I feel like you don't really trust me. I am done with all of that and I'm not thinkin' about anybody but you. I got the man back that I wanted. Anybody else was just collateral damage."

"And you don't feel no type of way toward Tre for how he embarrassed you?"

"Baby how do you embarrass a millionaire exactly?" She played around with the huge diamond-encrusted ring she bought for herself.

"I feel that." I laughed.

"How do you embarrass a bitch that had three brothers in love at the same time?"

"I wouldn't say all that. Tre was in it to get back at you."

"If you think that nigga never loved me, you stupid. If you think he doesn't *still* have feelings for me, you crazy."

"Well why you wit' me then? Since you got all these niggas that love you and shit."

"Aww shit. Here this nigga go. First, you're constantly accusing me of setting your stupid-ass brother up, who deserves it by the way, now you're suggesting I go be with one of them because of the feelings they had for *me*? Make it make sense bae."

"I'm just sayin', since you boastin' and braggin' about the shit go suck one of they dicks then." I ain't like that shit at all.

"Bye dumbass." She left me sitting there salty and stupid.

"I'm serious, Isabella. Some of my shit came up missing and now I'm affected by all of this."

by Santana

"You the only man I know that's dumb enough to do some shit like that." She laughed then went back to cooking.

"I'm not done talkin' to you. Get yo ass back in here and don't walk off again 'til I'm finished," I demanded.

"Nigga who the fuck you talkin' to like that? What else you gotta say Chase, huh? That you gonna kill me if you find out I'm involved? Yeah, I know, I've heard it several times before."

"You think it's a joke or a game? Do you know who you fuckin' wit'? Them niggas you see missin' on the news and social media, a body ain't ever been recovered. Don't get crazy just cuz I tell you I love you and put my dick in you. You not exempt."

"I know I'm not. You tried to kill your own wife. And your unborn."

Then I snapped.

I jumped up from that couch so fast, I was like Quicksilver from X-Men. Before I knew it, I had both my hands around her throat.

"Fuck you say to me?" I barked as I squeezed the life outta her ass.

"Chase! Stop!" she screamed but I was seeing red.

I couldn't believe she had brought that shit up. I made the biggest and worst mistake of my life, aside from being with her, when I shot my wife and ended up causing her to miscarry the child I had no idea she was pregnant with. I wanted to beat the blood out of Isabella but I don't hit women. I will strangle the shit outta one though.

I stopped when I realized she wasn't moving or fighting back. The veins in my arms were bulging as well as the one in the middle of my forehead. I let go of her neck and her lifeless body sank to the floor.

"Isabella? Isabella?" I panicked as I shook her.

She wasn't responding. I had fuckin' killed her.

KIA

Regardless of how good Rico was in bed, and he was amazing, I still had him blocked. I really was trying to get over him. It had been about two weeks since he tried to fuck his way back into my heart and I wasn't having it this time. He hurt me one too many times, then I found out he was fuckin' my sister behind my back. I didn't say anything about it because I didn't care anymore. I was done with him and Dro. I was done with men period.

That was until I stepped outside in my silk shorts and bunny slippers to get the mail and Dro pulled up in front of my house like he lived there. Nigga was all on the curb. He deaded the engine and hopped out so fast I didn't have enough time to try to run inside. These flat-ass bunny slippers wouldn't allow me to move fast enough. Then I tripped over a lump in the pavement and went crashing onto the ground, skinning my leg. I was so embarrassed, I just sat there crying and holding my knee like a toddler.

"Need some help baby?" Dro walked up holding in laughter and offering me his hand.

"Fuck you," I spat as he picked me right up off the ground as if I weighed nothing.

"Still mad at me huh?"

by $Santana$

"I'm not mad, I'm done." I folded my arms as he carried me inside and sat me down.

"You got some band-aids around here?"

"Thanks, Dro but I got it from here. You can go." I ushered him away. He, aside from Rico, was the last person I wanted to see.

"I'm just tryna help you baby." He walked off to the bathroom and fished around until he found what he was looking for.

"Dro, just leave okay? I don't need your funky-ass help." He was so stubborn, he did whatever the fuck he wanted.

"Damien. Call me Damien. My wifey don't use my street name." He corrected me as he got down on his knees and cleaned my scrape.

"Damien, I don't want anything to do with you. Keep that wifey shit."

"You don't have much of a choice in the matter, Kia."

I let out a deep sigh, "Listen, you have a woman already. Leave me be."

"Stop sayin' that alright? I already told you the deal with that. She outta there. I want you and I will have you. Now come here." He grabbed my chin and pressed his lips against mine.

I couldn't even lie, it was something about him that made me want him in the worst way. His dark, ebony skin made me hot with lust. I loved chocolate, despite being with a light-skinned devil for the past two years. I caressed his wavy-textured hair as he flicked his tongue in and out of my mouth. He tasted like caramel. He hungrily sucked on my bottom lip until I was sure he left a bruise.

"Dro," I pleaded as I broke the kiss.

"Damien," he corrected me again.

"Damien, let's just stop this. It won't work."

"Yeah, cuz you wanna be stubborn. You got the perfect nigga tryna make you his girl and you still wanna act stupid."

Then he ripped my dainty silk shorts off and went straight for my pearl.

"Wait, Dro, stop." I panted as he sucked away.

"Damien," he insisted.

"My friends, Dami…"

"Fuck yo friends." He just kept going despite the fact that Jas and Simone were making their way up to the door.

Now the locks were turning but he was slurping so loud he couldn't even hear. I tried so hard to get away but my leg was sore and busted up and the strength he was using to hold me still was far too much.

"Oh shit!" Jas hollered as she sauntered into the living room with Simone right behind her.

THE OTHER SIDE OF A THUG
SHE WAS A THUG'S WEAKNESS 2
by Santana

And he *kept* going. The fact that Dro, I mean Damien, gave not one fuck gave me all the motivation I needed to make a mess of his face and beard. I gushed everywhere and he still kept going. I was seeing, stars, planets and asteroids instead of the ceiling he had me staring at. I thought about marriage and kids. The whole kit and caboodle. When he finally finished, I was sitting in a puddle of my own juices, basting like a damn thanksgiving turkey. Why God?

"You ready to stop being so stupid?"

I placed my head in my hands and sighed. I was more than ready to stop being stupid. Shit, I was ready to get my heart broken again. He took me to my room and finished the job. Long story short, I was claiming that wifey title after that. He was mine. That nigga was unnecessarily good in bed and I hated to admit to myself that it was over for me, my pussy, and Rico. He couldn't come nowhere near me after this.

Part of me wondered why Damien wanted me so bad. See, I check into niggas, and he isn't exactly the chasing type. He will literally drop a chick for close to nothing. Something made me think twice about this whole thing. He unapologetically barged into my life and flipped it upside down. I went from being attracted, to being infatuated, to hatred and now I don't know what the fuck I am. I fall entirely too fast and if Rico finds out, somebody gon' die.

KALIEF

I had sent the test results in and they came back saying that Jayla was indeed mine. However, Kema had cheated. I was done with her. I was a good nigga and didn't deserve to be treated that way by anyone. She wanted a grimy, loud-mouth hood nigga and that wasn't me. I had popped a couple niggas but I was the behind the scenes type. Never on the forefront. She couldn't handle my laid-back persona despite the fact that niggas knew not to fuck wit' me, it just wasn't enough for her. But I knew who it *was* enough for.

I had been thinking about Simone more than usual. I stayed away though because I didn't want to seem like I was rebounding. I decided now was a good a time as ever. Plus, lately I had been having this weird feeling about Simone, so I checked into it to see if I was the only one that noticed. I could always feel some shit coming and something told me Simone needed someone.

"Hey, baby Jay," I greeted Jas as I stepped inside Kia's house.

"Hi boo." She kissed my cheek.

"Where's Kia?"

"Out," she said quickly trying to conceal a smile.

"Uh huh? Let me find out you keepin' secrets." I smiled.

217

"Mind yours," she warned with a half-smile.

"I been meaning to ask you, Simone been a'ight? She don't seem like herself and you know I'm always sensing some shit."

"I've been feeling the same. Ever since that day she came from her mom's house, she's been like super depressed. She's been drinking more than normal. But you know what happened with that situation with her nigga right?"

"Yeah, I was there. Y'all some gangsta bitches." I chuckled as she handed me a cold beer.

"Listennn, I didn't know she had it in her. He must have really flipped out. She hasn't talked about that since it happened so it may be what's really bothering her. She been in that damn room for two days. I think I heard her crying the other night."

"I'm gonna check on her."

"Alright, I'll see you later okay?" Jas waved as she exited the house and pulled off.

I finished my beer then headed towards Simone's room. I knocked a few times and she didn't respond. Fear started to seep in so I turned the knob and it was locked. I pulled out a key and picked the locked that sealed her bedroom door. When I stepped in, I still didn't see her. What I did see was a note on her bed along with a duffle bag full of money. I didn't even take time to read the note. I searched around frantically, calling out to her several times until I saw the balcony window open. I ran to the fire escape and there she was, standing on the edge with her face drowned in tears.

"Simone, what the fuck are you doing?" I inched closer to her.

"Leave me alone, Kalief." She sniffled.

"No, Simone, are you really about to do some shit like this? Did you think about how it would affect your friends, who love you?"

"I left them a million dollars. They'll get over it."

"What? No, they won't. Can't no money replace you." I stepped a little closer.

"Get the fuck back!" she screamed, startling the birds that nested in the tree outside the balcony.

"Simone, you know damn well I'm not gone let you do this in front of me."

"Why not? You or nobody else gives a fuck. Nobody!"

"Simone, baby please. Just come here, I swear it'll be okay. I promise that whatever happened, I'll make it better. I won't let nobody else hurt you." I was serious as fuck.

I have always loved Simone. She and I had never been intimate but if I hadn't been in a faithful relationship with Kema, Simone and I would be together. The first time we met, I knew I had to have her but back then I know I would've hurt her. She would've been a side-piece but now that things with Kema and I have been nothin' but a headache, I was willing to risk it all to save her.

"Kalief, just let me go. I need peace. I need to die." Then she let go of the railing.

I had never moved so quickly in my life. I grabbed her so fast, I still have no idea how she didn't fall. I strained every muscle in my body to snatch her ass back over that railing. Once I got her to safety, I held her. I held her until she soaked my shirt with her tears.

"Why didn't you just let me die, Kalief?"

"Cuz I care about you Simone. You not gone die on my watch. Plus, that's not a high enough fall to kill you."

I cleaned her up and kept a close eye on her for the rest of the night. I texted Jas and let her know what happened. She rushed home immediately.

"Simone baby, are you okay?" She burst through her room door in a panic.

Simone was sitting on the edge of her bed, face in her palms, still crying. I was about to walk out and give them some privacy, until Simone gently tugged my shirt asking me not to leave.

"Can we talk tomorrow? I can't do this right now."

"Sure." She hugged Simone then turned to leave.

I sat next to her and put my arm around her then pulled her into my lap.

"It's gon' be alright baby, I promise," I reassured her and kissed her forehead.

"No, it's not. I will never be able to live with myself. Nobody will ever even look at me the same."

"You didn't know. You can't blame yourself for that."

"Everybody got somebody they love or fuck wit'. I never have anybody for long. Something bad always happens."

"You got me, I love and fuck wit' you."

"You know what I mean, Kalief. You with Kema, y'all all happy. Kia got Rico, Jas got Tre, who the fuck I got?"

"Me," I said as I grabbed her face and kissed her.

I had been feelin' Simone for a while and seeing her all broken down, broke me down. I had to do something to make her feel better. I didn't feel bad about fuckin' around on Kema because Kema wasn't shit herself. She ain't appreciate me unless I had a gift for her, and yeah, I could afford whatever she wanted but she all she wanted from me was money. I wanted someone who wanted me for me. All bitches saw was dollar signs when they looked at me, but the way Simone's eyes lit up anytime I came around showed me that she was feelin' me for me. Or maybe my dick, but I would soon find out.

We made love that night. She opened up to me in a way that I knew she had never opened up to anyone else before. She told me things about her life and past that made me understand her better and love her more. She was a beautiful but broken soul and I was going to fix her. Chance the Rapper lyrics popped into my head: *"I'ma fix you, I'ma fuck you, I'ma get rid of them demons."* That's exactly what I planned on doing. I had to handle Simone carefully, she was fragile and anything could set her off. I wasn't in the business of hurting women but at this point, someone could simply miss a call from her and she'd be right back on that ledge.

TRE

I don't know what the fuck I was thinkin' getting back with Liyah like I could just get Jas off my mind that easy. My thoughts of her literally consumed me for these last few weeks. I knew she was done wit' me by now and that shit made it even worse. There was likely nothing I could do to get her back, cuz she was never mine to begin with, but then something inside me wouldn't let it go. Torture. I knew I had to and was gonna try just because.

I sat there thinking of how I could get her in my presence by accident when an idea came to me. I jumped up immediately to look at the events for this week that were to be held at Club Lit and thank God, we had some local rapper having a release party there. If I had Rico invite Jas, she would come so I called him and put him up on my plan. Even though I was goin' through hell at the moment with my depleted bank account and all, I still had time to chase some pussy. Some shit never changes. A nigga wasn't broke by far but there was a dent in my pockets. Knowing me though, I *always* bounced back.

My brother, Marcus was in town this week too. I had him here helping me with this investigation. He was one of the only people I trusted and one of the two people that I know didn't hit my safe cuz they don't live here. We had been kickin' it all week and I was happy he was around. If he wasn't so crazy I would have begged him to move here but he was too much heat. He would have to come after I was more established.

"Bro, so this party finna slap on Saturday, I know you gon' be there right?" I asked Marcus as I passed him the blunt.

"Hell yeah. I'm tryna bag me one of these fine Detroit hoes." He laughed.

"It is some fine ones, bro. This one chick I hit, she so fuckin' bad it's drivin' me crazy. And she single this time."

We both broke into laughter. He was surprised cuz I was notorious for stabbin' other nigga's bitches.

"You? Wit' a single bitch? Nigga, I know you lyin'. She got a husband somewhere."

"Nope. I swear she single and she crazy. Pussy dumb good too."

"Let me find out you goin' legit." He smiled.

"I just might have to wit' this one. I can't let her get away."

"Niggas in love?"

"Man, I might be. I can't shake this one and trust me, I tried."

I really did try. I guess after we had sex, all those texts and calls got to me. We got personal, we got deep. She told me about her life and I told her all about mine. Then when we saw

by $Santana$

each other again, I acted like I ain't know her. Petty shit. It scared me how fast I fell for her. I'd only been in Detroit a little over a year and most of that was spent in prison. So, over the course of a few months I managed to fall for someone already. I had to shake my head at myself.

"Well bro, you better treat her right. That's all I'll say."

"I got this."

*****

Today was the day of Rell's release party and the building was packed. I was fashionably late to this event because I ain't know this nigga, but judging by the attendance and the line outside, everybody else here did. I walked through the club with my eyes peeled, lookin' for my love. I needed to see her and now. I got the drop from Rico that she was coming so I was looking.

I continued around the dance floor cuz she wasn't in VIP. Nobody was. They were all scattered around, mingling with the other attendees. Then I spotted her in this tan skirt that made her ass look so fat it looked fake. She was grindin' all up on some fresh-ass nigga wit dreads. *Marcus!* My blood was boiling. I knew he didn't do it on purpose cuz he ain't even know Jas but damn. I rushed over.

"Jas, can I talk to you for a minute." I tapped her on the shoulder.

"Aye bro, dis you?" Marcus threw his hands up in mock surrender and backed up.

"Yeah, dis me," I told him and he walked off.

"Excuse me, I was enjoying myself." She frowned.

"Yo, we need to talk."

"Nah, we don't. Don't you got a girl? Fuck we need to talk about?" She pulled away from me.

"I see you drunk cuz you talkin' to me crazy right now." Wit' Jas, I had to be aggressive. That's all she understood.

"I don't wanna be talkin' to you at all," she yelled over the loud music then attempted to walk away again.

"Aye, I said I needed to talk to you." I snatched her ass back before she sashayed off in them heels.

"Go talk to yo fuckin' girlfriend, nigga!" she spat.

"Jas, I will embarrass yo ass in here. Come wit' me, I ain't repeating myself again." I grabbed her arm and ushered her away from the packed dancefloor and into a quieter area.

She plopped down on the couch in one of the conference rooms inside the club.

"So, what's up? Why you ain't been takin' none of my calls?"

"Because you have a girlfriend. We ain't got shit to talk about, Tre."

"But we do. You can explain to me why I haven't been able to stop thinkin' about you," I admitted. I didn't care about how it made me look, I just needed her.

"Hell, I don't know, pussy bomb as fuck. You need to be thinkin' about yo girl, though."

"I tried, can't seem to stop thinkin' about yo ass. Why is that? You put voodoo or some shit on me?" I was dead serious.

"Nigga, I'm not that desperate over no nigga to have to do that. You bit off more than you could chew when you decided to hit this pussy. Not my problem." She rolled her eyes and crossed her arms.

"Perhaps. So, what we gone do about that?"

"We? Nigga, you on yo own." She smirked and crossed her legs. I could taste the attitude.

"So, you don't wanna fuck me, Jas?" By the way her eyes lit up, I could tell she did. "You don't want daddy to dig in that pussy again?"

"You got a girl, Tre, so no, we not fuckin' again."

"I know that, I'm faithful too but I thought me and you had a friendship if we ain't have shit else."

"We did but…"

"But what? You don't want that huh? Then tell me what you *do* want."

"You know what the fuck I want." She looked me square in the eye.

That was all I needed to hear.

"You talkin' real crazy. You drunk, I'm finna take you home, come on." I signaled her to get up.

"Nigga, I'm good I'm not goin' nowhere with you." Then she got up and left the office.

I followed her.

"Jas, let's go before I embarrass you, a'ight?" Then I scooped her up and put her over my shoulder, carrying her past security and out to my car.

She sat there with her arms folded, pouting like a big-ass kid. She didn't say shit the whole ride so I looked over at her and she was sleep. When we got to her house, nobody was there so I got out and walked her to the door.

"Thanks for ruining my night," she said as she fished around in her Chanel bag for her keys.

"Anytime, baby."

Once she got the door open, I pushed her inside and attacked her with sensual kisses she couldn't say no to.

I backed her into the foyer door making her kick off her Louboutin pumps so she wouldn't fall.

by $\mathcal{S}antana$

"Tre, what are you doin'?" She stopped me momentarily.

"I'm givin' you what you want," I told her and grabbed her face, kissing her more aggressively.

"Tre stop, we not doin' this."

"Yes, we are. Now where yo room at?" I glanced into the hall wondering which room was hers.

"I'm not tellin' you that."

"Either show me your room or I'm gon' fuck you right here against this wall." I pushed her back against the hard wall that connected to the kitchen.

"Ok, damn." She finally gave in when she saw I wasn't playin'.

She led me down the hallway to her bedroom which was at the end. Soon as we were inside, I closed and locked the door. I didn't want Kia or Simone coming in and ruining what I had planned for tonight. I was about to completely own her ass. She had played around enough wit' a nigga. Ignoring my calls and frontin' on me was punishable by law and that's exactly what I was about to do; punish that pussy.

I shoved her into the door and pinned both her hands above her head with one of mine. I used my free hand to grab her ass as I kissed and licked her left ear.

by Santana

"You missed me?" I asked in her ear making her quiver. I knew she loved that shit.

"No."

"No? Why not?"

"Let me go, okay? Go home to yo girl."

"You know you don't want that, do you Jasmine?" I looked into her lyin' ass eyes and she looked away.

I passionately kissed her mouth again and as usual she tried to hold back moans.

"You know you want it," I egged her on.

"No, I don't." She struggled to get loose but it was nothin' she could do. I had her pinned.

"Yeah, you do. I bet that pussy wet as a muhfucka." I used my knee to part her legs.

My free hand slithered under her skirt and of course she didn't have no panties on.

"Damn Jas, no panties?" I asked as I squeezed her bare ass. It was softer than I remembered.

"Fuck you, Tre," she spat.

"You about to. Now let me see if that pussy is as wet as I think it is." My hands felt around to her kitty.

My finger grazed her swollen clit and I felt her flinch. I rubbed it while staring at her, daring her to make a sound.

"Pleaseeee," she begged.

"Please what?"

"Stop."

"Nope," I told her, then I finally found her opening and it was drippin', just like I thought.

"Damn you wet as hell, Jas. Which makes you a liar."

Playin' around in her juices had a nigga breathing hard as fuck. I was panting like a damn dog and I finger fucked her against the door.

"Fuck! You wet as hell," I exclaimed. "Let me taste it." I made eye contact again forcing her to look me in the eyes, which she kept trying to avoid.

By now she was moaning like crazy as her sweet juices dripped down her legs.

"Tre, just please stop."

"Mannn, bitch listen, let me eat this pussy."

I sped up my pace as I felt her walls tighten. Her ass up here protesting but was finna nut all over my fuckin' fingers.

"Fuck Tre, I'm finna cum!" she panted.

"Let me eat that pussy!" I demanded as I felt her explode all over my index and middle fingers.

"Okayyyyy!" She finally gave in as her knees gave out.

I lifted her skirt and bent her over the dresser. I got on my knees like I was praying to the pussy and dove straight in. I tongue fucked her into submission as her loud moans filled the

THE OTHER SIDE OF A THUG
She Was A Thug's Weakness 2
by Santana

air. Her moans turned into screams as soon as I latched onto her clit and sucked it dry. I stopped right before she was about to cum again, got up, and slammed her onto the dresser. I put her legs in the air then went back to suckin' the life outta her. Then I slipped my tongue into her ass. She sat straight up with a look of confusion on her face.

"Tre, what the fuck?" she whined as my tongue circled her asshole and hit her taint at the same time.

"You like that shit?"

"Hell yeah," she said as her head fell back.

I stuck my whole tongue up her ass. I wasn't for no games tonight. She was gone quit wit' the bullshit after I was done with her.

"Oh my Godddd, Tre." She sat up again but this time her eyes had fresh tears streaming down.

I continued assaulting her ass and pussy with my thick tongue until I felt like she had enough. She was shivering, shaking and begging me to stop and my face was covered in her juices.

I lifted her damn near lifeless body off the dresser and carried her to the bed. But instead, I picked her up and shoved my dick up in her. I held her legs over my shoulders as I drilled her. She couldn't handle it and I didn't give a fuck. She held onto me tightly, burying her tear-drenched face into the crook of my neck as I went full-force, tryna knock the back out her pussy.

"Goddamn Tre!"

"Goddamn Jas!" I replied letting her know her tight-ass twat was just as good as she felt the dick was.

I laid her down on the bed, pushing her legs back as far as they could and plunged every inch of me inside her. Her expression had love, hate and admiration all mixed together.

"Tre, oh my God, why you fuckin' me like this?"

"Cuz you been dodgin' a nigga. This what happens when you don't give it to me."

"I'm sorry." She cried out as I grabbed both legs and sped up.

"Sorry what?"

"Sorry daddy." She knew the drill.

"This shit mine?"

"Hell yeah. You can have it, Tre." She cried out.

"That's what daddy wanna hear. You know exactly what to say to get this nut don't you?" I asked as I flipped her over to hit that fat ass from the back.

I grabbed a handful of her hair, which was messy as hell by now, and pounded her doggy style until all she could say was, "Oh shit!" Her submitting to this dick was a major turn-on.

by **Santana**

I loved makin' her mean ass squirm, it was a pleasure to break her down.

"Uh huh, daddy. Fuck me! Fuck me like that daddy!" She held the perfect arch and her beggin' for this dick had me ready to blow.

"You can't be talkin' to me like that Jasmine." I slowed down a bit. It was finna be over.

"Fuck that pussy! Gimme that shit daddy!" And that was it. It was over. I bust all up in her shit.

"See what you did? You can't be doin' that. Now you gon' be pregnant," I said as I pulled my dick out and fell in a sweaty heap onto her bed.

"I'm on birth control."

Then my phone rang and it was Liyah. I had her saved as "Liyah" with them gay ass heart emojis that she insisted I put next to her name.

"Wifey callin'." Jas smirked as she went to clean herself up.

It was a FaceTime call too so I definitely couldn't answer.

"I want you to be mine and mine only," I told Jas as soon as she came from the bathroom.

"Nigga, did you not just get a call from bae?"

by Santana

"Listen Jas, that ain't nothin' serious. I don't wanna be with her. I want you. Liyah is and always has been something to do," I admitted ,finally being honest with my damn self.

"So why you wit' her then? Why waste her time?"

I hit her with the whole story about Liyah and I and left out no details. All she could say was "damn."

"So, you understand now?" I quizzed while stroking her hair and planting small kisses on her forehead.

"Yeah, I guess but you really expect her to just be okay with this? She seems like the type that would get out of line and I'm letting you know I will *not* hesitate to lay that bitch out."

I believed her too.

"Okay gangsta. You ain't gotta worry about her," I assured her.

Then she turned over and I rubbed her butt until I heard her lightly snoring. Finally, I had gotten my baby to stop runnin' from me. Even wit' all my problems, I was the happiest I had been in a while.

by *Santana*

CHAPTER NINE

The Calm Before…

KIA

Dro and I had been enjoying each other. He was the same nigga that I had been falling for from the beginning. I had damn near moved in with him. He was everything I had been missing. He was affectionate, a good listener, sex was stupid wild and he didn't have no bitches in his face. Total opposite of Rico. Speaking of Rico, I hadn't seen him in a while and I hadn't noticed either. Dro had successfully stolen me away and I wasn't ever going to return. My heart had been broken enough.

"Bae, I'm gonna run home and check the mail and get some more clothes," I told him and left.

When I got home, the girls were there and I was happy to see them. It had been over a week since we'd seen each other.

"Simone, who is this bitch that just barged up in here? Hand me my 9." Jas laughed as I strolled in.

"Chill on me."

"Bitches glowin' out here. Dro must be givin' you some golden peen." She stood to survey my appearance.

"Girllll, if you don't get the fuck." I burst into laughter. She was on the money though.

236

"He's giving me more than that boo. How have you bitches been? I hope you ain't been on no more ledges, Simone."

"Wow bitch, that was low." Simone rolled her eyes.

"You know how I feel about that suicide shit. If you would have done that for real I would've killed you."

"I know. I'm sorry y'all. I was just devastated."

"Yeah, I know. I'm so sorry about that too. That was some fucked up shit to find out."

I hugged her tightly.

"Well at least I got some money. I'm moving soon."

"Me too, bitch! I already got a condo in mind. I went to look at it today and I love it," Jas chimed in.

"Simone broke you off?" I asked Jas.

"Nope. If you would've been here you would know that I won my lawsuit. A cool mill, bitch. I'm rich!"

"Aww shit, so it's two millionaire heauxs in my house and I'm still broke? Y'all gotta go today," I joked.

"Well we left you a gift."

When I went in my room there was a red balloon that reminded me of the movie "It" but when I saw a pile of money on my bed, I almost passed out.

"That makes *three* rich bitches," Simone said.

We all screamed and jumped into the pile of money, twerkin' and throwing it at each other like we were strippers.

"Damn, I love y'all," I said as I hugged them both.

I bagged up my money so I could go deposit it in the bank the next morning then I heard the doorbell ring. I slid the money under the bed and sat down, contemplating my next move. I let one of them get the door cuz this money had my mind gone. Then my bedroom door creaked open and in walked Rico. My heart sank.

"Well damn Ki, you just disappeared. I had to come see if you were still alive."

"If I disappeared, then that means I didn't want to be found," I snapped and went to grab some more clothes.

"What the fuck is yo issue?" He raised his voice and I could tell he was getting angry.

I was scared he was gon' try that shit he did at his party, so I hurriedly packed my shit.

"Put that shit down and talk to me." He slapped my bag to the floor and turned me to face him.

Then he saw the passion marks that covered my neck. Marks left by Damien when he held me down and sucked my shit until I was purple with bruises. He said he was marking his territory, and that he did.

by Santana

"The fuck is that on yo neck?" he barked once he saw I was covered in hickeys.

"Don't worry about it." I pulled away.

"You out here fuckin' another nigga? You serious?" His light-skinned ass was turning beet red. I grew even more afraid.

"Rico, just go. I don't want no problems."

"Where you packing to go to? That nigga house? You livin' wit' that nigga huh?" By this time Rico had his .45 out and was wiping his forehead with it as he paced the floor.

"Put the fuckin' gun away, Rico."

"I swear to God Kia, I'ma kill that nigga! Who the fuck is it? And you better not lie! Matter fact, gimme yo phone!"

I complied. Rico was a psycho. Everybody knew that but up until now he never had a reason to unleash that crazy side on me. Bitch, I was shaking. Tears immediately started to pour when he asked me to put the code into my iPhone with his gun resting against his temple.

"Dro!? That's who you fuckin'?!"

Fuck! I screamed inside my head.

"Rico, just calm down please." I fell to my knees hoping my crocodile tears were enough to sway him. They weren't.

That nigga grabbed me by a patch of my hair and lifted me clean off that damn floor. When I tell you, I'd never been so scared in my life. Rico had blood in his eyes and I knew Dro was good as dead.

"You fuckin' my enemy?" he seethed through gritted teeth as he held my hair.

"Bitch, you fucked my sister! You think I didn't know about you and Cedes?" That caused him to let my hair go.

"I never fucked her. I dated her and even cashed her out but I never stuck my dick in her. When I found out she was your sister I left her alone. Call and ask her if we fucked."

I felt like shit.

"I'm sorry, Rico."

"Nah. When that nigga break your heart, don't fuckin' call me, bitch," he barked and stormed out of my room.

I sank to the floor and cried my eyes out. I was supposedly over him but why did it still hurt? Why did his words matter? I couldn't pull myself to go back to Dro's house tonight so I turned my phone off and cried myself into a headache.

RICO

This bitch really out here getting' dicked by my fuckin' enemy though. I bet Jas and Simone hoe-asses knew too. I gave them a death stare as I walked through the living room toward the door.

"Yo,' y'all knew she was fuckin' that nigga? Huh? Jas, you supposed to be my sister but you ain't even tell a nigga shit? Fake-ass bitch." I shook my head at her.

"Rico, don't call me no bitch." She stepped to me.

Now usually I back down but I was heated and I wanted to choke her ass for not even givin' a nigga a clue.

"I called you a fake-ass bitch. And you are. A fraud-ass hoe!" I was wrong but I was takin' all my anger out on her.

"Call me one more name, Rico. You mad at me cuz yo' bitch finally left you after all the shit you put her through? And you gone stand in my damn face, the person who always had yo' back, and cuss me out cuz she went and got her some new dick? Punk-ass bitch!" She pushed me so hard I fell into the door.

I lost it. I grabbed her neck and threw her into the wall. She lit me up with a barrage of punches and all them bitches connected.

"Fuck off me!" she yelled when I backed up.

by *Santana*

I grabbed her again but not to choke her. I simply looked her square in the eyes and told her, "You dead to me." With that, I kissed her forehead and walked out.

She was no sister of mine anymore. I couldn't believe she actually let that shit go down. She of all people knew the relationship between me and Dro was hate. I mean, there was hella respect mixed in too but we ain't fuck wit' each other like that. Dro got respect from me because although I ain't like the way he moved, he has never lied to me about nothin'. I ain't trust his actions but I trusted his word. If he did some shit he owned up to it. I think that's why he was so respected with any and everybody he came across. He took territory, custos, plugs, shit he even tried to take my life, and now he wanted my bitch.

I was gonna have to pay him a visit. It's some shit you just don't do and makin' a move on my bitch was one. I pulled up to one of his spots on the westside, killed the engine, and hopped out. He was there cuz his car was parked crooked in front of the trap. I walked past the fiends that were outside the house and went straight in.

"Clear this shit out. I need to rap wit' Dro for a minute," I told his flunkies.

They looked like they wanted to challenge me but Dro dismissed them.

by Santana

"I got it. I'm good." He smirked and they cleared the room.

"So, what's up nigga? You got some shit you wanna get off yo chest?" I eyed him as he rose to his feet.

"Nah, but you seem like you do. You dressed in "kill a nigga" gear. Is this about light-skin?" he asked, referring to Kia.

"Hell yeah it is." I shook my head.

"Come on Ric, two light-skinned muhfuckas together don't even look right."

"You funny, man." Nigga was funny. I had to laugh at that goofy shit.

"Besides, it ain't like I knew y'all was together. The way you switch hoes, I thought she was just some li'l freak you hit here and there. You know, fair game and shit. Although I do step on toes, I wasn't tryna step on yours. We got enough beef. Kia is a good woman though, Ric. it's a shame you couldn't see that."

I snapped. I had my gun out before I realized it.

"Nigga chill a'ight? You a real nigga and me nor you finna die over no pussy. Put that shit up before you get yoself killed boy." He pushed the gun down.

"You love her?" he asked me in all seriousness.

"Yeah, I do."

THE OTHER SIDE OF A THUG
SHE WAS A THUG'S WEAKNESS 2
by *Santana*

"If you love her, why you treat her like shit then? And I'm bein' a hunnit wit you, li'l nigga. You know I respect you regardless of this street shit but don't lie to yourself. Love is an *action,* and the way you treated her ain't love, nigga. I'm older than you, not by much but I done thought I loved a lot of women, turns out that shit wasn't real at all. My actions ain't reflect my feelings. If you feel like you can treat her better than me then I'll walk away from her. But you need to work on yoself, young dog. You niggas got this love shit twisted."

Damn ,I felt stupid. I came over here wit' every intention of splattering this nigga brains and ended up getting a lesson in love. Another reason I hated but respected this nigga. He could talk himself out of anything.

"Cool, I'm out." I threw my hood over my head and dashed back to my whip. I had a lot to think about. This nigga was in her head and it was truly over for me, for us. He was the best and worst thing to happen to her. It seemed like it was nothin' I could do anymore.

THE OTHER SIDE OF A THUG
SHE WAS A THUG'S WEAKNESS 2

by Santana

LIYAH

The divorce proceedings were going in my favor. I was about to take everything I could from Chase. I was sick of being dogged by men. I had just left the last hearing before everything was to be awarded to me. I smiled inside seeing Chase crumble knowing he had to dissolve his estate and give me half of everything. Although he had money that wasn't accounted for, this shit hurt him right in his pockets. I was surprised he didn't bring his little side bitch with him. Once the hearing ended I caught up with him outside the courthouse to rub it in.

"Well Chase, I hope you're happy," I said when he turned around.

"Nah I hope *you're* happy. You gone be broke in no time and you still ain't got no man." He laughed in my face.

"Where's your whore, the one you were cheating in my house with?"

"Not worried about you. Don't you have some nigga to chase behind, a nigga that don't want yo ass and already got another chick? Miss Attempted Suicide."

That shit hurt. How did he know what was goin' on in my personal life? Tre must have told him.

"You don't know shit about what I'm going through," I spat.

by Santana

"But I do. You thought my brother was finna settle down wit' you, right? You really thought you was about to be Mrs. Carter? You really are craz,y Liyah. That man don't want you, he felt sorry for you. He gave you pity dick cuz you a pitiful bitch." He chuckled and walked off.

I needed to see Tre immediately. I needed him to clear this shit up because if Chase was right, somebody was about to die. I got a plane ticket and was on the first thing smoking back to Detroit. When I arrived, I went home, changed, and went to Tre's house. I didn't call or text. I showed up unannounced as fuck. When I pulled up, to my surprise Tre was walking out of the house with his arm around some light-skinned bitch. That must have been the bitch Chase was referring to.

I stopped and parked in the street, blocking his driveway. "So, this is what the fuck we doin' now, Tre?" I screamed as I approached they happy couple lookin' asses.

"Liyah man, don't come over here wit' that dumb shit," Tre warned but I didn't give a fuck.

"Who is this bitch?" I pointed to the girl that was standing there smiling like she was happy to be a side-bitch.

"I'm Jas and you are?" She held her hand out like I was about to actually shake it. Smug-ass bitch.

"You better move that hand before I cut it off!" I threatened her.

THE OTHER SIDE OF A THUG
SHE WAS A THUG'S WEAKNESS 2

by Santana

"Tre, you better get yo hoe in line before she don't have a mouth to talk shit from."

"Liyah, go home. That shit dead, a'ight?"

"Really, Tre? This is how you do me?" I wasn't about to cry and go out like a punk so I lunged at the girl, Jas, full force.

She grabbed my hair and started throwing me around like a rag doll. Tre had to pull her off me. That hoe was strong. I was so embarrassed. I got back into my car and pulled off so fast. I had just taken not one, but two blows to my ego, and now this made it three, all in one day. I was thirsty for blood. I paced the floor in my bedroom plotting revenge. Then I thought of something that could help give me some leverage.

MARCUS

I was in line at the soul food restaurant picking up my order when my phone rang, it was Liyah, Ava's friend.

"Hey, what's good?" I greeted her, confused about why she would be calling me.

"Hey, I need to talk to you as soon as possible, but it needs to be in person."

"Uhh, sure, you can meet me at my brother, Tre's house if you want."

"No, it can't be there. Come to mine. I'll text you the address. You're gonna wanna hear this."

"A'ight. I'll be on my way."

As soon as I got the text I input the address into my GPS and headed there. I was glad I decided to stay in Detroit for a while cuz I needed to know what this girl wanted. I bet she wanted some dick.

When I pulled up to some nice area outside of Detroit, I saw someone peek through the window. I always kept my burner on me so I grabbed it and approached the front door.

"Come in, hurry up." She startled me as she snatched the door open.

"What's this about? And get straight to the point, lady," I demanded, taking a seat in her dining room.

by *Santana*

"I got some news for you that I know is gonna crush you, but you have to proceed with caution and you *can't* tell him I told you."

Whatever this bitch was gettin' at she needed to spill before I spilled her damn guts all over her nice marble kitchen floor.

"Get to the fuckin' point," I urged, losing patience.

"Well, word is Tre was fuckin' your baby mama, Ava a while back, around the time she got pregnant with Hope. You didn't hear it from me though."

"How long you knew?"

"Why does that matter?" She got defensive.

"Cuz if you knew why you just now tellin' me? Tre told me about you and his relationship. How I know you ain't just lyin' to get revenge cuz he left you?" I drilled her.

"I am trying to get revenge, but I'm not lyin'. Tre isn't even the one that told me, Ava did."

That was all I needed to hear.

TRE

After that run-in with Liyah I decided to drop Jas back off at Kia's. I had to meet up with Rico anyway so cutting our evening short was in the cards tonight. I walked her inside and noticed Kia sitting around all red in the face watching romance movies.

"Kiwi, what's up baby? You a'ight?" I asked when I saw tissue coupled with a box of ice cream and half-eaten birthday cake. This broad was over here stuffing herself with comfort food.

"No, nigga." She kept her eyes fixed on the TV.

"Anything I can do?"

"Yep, tell Rico to stop being mad at me." She looked at me with puppy dog eyes like I could make that nigga take her back.

"I'm on my way there now. Come wit' me, you can tell 'em yourself." I saw Jas give me a thumbs up and a smile.

She got up and cleaned herself up. The whole ride there was her sniffling and telling me how she fucked up. I ain't wanna hear that shit at all, but I listened because she was cool people and I knew my nigga loved her rat ass.

"Now listen, you know who you fuck wit' right? A made nigga. Women who fuck wit' niggas like us don't have many options when it comes to men, so I get why you got you another drug nigga. I even understand how you felt after all the shit Rico put you through but that nigga Dro was the wrong move."

"I knowwww, damn! But I didn't know who he was. I hadn't done no research on him. We were having too much fun for me to even be thinkin' about who this nigga was affiliated with. Don't act like you ain't never been wrapped up in a chick you ain't investigate before it was too late."

She was right. I couldn't argue there.

"I understand, trust." I did the same thing with Liyah and she ended up being the wife of my brother, so I couldn't judge Kia at all.

We arrived at Rico's house and Kia stood behind me quietly as we entered.

"Fuck she doin' here?" He pointed in her direction but never even looked at her.

"Can we talk please?" she begged.

"We ain't got shit to talk about, Kia. I don't even know why you came here. Tre, let's get this shit over with." He took me into his back room and immediately started to cut into me.

"Dog I know you playin' wit' me right? Why the fuck you bring her here?"

by Santana

"She wanted to apologize. Don't act like you ain't never made a mistake before nigga."

"I don't give a fuck. I'm done wit' that shit. Dro can have her." He scoffed. Nigga was real-life hurt.

"You don't mean that, you just mad right now." I was hoping he wasn't for real.

"Nah, I'm done. This gon' take a while so I'm finna have Kalief take her home. She don't need to be here. You know we got shit to do." H unloaded bags of cash onto the dusty wooden table next to the money counter.

"Shit is short." He looked up at me.

"Let's get to it." I sat down ready to get my hands dirty.

About thirty-minutes into count money and chill, Kalief came to collect Kia and take her home. He had Ubered there cuz he let Simone keep his car, so he had to use mine. She reluctantly left with him with the saddest look on her face. I felt bad for her. Her eyes were pleading with me to do something but shit, I couldn't convince that nigga to even look at her right now.

"Yo, I'll come check on you a'ight?" I told her before she got into my car and closed the door.

Just seconds after his front door closed, *Pop! Pop! Pop!* We heard gunshots right outside the house. We strapped up and darted outside to the scene. It was Kalief, my car wrapped around a light pole.

"Oh my Godddd, help!" Kia screamed as she held onto Kalief for dear life.

The car was gone by the time we got outside. I pried the smashed driver's door open as Rico assisted me with pulling Kalief to safety.

"You a'ight? you got hit?" I asked Kia frantically, but she was untouched.

"Who the fuck did this?" Rico screamed at Kia.

"I-I don't know. It was a black Charger, tinted windows."

By now, the police were on the scene being that Rico lived in a suburban area. One of them nosy-ass white neighbors had called them. The ambulance struggled to keep Kalief conscious as we stood there confused and soaked in blood. The three of us ran inside, changed, and went straight to the hospital. I called everybody and let them know the bad news. This was the craziest shit. I had a feeling that whoever had shot up Kalief wasn't after him. That was *my* Maserati. Niggas knew who it was when I pulled up in it. I was the only nigga in the D that drove one. So that hit was indeed intended for me. Shit was gettin' out of hand.

First, somebody tries to get me locked up for drugs, then Silas shoots up the club, which now I was starting to think that it was so I would get caught shooting on probation, sending me right back to prison. Then somebody blew my safe and took drugs and money. Now somebody straight up tried to kill me tonight. I still had no idea who but shit was about to get real. Whoever this was, they were out for blood. I had to get to the bottom of it cuz now my niggas were getting hurt, and I couldn't let that happen on account of me.

Pacing through the hospital, we waited for someone to come and give us some news on Kalief's condition. We all gathered in the waiting room. Everyone huddled around Simone, trying to console her because she seemed to be taking it the hardest. I knew it was cuz he had been stickin' dick to her lately. I hoped like hell no one called his baby mama, Kema, cuz all hell would break loose and we ain't need no drama right now.

I sat there thinkin' hard about who could be behind this and against my will, Rico popped up in my mind again. I needed to clear my head so I excused myself to the car for a blunt. When I came back in, my high was blown immediately when I hit a corner to use the bathroom and saw Jasmine and Rico hugged up in the hallway. I'll be damned!

254

JASMINE

I rushed straight to the hospital when I found out Kalief was shot and had been in an accident. He was my heart. I can't name no other nigga in the world who I didn't feel deserved this shit but Kalief. He had so much love for everybody, he literally fed the whole hood. He saved lives, nd was indeed the black Jesus of the ghetto. I raced to the hospital and immediately felt nervous when I realized Rico would likely be here. Once I saw his truck in the parking lot, I knew it for sure.

I jumped out and took a deep breath, trying to relieve some of my anxiety before stepping inside the automatic doors into the waiting area. Everyone was there, including Simone. She was broken up. If I didn't know they were fuckin' before, I surely knew now. I couldn't imagine how she felt. If I knew Kalief, I knew he was nothing short of a gentleman to her. And to keep it a G, I knew he was tearin' that ass up too. That nigga was notorious for his dick when he was younger. I couldn't imagine he was anything less than a monster now.

I looked around and didn't spot Tre, which was odd. I didn't see Kia either. The last person I wanted to talk to was Rico but he was trudging his ass toward me anyway.

"Sup sis?"

THE OTHER SIDE OF A THUG
She Was A Thug's Weakness 2
by *Santana*

I didn't respond, just rolled my eyes and avoided direct contact.

"We need to talk. Come on." He pulled my arm and led me around the corner next to the bathroom.

"I know what I did was whack but you don't understand the shit that was goin' through my mind. I lost my bitch, Jas. To a rival nigga. I'm fucked up," he finally admitted.

Damn, I know he was hurting. From what Kia had told me, Dro was indeed the better man. Nothing to do with looks or money; it was the absence of lies and bullshit. Dro not only was brutally honest, he immediately fixed any issues he caused. Dro was a real man.

"Damn bro, that was real," I responded. It took a lot for him to say that shit out loud.

"Jas, you have no idea. I wanted to cry almost. I mean regardless of how I treat her at times, I love that girl so much. I'm just an ain't shit nigga. But I really was tryna change for her."

"See, that's the thing. Don't change for her, change for you, Ric. It ain't real if you ain't do it for yourself, cuz *you* thought it should be changed."

"That's why I fuck wit' you. You always spittin' some deep shit. I'm sorry for how I acted, man. I was bein' a hurt-ass bitter nigga. Take me back, sis?" He held out his arms and I obliged and hugged him back.

Rico needed a hug. A long one. He lost his girl and one of his closest homeboys was fighting for his life a few feet away. I held him until he let go. Then he kissed my forehead as usual. When we let go, Tre was standing there looking perplexed.

"Sorry to interrupt," he said and then he just walked off.

I was hardly in the mood for any of Tre's shenanigans. He had these mood swings that were hard to deal with at times and this was one of those times when shit could get very heated. We were in a hospital after the shooting of one of our closest friends, so everybody was on edge. I tried my damndest to keep a level head until we knew if Kalief was even alive.

I stepped back into the waiting room where I saw the doctor announcing Kalief's condition. He was in surgery but they said he would make it. The bullet didn't hit anything vital. I could relate and I was silently thanking God that She decided to spare his life. I had been in the same hospital months earlier, so memories started to flood my mind. I was so emotional that I simply wanted to disappear. I refused to let anyone see me cry. I went into the ladies' room before the tears overwhelmed me. Once I was done crying, I went back into the waiting room until it was time to see him.

Tre was still avoiding me for whatever reason but I wasn't concerned with that. I just wanted to see my bro. As soon as the doctor came to get us, I went in first. He was up but he was groggy and incoherent. The morphine had him nodding in and out. I told him I loved him and kissed his cheek. I left after that. I couldn't handle all the emotional stimuli. My legs were starting to ache because of that empath shit. I waited in the hall until Tre came out. Despite his attitude, I wanted to talk to him. I needed him to hold me, at least for tonight. I was having flashbacks and shit.

"Tre, can I come home with you please?" I asked him when he left the room.

"Nah, go home with Rico," he spat.

"Tre, you serious right now? This what you on?" I stepped back, partly shocked at his stupid comment.

"Hell yeah, I'm serious. Y'all was damn near kissin' a minute ago. Y'all got unfinished business. Get that shit off, li'l baby." He smirked, pleased with his blatant stupidity and jealousy.

"Listen, I'm tired and I just wanna lay with you tonight. You know damn well I don't want Rico and he doesn't want me. Whatever you think is goin' on is in your head, and is probably a manifestation of all the fucked-up shit you've done in your life. Don't project that onto me, Tre."

THE OTHER SIDE OF A THUG
SHE WAS A THUG'S WEAKNESS 2
by *Santana*

"Do you wanna fuck that nigga?" He got close to my face.

"No, and I don't wanna fuck you either, piece of shit." With that, I walked away. Guess I'd be sleeping alone after all.

Even though I had moved, I went back to Kia's house hoping to get some comfort but she wasn't there. Simone stayed at the hospital with Kalief so I was there by myself. I was shook, to be honest. I wasn't in the best frame of mind to be alone which was why I didn't go to my house. I wasn't used to it yet. I showered and changed into a sports bra and biker shorts, preparing to take my "medicine' and lay down when I heard the doorbell.

When I peeped out, it was Tre. I was relieved and happy that he came by.

"I see you changed your mind," I said and let him walk in.

"Nah, I still don't like what I saw but…"

"But what? Do you know Rico choked me and cussed me out a few days ago?" I got defensive.

"What? Why?"

"Cuz he was mad that Kia found her a good man and thought that I should've told him. He went off on me and we got into it. He was apologizing. Then he got all emo and shit and he needed a fuckin' hug, Tre, damn. The man lost his girl and his fuckin homey is in the hospital. The nigga was hurt! He wasn't coming onto me."

"I'm sorry, baby. But who this "good man" Kia done found?" he asked as if that were unbelievable.

"Some nigga named Dro." I shrugged and sat down with him.

"Dro? That nigga ain't no good man." He chuckled. "He ain't shit but a drug dealing, murdering, goon-ass nigga. Fuck you mean a good man? I thought she had two niggas cuz I knew about Dro and ain't shit good but his cash flow."

"Well, he treats her better than Rico did." I folded my arms, prepared to defend my best friend and her decision.

"For now, Jas."

"You know him personally?"

"Hell yeah, I do. Dro ain't never did no hoe shit but if he don't want a bitch no more, ain't no arguing. It's done. Don't matter if you crippled or goin' into labor. I wonder how long Kia gone last. That nigga ignore game would drive her crazy. I used to work wit' the nigga years ago. He a muhfucka, man."

"Well, he sounds no different than y'all." I ended the conversation.

The nerve of him to sit here and act like he was any better when he was also a piece of shit. The way he did that chick, Liyah was bold as hell.

RICO

I wanted blood! That was the only thing that was on my mind at this point. Somebody done tried to body my nigga? Somebody was as good as dead. My bets were on Dro. Because I thought it was him was the only reason I was sitting here plotting instead of out here slaughtering niggas. Tre told me he ain't think it was Dro but something told me it was.

Tre's judgment couldn't be trusted right now. That nigga thought *I* blew his safe and robbed him. I couldn't count on him to think straight now. The saving grace was that all I had to do was simply ask Dro did he try this shit. I know that haughty nigga would own up to it if it was him. This ain't the first time he done tried to kill somebody in my camp. The only thing was, I needed to get him alone, or at least somewhere I had hella backup cuz if he really was out for one of us, he'd have no issue killin' me if I came to one of his spots again, like the other day.

I sat there steaming, my skin was hot and red with rage. I couldn't let this shit slide. All that kept coming to my head was, "Damn, Kia pussy *that* good to where this nigga gone go back on his word?" That fact alone had me amped. We decided a while ago to just stay out of each other's way, and now this nigga done had a taste of some twat and said fuck the treaty. I couldn't hold it in any longer.

by Santana

I punched a couple walls hoping that it would calm me but it only made me angrier. I replayed all the times where my school teachers and friends said I needed anger management. I knew I did but I let it take over me this time. I grabbed two of my favorite guns, which included my desi, jumped into my all black "kill-a-nigga" gear, bulletproof vested-up and dashed out to my car. I drove to my spot, which is where I kept a towaway. It was a hot car that I used when I needed to ice some niggas. I parked my whip there, hopped in the stoley, and sped off to the block where I knew Dro's most valuable soldiers would be.

I creeped slowly behind tinted windows, holding my gun closely with my finger tight on the trigger. As soon as I spotted them niggas, I let a hail of bullets rain. They all fell in a heap and that was the end of them, but the start of a war.

I quickly left the scene and parked the car where I knew it would be taken away by my contractors later, then I hopped back in my car and sped home. When I arrived, I spotted a familiar truck in my driveway. I pulled up slowly and deaded the engine. It was Kia. I grabbed my pistol and approached the car. My trust was on zero. She could've been here plotting with this nigga, Dro, so I was prepared to dump. But as I got closer, I saw that it was only her and I sighed relief.

I tapped the window and she jumped. She looked tired and worn out as she exited the car. She fell right into my arms.

THE OTHER SIDE OF A THUG
SHE WAS A THUG'S WEAKNESS 2
by Santana

And my dumb ass caught her. Even after all the shit she caused, I still felt for her. My feelings were still there and that ate at me. I walked her into the house and to my room where she removed her jacket and shoes. I turned the heat on, lay next to her, and held her. She cried and apologized, and cried some more.

"It's gone be okay. I'll fix this shit," I assured her as I rubbed her back.

"I can't believe what happened to him." She sobbed in a high-pitched squeal.

"I know, Ki, neither can I but trust me, I'm gonna deal with yo' boyfriend."

"So, he *did* do this?" She rose up, the realization that she was sleeping with the enemy made her eyes bulge.

"Yeah, that's what its lookin' like."

"Oh my God! It's all my fault." She curled into the fetal position as the truth about her nigga being responsible for her bro almost dying set in.

I knew how Kia felt about Kalief. Hell, how we all felt. Kalief was that guy. Nobody, even niggas we beefed with, disliked him. That was why this was so hard for everyone. Kalief was a godsend. He always got niggas out of trouble, caught our mistakes, and saved our asses a many of times. Just having to imagine losing him cut deep.

"It ain't your fault. If it wasn't for me, you wouldn't have been in the position to get caught up with that nigga. That's why I'm gone handle it. Let me handle it baby." I squeezed her tighter to let her know I was here for her.

As many times as I'd hurt her, I felt like this may have possibly been the worst. I had pushed her into the arms of another man and the result was some straight bullshit—someone we all loved getting hurt. I was just happy that it didn't take him out. But Dro was gone get his. I wasn't done with him by far.

.

CHAPTER TEN

Wildfires

CHASE

It had been damn near three months since I had seen Isabella. After that day I choked and almost killed her, she ran off and I hadn't seen or heard from her since. A nigga was sicker than a bitch in her first trimester. I mean literally, just imagining her never coming back made me nauseous. I was up to my neck in tears. Like, I really cried over this bitch.

A nigga spent so much time in a slump I hadn't even considered the fact that my brother might be able to help me locate her. I gave bro a call immediately.

"What's good, bro?" he answered the phone, sounding irritated.

"Shit, what's good wit' you?"

"Nothin' and I mean that literally. Some niggas tried to kill Kalief, but the thing is, I think the hit was for me."

"Word?" I shook my head in disbelief.

"Word. Now this nigga, Rico thinkin' it's this one nigga named, Dro and he plannin' a fuckin' war as we speak, but I don't think it's him."

"You gone let that shit pop off?"

by Santana

"Shit, I might have to. Ain't no stoppin' this nigga, Rico when he mad."

"Let me know if you need me. You know I got hittas. You better use me while you can," I offered.

"Fasho. But you got business, what's up?"

"A'ight man, now I know you and Izzy ain't always seen eye-to-eye but I need your help. Long story short, I did some fucked-up shit and she ran off. I haven't seen her in damn near three months and to be real, I can't take it no more man." Shit was truly killin' me.

I knew I could admit it to him cuz that nigga did hella sucka shit over pussy.

"I understand. I can have my nigga, Drew get a location on her. He in Cali too, so it's your lucky day. I'll send you his number and tell him to do everything he can. I know that's yo' heart, nigga."

"Thank you, dog. She really is."

When we ended the call, I waited patiently for this Drew nigga to call, text or something. After a few hours, he finally called and I gave him every piece of information I had on Isabella. It wasn't much but it would do.

"I'll pay you whatever you need, just make this shit happen, and fast," I urged him before ending the call.

He said he would do what he could and would get back to me as soon as he had something. I bit the inside of my jaw as I sat there pondering on where she could be and what the fuck she was up to. I couldn't help but think she had found a new nigga and moved on. I was really losin' it just imagining another nigga fuckin' her like I did. That shit had me so upset I didn't even realize my nose was bleeding.

See? I was completely out my shit and nobody was safe until I found her. Whoever these niggas was that my brother was finna go to war with was gone get all of this rage and anger taken out on them, and whoever else that wanted to be involved. This state I was in mentally and emotionally couldn't possibly be healthy, and it was now affecting me physically. My head was pounding as I tried to stop my nose from bleeding.

Aside from not seeing Isabella in three months, I also hadn't fucked in three months either. A nigga was hella backed up. I battled against my weak flesh, the same weak flesh that had me cheating on Liyah with Isabella. I couldn't help it. I needed some pussy and I was gonna get some. Yeah, I coulda jacked-off but I needed to feel a woman. The only woman I truly wanted was nowhere to be found so I searched through my phone for the answer to my problem. I found Kalani's number and dialed it.

"Hello?" she answered softly.

"What's up, Kalani?"

"Chase?" She sounded unsure.

"Yeah it's me."

I heard her smack her lips.

"What you want?" she asked. Her attitude was apparent and understandable.

I fucked her at the club then was in VIP cuddled up with Liyah right after. I know she felt used but when I say she owed me some pussy, I meant that. Kalani played unnecessarily hard to get. I mean, she really acted like she ain't like a nigga and like she ain't wanna let me fuck. I can't stand a woman that plays that role wit' me. That's just gone make me fuck and dip. Now I needed something to hold me over 'til I could have my girl back and she was it.

"I want you. What you doin'? I wanna go somewhere," I told her hoping she wouldn't put up a fight. With the way I was feeling, I would just pull up and take that shit. I wouldn't be nice and take her somewhere to eat first and throw her ass some money.

I felt like I was cheating, but shit, it wouldn't be the first time and Isabella left *me*. I didn't have any obligations to be faithful to someone that didn't even want to be with me.

"Where?" she asked, snapping me out of my battle with the devil.

"Let's go eat, get a room, and go swimming. I wanna see yo ass in a swimsuit. That muhfucka still fat?"

"Don't worry about it."

"Why you so difficult, Kalani?"

"Cuz you think you can fuck wit' me whenever you want and I'm supposed to be okay with being the bitch you call last minute," she fussed.

"You know I been dealin' wit' a lot of shit! You part of the reason I'm getting a fuckin' divorce now. Chasing you down for some pussy you wasn't even tryna give me," I shot back.

"Really, Chase? You blaming me for your divorce? For you cheating?"

"Yeah, sure fuckin' am. I couldn't help it, I wanted you too bad. You made it your business to be somewhere close every time I made drops to your brother. You ain't have to be there, especially dressed like that. You knew what you were doin,' Kay."

"You are full of it." She chuckled at my blatant stupidity.

"I want you to be full of me."

"Chase, come on. I don't have all night," she said, then I heard the beeps signaling she'd hung up on me.

by $\mathit{Santana}$

I got myself together and grabbed my overnight bag. I
scooped Kalani from her apartment and we were on our way to
eat. I was gonna take her somewhere nice because although she
wasn't my girl, she still deserved the best. Kalani was a bad
bitch and if I wasn't already head over for a badder bitch, I
would be chasin' her fine ass down tryna wife her.

As we headed into Iridescence, I couldn't keep my eyes
off her round ass that she squeezed into that tight-ass dress.

"Shit Kalani," I moaned as I smacked it and it jiggled.

"Chase." She smiled at me seductively.

Words couldn't explain how terrible I was about to fuck
her tonight. It should be a crime. She was finna get all this dick.
Three months' worth of backed up nut was finna be all down
her throat in a couple of hours.

I ain't gone lie, I was feelin' vulnerable as fuck with her.
Kalani had always been someone that I couldn't resist. She
always escaped my grip though. Every time I was about to
move in for the kill, something would come up. When I finally
got her ass that day in the club, I had to make her pay for lost
time. But leave it to me to be the typical nigga and still play her.
After that, I rarely saw Kalani. We had only snuck around to
fuck a few more times and then I was with Isabella. We hooked
back up a few more times but by then, all the drama had ensued

by Santana

and I had to leave Kalani again. I knew she was sick of me, but not sick enough obviously.

Looking at her sitting there, breathtakingly gorgeous, made me realize one thing: I was a piece of shit. I had all these beautiful women, including Liyah, and still was never satisfied. I had hurt every last one of them and they still fucked with me, and I *still* hurt them again. It was like I was addicted to causing other people pain. None of them deserved it and that was the part that fucked with me.

Aaliyah, my soon-to-be ex-wife had been the sweetest girl at one point. She was always mine and I took that shit for granted. She never gave me any problems, other than small misunderstandings with her. It was always me causing the drama; me and my dick. My big-ass dick. Liyah was the perfect fucking wife until I started to slowly break her down with all the side-bitches and lack of attention. She knew the game had its unpredictable moments but on some real shit, it was a business and businesses for the most part had operating hours. All those impromptu "meetings" I made up was just my cover for fucking countless other women. She wanted to leave me so bad, but I constantly played with her emotions and used my dick to keep her with me. Now we were going through a nasty divorce that was gonna drain the shit out of my accounts and cause me to have to move. Although I kept a rather large stash, I couldn't lie and act like this shit wasn't hurting my pockets and my feelings.

Kalani was one of my partners' sisters and he didn't want none of us even looking at her, but she made it hard as hell not to. When I came to Ronnie's house to bag up, count money or chat, she'd be there and she made certain I saw her every time. She was always subtle, making sure she acted in a way that pulled me to her instead of her ever approaching me. She did little shit, which I may have blown out of proportion, to get my attention but she never made a move. Even though she was grown, she knew better than to fuck wit' any of her brothers' partners. It was just an unspoken rule, but I had to have her. A couple years later, she was still on bullshit until one day I cut into her and told her the next time I saw her, it was mine. I just happened to see her at the club but a promise was a promise. And even though she was someone I had a great deal of respect for, it didn't stop me from stickin' my dick in her and leaving her a mess in that bathroom.

Then there was Isabella, my fuckin' heartbeat. That little evil, good pussy, pretty muhfucka meant everything to me, even more than my wife. She was freaky, feisty, and fun as hell to be around. She was truly my best friend. That childhood shit created a bond between us that I felt could never be broken. So much shit occurred that I knew would've torn the average couple apart, but it did nothing but add more fuel to the fire that burned inside me for her. Yeah, even after she tried to get me murked, I loved her no less. That is possibly the most foolish shit ever spoken but I now understand how bitches be letting niggas dog them in the name of love. That shit was not a joke. It was real.

I sat there admiring Kalani as she played with her food. For some reason, I was enjoying watching her. She had this innocent air about her but she was a nasty li'l bitch wit' some fye-ass pussy. She was the embodiment of a lady in the streets but a freak in the bed. My feelings were becoming more conflicted with each moment I spent watching her in a trance-like state. The way her lips looked as she slurped her spaghetti. Her long eyelashes fluttered as she savored the sauce. She was like a cute little kitten and it made me wanna love her instead of dickin' her down all stupid, but I still was though.

I couldn't wait until we were back at the hotel so I could get deep in her guts. I missed her energy and I missed her tryna run from this dick. I loved her attitude and how she tried to be so mean 'til I had her bent over.

Speaking of having her bent over, Kalani was now takin' these backshots like a pro, like she missed me just as much as I missed her. I watched her face through the bathroom mirror and she was in a state of bliss. I had to smile at myself. My dick was the shit.

"Goddamn, I missed you baby," I panted as I tried to hold my nut.

"I missed you too daddy," she purred as I repeatedly hit her spot.

Her knees finally gave out as I caught her just as she was about to hit the floor.

"Keep up, girly," I whispered in her ear as I squeezed and smacked her fat ass.

Grabbing her throat, I pulled her into me and kept my pace and she begged for mercy. There was none. She had to get all of it and this was only round one. By round three she was crying, and barely audible moans filled our suite. I just stared into her deep brown eyes with a fistful of her hair held tightly in my hand.

"You gone make me love you, Kalani," I slipped and said. I tried to stop myself but there were too many emotions running through me.

"Chase, don't do that." She was losing her voice from all the screaming I had her doing.

"Do what?"

"Don't make me love you too." That was her way of telling me the feeling was mutual.

THE OTHER SIDE OF A THUG
SHE WAS A THUG'S WEAKNESS 2
by Santana

Man, what the fuck was I doin'? I had no idea but the shit felt good. I felt like I could fuck her forever. I loved her submissive side. It balanced out her snappy attitude. Once we finished, we got in the shower and just kissed. We didn't even fuck again cuz we were both spent, but we couldn't keep our hands off each other. I couldn't explain what was happening. Now usually a nigga would be thinkin' about his girl but Kalani had me invested. She took my mind completely off the situation.

Matter of fact, she was the best distraction I had. So much so that I spent all my free time with her. I didn't know if I was rebounding cuz the feeling had always been there, but I was happy that my heart had healed a little and the void had been filled, somewhat. Kalani was invading the fuck out of my space and I genuinely loved it. Now I don't fall easily but damn, she made it hard not to. I never noticed how sweet she was, partly cuz anytime we spent together was punishment for her not fuckin' me soon as I would've liked. Kalani was wife material and I'm not sayin' that cuz I was missin' Isabella.

Kalani cooked for me, kept my house clean, gave me back rubs, and stayed givin' me stupid-good neck and pussy. She even waved me off when I told her about my possible shortage of funds and me having to relocate. She was around through my depressive episodes after going to court. That shit was truly killing me inside and if I didn't have the little ounce of love I did have for Liyah, I would've killed her ass for real. She was straight rapin' a nigga pockets. But Kalani didn't care about the money. She knew I'd bounce back so she stuck around and held me down through some of my worst moments.

I shuddered thinkin' about Isabella comin' back in my life. How the fuck was I supposed to let Kalani go and she was doin' a nigga so right? Plus, she was fine as hell wit' a fat ass. I wanted to stop her from giving me all this attention and love but she insisted. I was being treated like a king. Kalani was treating me so good I thought about paying them both to be polygamous just so I wouldn't have to give her up. My Capricorn side had me feelin' like Peter Gunz.

TRE

I still hadn't been able to get any closer to solving this case. I was completely in the dark about who had it out for me, but I wasn't gonna give up until somebody was no longer breathing. I still hadn't been able to find that bitch-nigga Silas since he shot up the club that night, and I knew Dro wasn't gone give up his uncle for nobody, no matter how much wrong he did. Dro protected that nigga like it was his son cuz Silas definitely acted like a child. He never had much sense but out of respect for Dro, niggas let him be. But I wasn't. As soon as I located that clown, I was gone have Marcus kill him.

I could've landed back in prison had I been stupid enough to get into that gun battle at the club that night. It almost cost us our business as well. Thank God for connections. We reopened shortly after that but even that time off had fucked with our cash flow and cost us some customers willing to pay big for that venue. I didn't let it bother me, but this shit here had been nagging at me since the day it happened. I didn't care what nobody said. Those bullets had been meant for me.

Luckily, I had Drew on the case looking into some shit for me. He was gonna find me a location on Silas so we could put an end to at least some of the shit that was plaguing my spirit. This mess was affecting my relationship with Jas. I had to distance myself from her because if anything happened to her because of me, I'd lose my shit. I was even dreaming about a bullet hitting her. That was why I knew I had to cut her loose for a minute and I knew she wasn't gonna like it.

"Jas, I'm not saying we done but we need to chill for a minute." I tried to convince her but she wasn't havin' it.

"Nah, just tell me you're having second thoughts. I can handle it. You've been nothing but bullshit since we met."

"Jasmine! Just listen to me."

"You listen to *me*, just leave me alone this time. I knew this was a bad idea." She was trippin'.

Ain't no idea felt better than the day I stuck my dick in her. I desperately wanted to choke her for being so stubborn but that just meant she cared. That made me happy. For a while I sincerely thought Jas couldn't fall. I thought she was as tough as she seemed, but this last month really showed me the real her and she was soft as baby shit. My mind dragged me to a place I would have liked to stay away from, but I couldn't help but to imagine all the ways I could make her crazy. All the ways I could make her succumb to me. But later for that. I had to keep her out of harm's way until this shit blew over.

"Listen baby, I got a few things to handle and this will all be over soon. You can come back to daddy then. It won't be

long, I swear to you. But for now, we gotta keep our distance."
It pained me to have to do this to her.

I saw the way she looked at me, like I was the most handsome nigga she ever laid eyes on. The way she kissed me made my body hot. She was so fuckin' sexual. I even loved the way she talked crazy to me. I loved how she responded to me sexually and how she was giving me a hard time about this temporary break. Jas was what I needed. She kept me in line, kept me disciplined, but also fed the hell out of my ego.

"If I leave, I won't be back. I have a feeling this ain't about what you tryna make it about, so I'll save myself the trouble. Bye, Tre."

"Don't leave yet." I had to get some of that good shit before she tried to cut me off.

I grabbed and pulled her close to me. She tensed up but once I started kissing and sucking her neck, she relaxed. I undressed her beautiful body and just gawked at her. She was perfect. I watched her eyes beg me not to do this, not to leave her, and not to stick my dick in her and destroy her. I took my time though. I touched her everywhere, almost like a massage but with kisses, biting, choking and ass-smacking, the shit she lived for. By the time I was done teasing her, she was dying to get my dick inside her.

She was so wet and warm, I could've lain there forever. I heard her whimpering. This girl cried every time I fucked her. It was lowkey a major turn-on. Watching her tough ass go from gangsta to bitch was everything my ego needed. I slid in carefully, filling her up with all of me, while she panted and moaned beneath me.

"Jas, I swear to God, we'll be back," I said as I plunged deeper inside.

All she could do was cry and try to cover her face. I quickly pinned both her wrists. I wanted to see her in all her beautiful vulnerability. Those tears had meaning.

"You love me, don't you?" I asked her.

"Tre, don't, not right now. Don't do this." She struggled to get loose but I wasn't gonna let her. I needed to know how she felt.

"Do what?" I pounded her harder to get it out of her.

"This. Don't do this to me right now," she begged.

"Do you fuckin' love me?"

By now she was on the brink of orgasm. I repeated myself and went harder until she screamed out, "Yesssss!"

I knew it. Jas was mine.

I left her there in a mess in the middle of my bed as I went to get a warm cloth. I cleaned her up then went back to the bathroom to pee. When I came back, Jas had dipped. That shit stung. I tried calling her but to my dismay, she blocked me. I didn't know where her new place was cuz she had just moved and hadn't given me the address.

I couldn't believe she didn't believe me on this even though her homeboy was recovering from the aftermath of someone tryna get at me. She was being unnecessarily stubborn. I was steaming because she blocked me but I knew I'd get her back. I knew she was just a little hurt right now, but she'd get over it.

After she dipped on me, I called Pulanko to see if he had any news and luckily, he did. I raced to my fax machine as he sent me the information as well as a blueprint of the building Silas was hiding out in. I shot him a "thank you" text and looked over the blueprints. I had to get Marcus on this nigga ASAP cuz even though this would soon be a dead issue, it still didn't account for the other occurrences.

"Yo, bro come through. I got a job for you," I told my brother. He automatically knew that meant a kill.

He was pulling up to the house in no time. He made it inside and sat down with me to talk business and plot Silas' murder.

MARCUS

I had found Silas and watched as his stupid ass walked around like he was good out here. He was good as dead. That was the only good he was. Silas was a drunk, a pill head and a fuckin' failure but the nigga had a mean trigger finger back in the day. I don't know what happened to him but he was a shell of the nigga he used to be.

As I walked up the steps of the rickety apartment he was cooped-up in, I startled him as he stood there jingling keys to let himself in.

"Sup homeboy?" I asked, making my presence known.

"Marcus, wha- what's good?" He jumped but calmed down when he realized it was me.

"Nothin' much. We need to have a talk."

He invited me inside thinkin' shit was sweet until he saw my attire and the Jansport backpack I was armed with. He knew what time it was. He started to plead his case profusely. He dropped to his knees, clasping his sweaty palms together in a praying motion. I stood there, playing with a toothpick, eyeing his pathetic attempt to beg for mercy with disgust.

"Silas, I'm sorry man but your time's up."

I started to set up the scene for the kill. I had been perfecting my technique for a while now. Absolutely nothing could ever be traced back to me. I was so good now that a muhfucka coulda watched me do it and I would still get away with it. I secured the premises making sure to cover any footprints. I had plastic on my shoes and had sprayed my clothes with repellant to keep any fibers from attaching themselves to me. I wrapped my locs in plastic all while wearing gloves that covered my arms up to my elbows. I laid a plastic liner on the dingy carpeting while trying my best to tune out his begging. I then hogtied him so he couldn't try to fight his way out of his fate. He would meet a timely death today by any means.

Anyone who came against my brother would get this type of treatment. I loved that nigga regardless of the shit we'd been through. The recent information I found about him fuckin' Ava admittedly burned me, but that shit was old. I asked her about it and she didn't flinch, she owned up to it. But I had been lost all feelings for her anyway so I wasn't trippin' too hard. It was just the fact that he never told me. This was his second time goin' behind my back but I had something for him.

I continued to safety-proof the area where Silas would meet the devil. At this point, I had completely tuned out his incessant whining. I saw the look of sheer terror in his eyes as the veins in his forehead bulged. He was red in the face as he cried so hard, the tears and sweat started to loosen the duct tape

by $Santana$

that secured his mouth. I kept a smile on my face as I happily prepared his deathbed. Silas had failed me too many times.

I snatched the tape from his mouth and he winced in pain, realizing pieces of his beard went with it.

"Marcus please, don't do this man!" he pleaded, but it fell on deaf ears. "Why are you doing this?"

But this time I answered, "Because you tried to kill my brother... and you missed..."

His eyes got bigger than saucers. "But you're the one who..." And a bullet between the eyes silenced him forever.

I chuckled as I swished my toothpick around my teeth. I called the cleaners and waited a few minutes for them to come. I suddenly didn't have the energy to mutilate his body anymore. Anxiety washed over me. I sat there sighing heavily to myself, considering the situation at hand. I hired someone to do a job, they failed, and now I had to do extra work to make up for their and my failures.

After they finished removing Silas' body, I made my way back to my car, but not before noticing a familiar car at the scene. I made note and proceeded to leave. I went to the burn house, which was where I took any evidence that I had from a kill and burned it. After I was done, I headed to Liyah's' house. That was where I'd been spending most of my time. Crazy she ended up just like Isabella, fuckin' three brothers. Regardless, she gave me valuable information so I was thankful for that. And the bitch pussy was good.

I noticed me and my brothers had the knucklehead gene. We would have these fine-ass women that fucked us good and treated us right but we just couldn't do the same in return. Shit was crazy but I enjoyed Liyah while I could. I knew after all this shit blew over we would probably be better off never seeing each other again. She ain't need to know that though. For right now, she was good fuckin' and suckin' me while I planned my brother's funeral.

KIA

Being stuck up under Rico for the last few weeks was toying with my emotions. I wanted to feel he had changed, but I couldn't help but think it was because he was under his own emotional distress. I had somewhat gotten over him but I still loved him, there was no denying that. However, constantly ignoring phone calls from Dro's snake-ass was eating at my sanity. The texts he sent me didn't reflect someone who had tried to take the life of my brother a few weeks ago. Dro struck me as the type to admit his fuck up so it was odd that he was texting me "Where are you?" "Why'd you leave?" as opposed to "Look I know I fucked up."

Rico had been treating me like a pregnant girlfriend the whole time. He was rubbing my feet and back, spending copious amounts of time with me and constantly checking the status of my well-being. It was scary almost but I couldn't say I didn't like it. I just wished he had been like this a long time ago. I would've never been exposed to Dro if Rico was treating me like I deserved.

I was fighting back the urge to text Dro. With Rico down my throat so much, I knew he would catch me sooner or later so I eventually blocked him and let it go. I trusted Rico's word to an extent, so I let things ride even though my heart was pulling me in another direction. Ain't it crazy how we fight tooth and nail for a man's love and when we finally get it, we don't want it no more? This was my situation. What made it so hard was that Rico and Dro were both attractive, had money and respect in the streets. I wasn't leaving some broke, whack-dick nigga for a good man. I was going from good to what I felt was better until he tried to kill my bro.

This was the hardest situation I'd dealt with in a long time. I had never been this torn. Dro was perfect for me. He was sweet, attentive, and took things serious with me. He didn't play games like other men. He was straight-forward and honest. You just had to ask him. He never volunteered information. I especially loved the way he handled me. He disciplined my ass and had me wanting to act right. My heart ached every moment I had to be away from him. I wished it didn't have to be like this but, unfortunately it was. I had to let him go and I knew it would kill me emotionally.

I knew I didn't have that same passion for Rico anymore but being with him was familiar for me. Sometimes I hated the sight of him. It brought back too many times I had been stupid as hell for him, too many times he took advantage of my feelings for him. But then other times, I was so happy he was around. I remembered the good times and things felt right. Still, Dro wasn't gonna leave my mind any time soon.

I rolled my eyes as I jumped up to get dressed and have a day with my girls. I pulled up at Jas' condo. This was the first time I really even got to see it. We had been so wrapped up in niggas and the shit that happened with Kalief that we'd barely seen each other, much less got to see her new place. I reached the door and rang the bell. It was loud as hell. A few moments later, she appeared at the large wooden door and let me in. Her place was laid out.

The whole front area of her condo was a sparkly white and the foyer was adorned with a sunroof and a beautiful crystal chandelier. I followed her up the steps to her living room that was nicely furnished with a black U-sectional and 70-inch flat-screen, with black, white and teal accent pieces. The lamps and vases that were scattered lovingly were silver, with glitter sequined throw pillows. It was gorgeous. She showed me her bedroom and I wanted to fall in the middle of her bed and stay there.

Her master was heavenly. Her champagne-colored bedroom set had me gawking. The cushioned headboard had huge rhinestones in the center of each square. It was so stately, it looked like something a queen would take up residence in. Everything was so neat and new. It had me ready to move immediately.

by Santana

"Bitchhhh, this is immaculate. I am jelly as hell right now," I exclaimed as I scoured through her closet, making note of a few bags and shoes I was gonna talk her into letting me borrow.

"Thank you. Maybe one day we can see Simone's. When she get her head out of Kalief's ass long enough to acknowledge we exist." We both laughed. We knew Simone would disappear for large portions of time when she had a man.

"Girl, we about to go get her now. We gone barge all up and through that bitch. I'm stealing something," I added as we fell out laughing again.

"I'm done with you." She pushed my shoulder before grabbing her coat and leading me to the door.

"No but seriously, I gotta find me a new place too. Too many memories in that old apartment." I thought about all the shit I endured with Rico, then my mind went to Dro eating my pussy on the couch. It was too much.

"Well I got a great realtor. This place barely cost me 100 grand."

"Really?" My eyes bucked.

Her condo was lavish, nothing short of rich-bitch status—three beds, two baths and that lovely lower area with a den, exercise room, and huge sliding glass door leading to a nice-sized backyard equipped with a deck. I hardly believed it was anything less than 200K.

"Yes girl. The real estate market is trash. You better hop in one before they gone. Simone got one a few streets over but she been with Kalief. She hasn't even slept there yet."

"Straight? And you heauxs ain't even tell me?" I popped the locks on my car as we headed out.

"Don't start. You know I mentioned it but you was too busy getting dog-fucked by Dro." She rolled her eyes.

"I was. I need some advice too. Just listen and don't make an opinion until I'm done talking," I instructed her. She was known to cut you off to cut into you.

"Don't do me," she warned.

"Okay bitch. Now you know Rico is accusing Dro of having Kalief shot, but then Tre says he doesn't think it was him. He thinks the person who has been behind all the other shit that's been happening to him is behind this too, and it ain't Dro cuz him and Tre don't have beef. Dro has been non-stop texting and calling and genuinely concerned about me not responding. And his texts don't reflect a guilty nigga conscience. That nigga has always been honest with me and I know if I just ask him if he had anything to do with this, he'd tell me. However, I'm scared to even ask, cuz if he did, that would hurt me so bad. I just took Rico's word for it cuz if I ask Dro and he didn't do it, then it's gonna seem like I'm being disloyal to the whole clique by doubting Rico and giving Dro a chance to clear his name." I sighed deeply after my long-winded speech.

I knew Jas wouldn't judge me for wanting to know for myself if Dro was responsible, but I thought she might flip because her feelings about Kalief were so strong. I was a little scared of her response but braced myself anyway.

"Ki, it's no harm in asking. If you trust he'll tell the truth, then it's only right you get to the bottom of this cuz if it's not him, and Rico is planning some shit, it's only gonna get worse. It's gone be two people coming for our niggas now." That was true and made a lot of sense.

"You right."

"You really like that muhfucka don't you?" She smiled and tickled my cheek, teasing me.

"Bitch yes. I'm damn near in—"

She cut me short. "Don't you fuckin' dare." She put her finger up to stop me from saying the "L" word.

Crazy how love and lost were both "L" words that could describe my situation.

"But anyways girl, guess what?"

I knew it was about to be something about Tre.

"Tre dumped me. Even though we not together, he said we need a break from seeing each other until this shit blows over. I mean, I understand he wouldn't want anything to happen to me but that shit hurt." I could tell she had fallen for him. She rarely ever talked like this.

"Wow, so what did you say?"

"After we finished having sex, I dipped and blocked him. I don't know why I don't believe that that's the only reason, I just don't." She shrugged. Trust was far and few for her but she had good reason.

"Jas, his car got shot up. Kalief could've been you."

"I know, Kia but you know how I am firsthand. That shit burned me. Like, I *just* let my guard down. I admitted some shit I shouldn't have. I risked it all for him and he just so easily says we need a break. He could have at least acted sad or something. He was too cool about it. Ki, this shit is hard. Look at him. He's like my dream nigga. His attitude and personality is exactly what I needed. He's soft and gentle but still will put a bitch in line. His sex is mind-blowing and he is patient with me and handles my craziness so well. This nigga didn't even flinch when I pulled a knife on him." She chuckled, flashing back to their first encounter.

"Everything moved so fast. It was all so wrong but so fuckin' right. This thug-ass nigga from a hood fantasy I tucked away in my subconscious, right in my face, challenging me, pulling at emotions I thought I no longer possessed. The shit is scary how open he got me. I cried in front of this nigga. Kia and now he's just throwing me away." Jas was speaking poetry right now.

She was singing my life as well as hers. That's exactly how I felt about Dro *and* Rico. I listened intently as she simultaneously described both our situations.

"After that shit with Monty, I was determined not to feel anything else again and you know I already have trouble with feeling and expressing emotions as it is. But then a couple months later I meet this nigga and I'm more open than I've ever been? What types of games is the universe playing with me?"

"Girl, now you see how I feel. I got two niggas I got feelings for. You should be happy you not in my predicament," I told her.

"Girl, bye. It ain't nothin' like having two men fighting for your love." With that, we pulled into Kalief's driveway.

We huddled at the door waiting for someone to let us in cuz it was chilly out. Fall had set in early in Detroit this year. Simone snatched the door open and greeted us with hugs and a huge, genuine smile. She looked happy, but who, aside from Kema's ungrateful ass wouldn't be happy to have Kalief?

"Boo, we missed you." Jas beamed as they embraced.

"I missed y'all. Kalief said come to the back and see him." She ushered us to his bedroom where he sat on the edge of the bed, swallowing pain pills.

"Brother!" Jas and I said in unison as we crowded him with hugs and kisses which he welcomed with opened arms.

"You feel any better?" Jas asked as she sat close to him. She could relate the most seeing as she had been shot just a few months prior.

"Gettin' there, sis. These pain pills and my baby nursing me is doing the trick," he said, referring to Simone. I knew she had been taking good care of him in more ways than one. She had been obsessed with Kalief for a while now.

"I'm happy to hear that. You gone be okay for a while if we kidnap Simone?" I wanted to make sure.

"Y'all go ahead. I'll be fine. I ain't paralyzed."

"You call me if you need me," Simone said as she kissed him and hurried out the door behind us.

Once we were situated in the car, Simone took notice of our huge grins from the backseat.

"Don't y'all heauxs start." She giggled.

"START!" I motioned, pressing a start button.

"Fuck that shit, how's the dick?" Jas asked in her usual blunt fashion.

THE OTHER SIDE OF A THUG
SHE WAS A THUG'S WEAKNESS 2

by Santana

"Everything I wanted and more. Even when he's in pain he puts it the fuck down. He's so gentle but rough too. Girlllllll, y'all just don't understand how long I've waited to get a piece of that dick," she bellowed with all these dramatic hand gestures. My girl was ecstatic.

"Oh yes we do, bitch," I cut in. Being her best friends, we knew better than anyone how long she waited.

"Anyways, we gotta plan my housewarming. I want it to be in about two weeks, on a Saturday," Jas informed us.

"Will do. We can have mama cater it and Simone can buy the liq since she rich now." We all cackled.

"I'd be more than happy while you volunteering me bitch."

We pulled up to Somerset Mall and left with too many bags to carry. Once we were done, we had lunch then I dropped the girls back off and returned to Rico's. I was honestly ready to go back home but after he text me several times begging me to come back, I caved.

When I got there, he opened the door in a white bath robe and slippers. He took my hand, ushering me up the winding staircase to his bedroom where he had rose petals trailing to the jacuzzi tub in the bathroom. He helped me undress and step in where he joined me with weed and champagne. We got so drunk and high that I momentarily forgot all the bullshit and drama, and let him weasel his way back into my pussy.

"Don't fuckin' leave me again," was all he kept repeating as he pounded me like a maniac.

"I won't, Ricooooo!" I cried out as waves of pleasure shook my body and had me questioning why I would ever leave.

The thing I hated most about myself was my whirlwind of emotional turmoil and confusion. I now had no idea where I wanted to be, all because Rico had turned over a new leaf suddenly. He was being so attentive, romancing me and fucking my brains out. This was all I had wanted from the start.

CHAPTER ELEVEN

Hurricane Winter

RICO

Word had already gotten back to Dro about his soldiers that I personally killed about two weeks ago, and I was still plottin' on him. I had to at least rid him of those who could protect him the best. The ones I got that night were like some jihadis for Dro's organization. With them gone, a war would have significantly less casualties on my end.

In the meantime, I was spoiling Kia like I should have been. She looked happier and that was all I wanted. I had to try excruciatingly hard to forgive her for letting that nigga slide up in her but having her back allowed the good to outweigh the bad.

"Yo Kia, I'll be back. I got some shit to handle real quick but when daddy get home, he got something for you okay?" I said before stroking her cheek and giving her a kiss.

This simple shit was all she wanted and I felt really stupid for refusing to give her these small things the whole time. I walked to my truck, got in, and headed to my stash spot to count-up the new shipment that arrived. Whatever connect Tre's brother had given him was that nigga. He kept us supplied and our pockets were literally growing by the hour. With this new influx of cash, life was only lookin' better.

I pulled up and spotted a familiar car. It was Dro and my heart started to race. I grabbed my burner preparing for the worst as I exited my car and walked toward him.

"You real funny my nigga. Even after I said no beef, you go and pull some shit like you did." He shook his head at me disappointingly.

"Me? Nigga, you the one sending yo fuckin' goon Silas to try to get at me but ended up hittin' Kalief. Man, fuck you. *You* went back on yo' own word." I poked him in the chest.

"I sent who? Silas? Of all fuckin' people, I sent Silas pill-head, no aim havin'-ass to get at the city's most feared?" He chuckled. "You know I got better men. The ones you killed for no fuckin' reason." He flicked his blunt then passed it to me. This nigga was so weird.

"So, if you ain't send him, who did? Cuz that's who it was," I said matter-of-factly.

"Shit sound like an inside job wit' some framing involved. You know good and fuckin' well I don't move like that. If I want somebody dead, they get dead. I wouldn't send no damn Silas to get at you and secondly, we ain't got beef, nigga!"

"FUCKKKK!" I knew this nigga wasn't lying. I had allowed my feelings to blind me, now the consequences could be deadly.

"Yeah muhfucka so now what? Truth be told, I ain't in no position for this shit but..."

"Nigga, you took my bitch."

"You ain't gone use her for leverage in this. I know she been at yo' house lately cuz you made her think I had something to do with this, but this shit bigger than her. You ain't the only nigga here I gotta worry about. Shit, you was like the only nigga here I thought I *didn't* have to worry about. Seems I was wrong."

Niggas take losses in the game all the time but this was an unnecessary one, a big one. Street soldiers are an integral part of stayin' alive. It was like I disarmed him in a sense. This would've been a smart move had me and him had any ill-feelings for real.

"A'ight listen, how about we team up." I sensed his hesitation. "For now, until you get some replacements. I'll even throw in some work. Look man, I really am sorry shit happened like this but I really thought you set that shit up."

"If I *ever* hear..."

"Look dawg, we cool. I won't say shit. This stays between us. I just don't want to be lookin' over my shoulder," I assured him.

"You got my word." And with that he threw the tail and walked back to his car.

I felt like a weight was lifted off my shoulders. Silas was dead and this shit was solved. I was thinkin' this was a little too easy, but I realized it was when I walked into my stash spot and saw he had already taken three bricks and the cash I had waiting to be counted.

"This muhfucka," I said, chuckling to myself.

After I finished counting my money and tallying up my losses, I was still on top so I locked up and headed to the jeweler to pick up the surprise I had for Kia. I was finna make shit hella official.

Baby, get sexy and meet me at the Westin. I wanna take you somewhere nice.

I shot her a text and went to get myself together for tonight. I showered, dabbed on some Gucci cologne, and hopped into my navy blue Tom Ford Windsor suit. I was never really a suit guy but the occasion called for one and I kept a few tailored suits on hand, just in case I ever needed one. Ever since Tre cut into us about looking more professional.

THE OTHER SIDE OF A THUG
SHE WAS A THUG'S WEAKNESS 2
by Santana

A nigga looked real classy tonight and when Kia arrived in a sheer, studded out fuck-me dress, she complemented the hell out of my look. Her hair was freshly curled and her makeup was flawless. She was flawless as always.

We headed out for a night on the town. We hit some expensive restaurant, drank to our hearts content, and then finally ended back up at the hotel. I opened the door for her and helped her walk in. She was staggering a bit but she made it to the bed. Her hands immediately clasped around her mouth when she read the message in rose petals, "Will you marry me, Kia?" and when she turned around, I was on one knee with that $300,000 rock twinkling in her face.

"Fuck yes," she said as she broke down crying. "You don't know how long I waited to hear you say that."

She kissed me hard, almost making both of us tumble to the ground, but I caught her. I always caught her. Then I slid the ring on her hand and she was already in stunt mode. Her eyes lit up with happiness and I knew she couldn't wait to show her girls.

They were gonna act an ass when they saw that and hopefully they would be happy for us, cuz not too long ago, Jas and I had fallen out. I had no idea if she was still holding that against me for hurting Kia. Nevertheless, me and my baby were engaged and we were gonna be happy.

301

KIA

"Damnnnnn!" Jas squealed as I showed off my big-ass rock in her and Simone's faces.

"That is fuckin' gorgeous, bitch!" Simone told me, fawning over it.

"I cannot wait 'til we plan this wedding. It's gon' be lit!" I squeaked as I finally put my hand back at my side. I had been admiring my ring since the moment he put it on my finger.

But Jas' next comment snapped my happy ass back into reality.

"So, I take it you didn't talk to Dro?" Leave it to her.

"No, I didn't. I don't think it matters now, Jas. Rico finally chose me after all this time."

"As opposed to a nigga that chose you the minute he saw you." She rolled her eyes.

She was right though. But I wasn't about to ruin my happiness with what ifs. I wanted to get on with my life and marry Rico. I couldn't stop to think about Dro because if he did do it, then I was getting married anyway. It was just the "if he didn't" part. That truly ate me up. I was throwing away a good man that saw my value immediately for someone who took years. I also felt like Rico was only doing this because he was afraid to lose me, and not because he truly wanted to love me right. Dammit! Leave it to Jas to get me thinkin' crazy.

"Well anyway heauxs, let's get it poppin'. We gotta celebrate. I can call and get a booth at Club Mix tonight. They supposed to be slappin'!" Simone exclaimed before pulling out her phone to make the call.

After securing us a table, we all got dolled up, took pictures to flood Instagram and Facebook with and headed out the door. We arrived in bad-bitch style, parking in valet and jumping the long line that was wrapped around the building. Typical envious eyes roamed our bad-ass bodies wondering who we were. We headed to our VIP booth and had bottles and shots delivered. I was so happy I even found a group of bad bitches who weren't in VIP and invited them up. We all toasted to me, got drunk as fuck, and danced on each other like the freak heauxs we were.

Jas and one of the girls were getting extra friendly in the corner. I was pleasantly surprised to witness them swapping kisses while trading lap dances. Simone grabbed her ankles as she bent over to jiggle her ass to "Skywalker" by Miguel and Travis Scott. It was such a feel-good song and a feel-good moment. However, I wasn't enjoying it as much as I should have been. I couldn't stop thinking about the conversation Jas hit me with earlier.

I excused myself to the bathroom where I hit my face with some water. Drunk or not, it didn't impair my thoughts at all. My mind was racing a mile a minute. However, when "Signs" by Drake hit the speakers, I couldn't help but dance my way through the crowd. I was winding my thick-ass hips, and mouthing the words to the song as I headed back toward my table. I was so fuckin' emotional and the damn DJ would turn on Drake. I held back intrusive thoughts as I tried to dance the emotion off, then someone grabbed my arm. When I turned around, it was Dro.

My whole heart dropped. I just stared at him. It was over. I knew he didn't do that shit. And that was the first thing he said after I wrestled away from the angry kiss he planted on my mouth.

"You know I ain't do that shit!" he scolded and grabbed my face again.

"Dro, please." I couldn't say nothin' else.

"Man, come wit' me." He grabbed my arm, leading me to the exit.

I went with him. Crying and all, I went. I hit Jas with a text and turned my phone off. I silently cried the whole way to his house, while he sat there smoldering with anger. I felt like my heart was ripping apart.

"Come on," he commanded after shutting off his car.

I unbuckled my seatbelt and followed him inside. There was still silence after we entered. I just stood there looking completely stupid.

"How'd you know where I was?" I finally broke the silence.

"Instagram, Kia." When I realized how he was dressed, I knew he didn't come there to party. He came to snatch me up.

"Okay so what's up?" I shrugged. I was terrified right now.

"Yo, why the fuck you been dodgin' me? You back laid up wit' Rico again right? You let that nigga get in yo' head," he yelled at me. I started backing up toward the door as he walked toward me with narrowed eyes and a menacing scowl. I was shook.

I covered my face with my hands and instantly knew I messed up.

"Kia, what the fuck is this!?" he demanded, pointing to the ring.

I immediately tried to hide my hand that was decorated with the fat-ass rock Rico bought me.

"Bitch, you finna marry that nigga? Over a misunderstanding? You *that* fuckin' desperate? Or you was lyin' when you said you was over him? Which one?!"

I melted into the floor and cried my eyes out while Dro punched the wall out of anger. The drywall shattered and fell into pieces next to me.

"Kia, get the fuck out!" he screamed at me.

"What? How? I rode with you." I pulled myself from the floor to plead my case. This nigga was not finna put me out in the middle of the night.

"*Fuck*! I fuckin' hate you!" He pushed me into the wall he just knocked a hole in.

"Dro, please don't hurt me." I was so small compared to him, he could've thrown my ass straight through that wall if he wanted.

"Who? This nigga got you back on that Dro shit, huh?" He chuckled.

"Damien." I sighed, trying to correct myself.

"Why shouldn't I hurt you? You scared to feel like me? Trust me, it hurts less." He let me go and walked off to his room.

I plopped on the couch and cried until I couldn't anymore. I went to the bathroom and cleaned myself up. I was about to call an Uber and just leave but something wouldn't let me. I tip-toed to his door and turned the knob. He hadn't locked it, so I let myself in. He was still up, lying across his bed scrolling through his phone and listening to heartbreak music.

He had on "Care" by Sonder. I knew he was deep in his feelings.

I expected him to protest when I got in bed with him, but he didn't. He laid his phone down and clasped his hands behind his head. I straddled him, just knowing he was gonna push me off but he didn't do that either. I searched his eyes for permission to kiss him and I found it. I removed his hands from behind his head and placed them on my ass, signaling him to touch all over me, and he did. He squeezed and massaged my butt while I slipped my tongue in and out of his eager mouth. This nigga was so open, it scared me. Him, the man of steel. Damn, did he love me? Nobody could convince me otherwise at this point.

He rose up and removed my dress, admiring my body. He hadn't seen it in a while and I could tell he missed me the way he ogled over my breasts and flat tummy. His eyes lustfully devoured me and he grabbed my throat and bit my shoulder. I winced as I felt tingles everywhere. Then the song changed to "Running on E" by Brent Faiyaz. I immediately started crying listening to those lyrics. A song I just randomly played cuz it was sexy had turned into a mirror of my life.

How did you get that way?

(Don't even hide how you feel)

How did it get this way?

by *Santana*

Make your decision

(You gon' regret it the rest of your life)

Now there's a consequence

Say you're seeing someone else

(Who can love you better than me?)

I'll leave you two alone

Now there's nothing left

(You messed up a good, a good thing)

So there's no coming home

Dro made me feel every word as he angrily but skillfully pounded my spot. All I could do was cry and apologize. He stopped all of a sudden and placed me on top of him.

"What you sorry for?" he asked between heavy kisses.

"This," I panted through tears.

He scanned over my body, using his hand to roam from my neck, to my shoulder, down the length of my arm, to my hand, where he removed my ring and set it on the nightstand. He then positioned me flat on my stomach, gently putting a pillow under me. He re-entered me, holding a fistful of my hair while he stroked me like he had a point to prove. He wore me out until I was hoarse from screaming his name. He made me call him Damien, call him daddy, and I told him I loved him, the whole nine. Long story short, I was sleep before he even returned with the warm cloth.

TRE

"Nigga, them li'l thotties prolly out somewhere turned up celebrating. You did just make her dreams come true. She good bro," I tried to tell Rico once he came over here trippin' at nine in the morning cuz Kia wasn't answering her phone.

"Nah, I don't think so. This shit don't feel right. I been by her house but she ain't there. Call Jas for me, bro. She ain't answer for me."

But I couldn't.

"Dawg, you know she blocked me? I told her we had to chill on seein' each other for a minute until I got this shit straight and she flipped out, blocked my ass and left. So, I can't help you there."

"Damn, that's bold. I told you she was crazy, nigga." He chuckled and lit up a blunt.

"Right and now that all this shit solved and that nigga, Silas dead. I'm good but my bitch won't even talk to me. This shit literally took less than a month. She a trip. And I don't know where she moved to either. It's all bad."

"Well I know where she live, and they prolly together but I can't even get her to answer. We could just do a pop-up but again I don't even know if they there."

by *Santana*

"Let's roll, nigga. I need to see where she live anyway so I can pop-up another time if they not home." We grabbed our jackets and got in his car like two bitches tryna find out if they nigga cheatin'.

We pulled up to some nice-ass condo in Royal Oak and her car was in the driveway. I knew she had to be here since Rico had told me Kia's car was at home. Them bitches in there just ignoring our calls? I wanted to see if they was gone ignore this loud-ass knockin'.

I let Rico stand in front cuz I doubted she'd open the door for me. Seconds later, her pretty ass snatched the door open with a scowl painted on her gorgeous face.

"Aye sis, Kia in there?" Rico asked.

"No. And why the hell you bring this nigga to my house?" She started goin' off as soon as she laid eyes on me. We both barged into her house not givin' a fuck about her protesting.

"So, where the fuck is Kia at then?" He looked around suspiciously.

"Nigga, she prolly at Simone house. You seem super mad. Relax, bro. She's okay. Have some coffee." She poured a cup and handed it to Rico but didn't offer me shit, or give me any eye contact. Evil bitch.

THE OTHER SIDE OF A THUG
SHE WAS A THUG'S WEAKNESS 2
by Santana

He sat on the barstool putting sugar in his coffee while I just stood there feeling left out.

"I'll be right back. Let me get my phone and see if I can get ahold of her." She sashayed off and I couldn't keep my eyes off that ass jigglin' underneath her satin robe.

"She actin' like I ain't even here though bro. Fuck wrong wit' her dog?" I asked Rico as he sat there sippin' that stupid-ass coffee and laughing at my misfortune.

"I told you, she a fuckin' pitbull." He shrugged.

She re-entered the room lookin' like she was ready to stab me.

"She ain't answer but Simone said she's over there. I called her. So there, you can all the way relax now nigga. And don't ever come to my shit like that again. The fuck is wrong wit' y'all?" She tried to shoo us to the door but I wasn't goin' no fuckin where.

Rico left but I stayed.

"Oh, hell no. Get yo' ass out."

"So, I can't get no coffee?" I made myself comfy at her kitchen table.

"Listen bitch, I don't want shit to do with you, okay? I don't have time to be wasting on no nigga that always got drama. You got hoes runnin' up in my face one minute then the next we gotta stop seeing each other cuz you finna get killed.

Sorry, I don't want that type of person near me. You bad luck and I've already had enough wit' the last nigga."

"I'm not listening to none of that bullshit you talkin' a'ight? I'm here now, the drama over with and you can come back to daddy." I stood up to hug her but she shut me down so smooth.

"Tre please, just leave okay? I'm not being put in harm's way for no nigga, especially one like you." She spat.

"One like me? Fuck that supposed to mean?"

"Some drug-dealing nigga that fucked his brother's wife." Damn, she wasn't playin' wit' a nigga at all.

"And what are you? A li'l pill-head bitch who gave up some pussy to a nigga cuz the molly had her out her shit." She had me fucked up.

"Bitch, fuck you."

"You did, the first night I got you alone, remember? You ain't shit special. You just a light-skinned slut wit' a fat ass."

"Okay, so why you here then? You pop-up at my house unannounced for a slut though." I could tell I struck a nerve.

I stepped closer to her and she stepped back. I could tell she was super offended. This was not going how I planned at all. I tried to grab her and you already know what happened.

THE OTHER SIDE OF A THUG
SHE WAS A THUG'S WEAKNESS 2

by Santana

She swung on a nigga so fast and busted me straight in my nose.
I forgot how quick she punched.

"Damn, I must have hurt some feelings huh?" I asked,
covering my nose with a napkin.

"Get the fuck out bitch. I regret all this shit! I knew I
should have never let you near my pussy. You whole-ass bitch."
When she grabbed that knife, I got the fuck on. I was not even
about to play wit' my life like that.

JASMINE

After that bitch left, I hurried and called Kia to make sure she got to Simone's cuz Rico was on his way. I was relieved when she said she had made it. When I got off the phone with her, I heard a knock on my door and I knew it was Tre's bitch ass again. I snatched the door open and there stood Liyah's crazy ass, and this bitch had the nerve to be holding a gun. Well guess what? I let the bitch right on in.

"What's up crazy?" I laughed as she stood there with a menacing scowl.

"What's up bitch? I see you still creepin' around wit' my nigga."

"Girl actually, I left that nigga alone a month ago." I waved her off as I slowly moved toward my kitchen cubby that had my gun in it.

"Oh really? So why he just leave here?"

"He popped up with Rico and tried to get me back, I bloodied his nose, and he ran outta here. So, you need to be mad at him, not me," I retorted.

"Nah, I need to be mad at the hoe that tried to take him." She raised the gun at me.

"No, you don't. Why do you dumb bitches come after the woman when he's the one who owes you loyalty? I didn't even want him. He came at me, stalked me, and damn near kidnapped me for some pussy. I didn't even know about you." I inched back until the gun was in my reach.

"Cuz if it wasn't for you…" Then I grabbed my gun and cocked it before she could even finish her statement.

"Bitch, get the fuck outta my house you crazy-ass hoe!" Then I grabbed my taser and shot her ass with it.

She fell to the floor shaking and convulsing. I immediately called Tre and he rushed back over. I didn't know what to do with this psycho bitch but she had to get the fuck out.

"What the fuck happened?" He panicked when he witnessed the scene.

"This stupid hoe must have been following you. I thought it was you when she knocked so I opened it without checking and it was her."

"A'ight, I'll do something with her and I'll be back, okay? Just please stay here.

He dragged her half-dead ass to her car and took off. I was so heated I wanted to cry. That's that drama shit I was talkin' about. Here I was about to get my ass killed cuz of a psychotic bitch he wanted to give that good-ass dick to. Why couldn't bitches be more stable and not let some dick get them all out of whack? Ain't nothin' in the world worth your freedom and especially not fuckboy dick. Some fuckboy dick that didn't even claim or want you at that. Some women would truly let a man be their downfall and that was the sad part. I would never be that girl.

I was so happy I was emotionally stable. I would never want to be the bitch poppin' up twice and getting dismantled each time. I don't know why these hoes thought they was gone be the death of me. My nigga couldn't even take me out, and I sure as hell wasn't finna die by the hands of some mad-ass girl with misplaced emotions.

I called Kia and Simone and dished to them about what happened, and they were on their way over with their weekend bags. When they arrived, I made sure to peek out before I opened up the door this time and I had my pistol ready just in case. Seeing it was them, I opened the door.

"Bitch, don't have us out there exposed to that creep-ass bitch," Simone cackled as she barged in and set her bag down.

Kia was smiling but I could tell she had a lot of tea to spill. I locked the doors behind me and convened at the U-shaped sectional, ready for all the juicy gossip.

"So, I need the rundown. I'm out here getting woken up out my life for yo crazy-ass fiancé. What the fuck happened?"

"Girl, so last night I went to the bathroom and when I came out, Damien was there and he grabbed me and kissed me and I just gave in. That nigga didn't do it y'all," she confessed.

"Wowwww, really?" Simone asked.

"No girl. He even played me a recording of Rico and him talking and they concluded that it wasn't Damien behind it. Yeah, it was Silas but he didn't put him up to it. Silas dead now so I guess it's over. But Damien ain't do that shit. So, we went to his house. Girl he was soooo mad at me. We argued. He went ape shit when he saw my ring. Long story short, he stormed to his room and I went in to talk. He had on all this sappy music but girl. You know that Brent Faiyaz song, running on E?" She looked to us for a response.

"Yes bitch." Both me and Simone's eyes bucked. We knew the fuck outta that song.

"Girl! It came on while we were fuckin' and it was my life. That nigga slid my ring off and went crazy. I lost my voice a little and went to sleep soon as he finished. Bitch, I don't know what to do anymore. Do I tell Rico and return his ring? Do I stay with him and get married? I'm so lost." She put her head in her hands and sighed.

"Marry Rico and have Dro as yo side nigga," I suggested, serious as fuck.

"Bitch, are you crazy?" She snapped at me.

"Yes, but shit Dro seems open as fuck for you. I'd do it."

"I don't think even you would do no shit like that Jas."

I laughed a little too hard cuz I really would.

I felt bad for her because of the situation she was in. I knew it was hard to have a nigga you loved for years who wasn't shit suddenly start treating you right after you almost got stolen. I just didn't want her to commit to Rico and his sudden display of love all be fake and stemming from jealousy. I wanted her to have someone who really loved her. I felt like that was Dro. Even though I loved me some Rico, I didn't feel like he appreciated or deserved Kia. I would let her make her own decision, though, cuz I didn't want psycho Rico down my throat again when he found out what happened with her and Dro last night.

CHAPTER TWELVE

Disappearing Act

TRE

After yet another incident with Liyah I felt personally
responsible for her, so I shipped her ass off to the nearest psych
ward and paid for her treatment. It was crazy how the dick
turned her into a stalkin'-ass maniac, but I knew it wasn't just
me. Chase had a hand in this too. I knew how rejection felt and
she had experienced that from both of us. With mine being the
latest, it was like the final nail in the coffin for her and she had
officially lost it. I had no idea what to tell those people when I
dropped her off at the hospital. "Dick sent her to the E.R." I
dipped as soon as they admitted her.

Even though the Silas thing had been deaded, I still had
a suspicion that someone put him up to that shit. I knew he had
been out his shit for a while, but it didn't add up for him to be
behind two hits against me on his own. That nigga ain't want no
beef unless he had a death wish. It really made no sense.
Someone had to have put him up to it so I still had Drew
looking into him. I had been waiting to hear from him all week.
He was in Detroit so I had no idea why it was taking so long,

319

but I continued to wait. I felt like the sooner I knew who was behind this shit, the better.

In the meantime, I texted Jas to check on her and ask her out to dinner. I was tired of playing games. She was gonna be mine whether she was ready to admit it or not. After her one-word responses succeeded at pissing me off, I was on my way to her crib to show her it was timeout for the bullshit. I pulled up and hopped out, trying my best to look as angry as I felt. I couldn't be mad at her at all but I was. I knew once I laid eyes on her angelic, fake-innocent face, all the tension I felt would go away.

I rang her doorbell several times before she brought her ass to the door. She finally opened it after I heard her gun cock. She stepped aside to let me in. She looked like she was on her way out. She stood there lookin' sexy as hell with a black ripped sweater dress that said "Fuckboy". It hugged her curves so terribly, it made my dick hard.

"Going somewhere?" I smiled and stepped inside.

"Yep, I have a date," she cooed like I wasn't about to snap on her already.

"With?"

"Not you, so don't worry about it." She patted my shoulder then went back to the kitchen table to drink her punk-ass tea.

by $Santana$

"Is it a dude?"

"Damn, you nosy. But if you must know, yes. Why you worried?"

"You ain't goin' so you might as well cancel." And I was serious as hell.

"Nigga, you got me and my date fucked up," she objected, then pranced off into her bedroom wit' them sexy-ass fuck me booties on.

I followed her back there. She wasn't going nowhere with no nigga lookin' all fuckable like that. She had her hair all perfectly curled, makeup all flawless, ass all poked out, and she thought I was letting her pass me to be with another dude? Not in that damn dress. It was damn near see through. She stood at her vanity, smiling wickedly, knowing that shit was killing me. She really thought she was goin' somewhere. That's what made me laugh.

"You know you not goin' right? So, you may as well call that nigga before he waste his time and gas."

"First of all, yes I am." Her defiant ass continued putting that rosy shit on her cheeks but it was finna get sweated off.

"No, you not." I came up behind her swiftly, lifting her dress and this bitch was bare-naked under.

"So, you not gon' put on no fuckin' panties to go out with this nigga?"

by Santana

"No! Now move, damn!" She shooed me away.

I couldn't take it no more. I started to unbuckle my pants and pull my dick out while she stood there oblivious to what was about to happen. In one quick move, I had her bent over the dresser while I slid my dick all up in her. I pounded her quick and rough. She wasn't about to play me again.

"Where you goin'?" I drilled her as I wrapped my hand around her throat.

"Out, Tre," she panted.

"Nah, you ain't goin' no fuckin where nigga." I grabbed a handful of her curls, hoping to make them bitches fall.

"Tre stop, you fuckin' my hair up." But she was bending over to get more of this dick. I knew her ass was long overdue. Her walls gripped the fuck outta me as I tried to control myself.

"Fuck yo hair! And fuck that bitch-ass nigga you not goin' nowhere wit'!"

"You a fuckin' asshole," she screamed as I gave her deadly backshots.

"Cum on that dick bitch and shut yo fuckin' mouth," I commanded. I could tell when she was finna explode cuz this was *my* pussy.

She did as she was told and I soon felt myself engulfed in her wetness. I couldn't take that shit no more so I pulled out and bust all over that pretty dress she had on. I told her she wasn't wearing that shit nowhere.

"Really, Tre?" she screamed as she realized what I'd done.

"Really, really," I said as I got undressed to use her shower.

Before I got in, I made sure to pull her ass right in with me. She was a slick li'l mofo. I had to watch her. I noticed she looked a little irritated so I asked what was wrong.

"I was going out with Kia and Simone." She rolled her eyes.

"Well, you should've told the truth. But the good news is, you got some dick. I know you missed that." I smacked her ass and she had no choice but to smile. I was gone dick her down for the rest of the night.

I ordered us some pizza and we stayed in and watched movies, talked, and remembered why we fell for each other in the first place. During our movie my phone started to buzz and it was an incoming call from Drew. *Finally*, I said to myself when I snatched the phone up to answer. However, when I answered, the voice on the other line wasn't Drew's. It was an automated robot voice.

"Sorry, Drew can't help you anymore. He's dead." Then I heard a gunshot go off followed by an eerie laugh, then the caller hung up.

Whoever it was had killed my nigga, and now I was right back at square one with even more to worry about. Whoever was behind this was still out there and still wanted problems.

"Fuckkk!" I yelled when the call disconnected.

"You okay, baby?" Jas rose up and rubbed my shoulder.

"Yeah, some shit came up. I gotta make a run but I'll be back." I kissed her and put my jogging pants on and left.

I had to get to Drew's hotel. I sped down I-696 until I reached the Marriot where he was staying, but when I got there he was already being carried out on a stretcher. None of the bystanders or paramedics would answer my questions, and I couldn't get into the room to survey the scene because the police had already yellow-taped it. This shit couldn't be real. I was *this* close to figuring this shit out but now I still had no clue. I got back in my car feeling defeated. I beat the steering wheel as I pulled out my phone to call Chase. He had Drew looking for Isabella too but now he was gonna have to find her on his own.

"Bad news, bro."

"What's up?"

by **Santana**

"Drew got got. I don't know who did that shit but somebody shot him and I think he's dead. You gone have to find Isabella yourself," I regretfully told him.

"*What?* Man, this shit getting' way outta hand. I'm gon' have to make a trip there soon."

"Who you tellin'? Muhfuckas getting hurt left and right cuz some stupid muhfucka got beef but won't show his face." I banged the steering wheel again with all my might.

"If I don't find her within this week, I'll be there and we gon' get to the bottom of this shit," Chase affirmed.

"Good lookin' bro," I said and disconnected the call.

The first place my mind went to was Jas. I didn't want to have to distance myself again but I swear if she got hurt behind me, I couldn't live with myself. I felt so helpless, like there was nothing I could do especially with Drew gone. Whoever this person was, they were smart, calculated, and a cold-blooded killer. They did that shit in a hotel room and escaped. If I didn't know any better, the muhfucka sounded like Marcus.

CHASE

In the halls of your hotel

Arm around my shoulder so I could tell

How much I meant to you... meant it sincere back then

We had time to kill back then

You ain't a kid no more

We'll never be those kids again

It's not the same, ivory's illegal

Don't you remember?

I broke your heart last week

You'll probably feel better by the weekend

Still remember, had you going crazy

Screaming my name

The feeling deep down is good- Frank Ocean, Ivy

The hunt for Isabella had turned up nothing. I was almost tired of looking. She was nowhere to be found and I had given up hope…almost. I still loved and wanted her but I did have Kalani and she was doing an awesome job filling the hole in my heart. I was about to spend the rest of the weekend with her because Monday, I would be on my way to Detroit to help my brother.

THE OTHER SIDE OF A THUG
SHE WAS A THUG'S WEAKNESS 2

by Santana

I had been packing and moving my shit to storage all week because Liyah won the house in the divorce settlement, and she immediately wanted me out. I didn't even have a chance to find a place. I didn't want to stay at Kalani's small place anymore so I got a room at the Island hotel and booked it for the weekend. She was meeting me there and had just confirmed her arrival by sending me a sexy picture of her waiting for me.

I sped all the way there cuz I couldn't wait to see her. I pulled into valet and let them take my car. I grabbed my bag and headed to my room. As I approached the door to let myself in, my eyes diverted to the left and came upon a beautiful sight. The person I'd been looking for for months. She stood there fiddling with her room key while holding a bucket of ice. She had on fuzzy slippers and a white gown covered her protruding belly. She was pregnant. I almost froze at the sight of her.

She didn't even look up as I approached her.

"Isabella."

She looked like she'd seen a ghost as I stood behind her once she got the door open.

I barged inside before she could protest.

"How'd you find me?" She put her ice bucket down and folded her arms.

"What? That's all you can say? Why did you leave?"

THE OTHER SIDE OF A THUG
SHE WAS A THUG'S WEAKNESS 2
by Santana

"Nigga, you almost killed me." Her eyes started to make tears. Mine did too.

"I'm so sorry, baby." I went to hug her but she backed away.

"Isabella, please. You carrying my baby this whole time and you weren't gonna even tell me?" I was crushed. She knew how I felt about the miscarriage I caused Liyah and about the one she had.

"I-I didn't want to tell you. We barely survived. You weren't even there when I came to." She was bawling her eyes out in the palm of her hands.

"I couldn't be. I was responsible for putting you there. I would've gone to prison for some shit I didn't even mean to do. I'm sorry, baby. Please, please forgive me." I dropped to my knees.

I hugged her around her waist and kissed her stomach. She finally let me touch her.

"If my daddy could see me now. I'm exactly what he tried to protect me from."

"Isabella, don't you fuckin' say that!" I stepped closer to her.

"You gon' choke me again, Chase? While I'm eight months pregnant with your daughter?" She stepped back. She was scared of me now.

"My what?" I know she didn't just say daughter. I wanted a little girl so bad.

"It's a girl."

I smiled so hard as tears came to my eyes I didn't bother to hold them back.

"Oh my Godddd, are you serious? I finally get my little princess?" I was overjoyed.

"Yeah, boy." She rolled her eyes and tried not to laugh.

She finally sat down since we'd been face-to-face. She had her guard up and it was understandable. I'd hurt her and she had every right to hate me right now, but what I didn't like was that it seemed like she was scared of me. It tore me up inside for her to think I put fear in her, even though technically I did.

"Izzy, baby I am so sorry for that shit I pulled. When you mentioned that shit about Liyah and my baby, I lost it. You have no idea how bad I wanted a daughter. Please allow me to be here for you for the rest of this. I already missed so much but I want to spend the rest of this time with you. Please, baby? I'll never do no shit like that again." I planted small kisses all over her swollen belly.

"I-I don't know," she stammered along, knowing she wanted to give in.

"Baby, this whole time I've been looking for you. I haven't been able to do shit without thinking about you." I got up and sat next to her on the bed. "Please?" Then I took hold of her cheeks. She had gained so much weight in her face but she was still as beautiful as ever.

I laid her on her side and slid behind her, handling her with much care. I held her while planting loving kisses on her neck. I'm not gon' lie, I wanted some of that pregnant pussy but I truly missed her and everything about her. I lifted her dress and rubbed her tummy while begging her to forgive me in soft whispers in her ear. She squirmed and moaned. I knew her hormones were out of whack and she prolly needed some, so I took the liberty and slid in slowly, massaging her slippery walls with my manhood.

"Oh my God! Oh, my GODDD!" she screamed out.

I thought I was hurting her as she dug her long nails into my arm, but when I felt her contracting tightly, covering me in her juice, I knew she had just had a premature orgasm.

"That quick, baby?" I asked as I continued to slip in and out of her.

This shit felt like heaven. I missed her so damn much.

"It feels so good. Fuck me, Chase. Please. Fuck me!" she begged, but I was not about to get crazy with her and end up hurting her.

"No, are you crazy?"

by Santana

"Chase, fuck me. Harder. Gimme that shit!" If I didn't know any fuckin' better, I would've did some dumb shit.

I bent her over the bed and entered her from the back. She wanted this dick so bad, her pregnant ass was tryna match my stroke and all. I finally found a rhythm where I could go a little harder but not so deep. I really wasn't trying to hurt her.

"Yessss! Oh my God, baby! Right there! Please don't stop!"

I played with her clit while gently pounding her spot. In no time I felt that shit again, her pussy tightening around this dick so bad that I couldn't even stop myself. I came so hard inside her I felt weak after.

*****

The next morning, I woke up to check my phone and saw I had hella missed calls from Kalani. I had honestly forgotten all about her but the reality was she was a few feet down the hall. Isabella was already up getting dressed to go have breakfast and she invited me to join. I couldn't say no so I braced myself for the worst and hoped we didn't see Kalani. All hope was immediately lost because as soon as those elevator doors opened, we came face-to-face.

She just stood there defiantly, looking hella offended and ready to pop off. But she took one look at Isabella's

stomach and knew better than to try it. Her face turned up with
disgust as she held back tears.

"I knew I should never have fucked with you!" she
yelled before stomping down the hall to her room.

I ain't gone lie, I felt bad. I expected Kalani to be upset
with me. After all, I did leave her in the room alone all night
while I was fuckin' my babymama two doors down. Why was I
always in these risky situations? Had all these years in the dope
game turned me into an adrenaline junky?

I looked over at Isabella who was scowling like a pitbull in a junkyard. Even though she technically had no right to
be mad, her craziness and the fact that she was pregnant and
hormonal was all she needed to be justified in feeling a way.

"Let me hear it." I sighed.

I knew she was about to cut into me something vicious.
Oddly, she didn't even respond. She didn't say a word during
breakfast or after. She was giving a nigga the silent treatment
for real. She acted like I didn't even exist. That was until I gave
her some head. She was talkin' then but immediately after, it
went back to silent mode. I couldn't take it so I kindly excused
myself from the room to go cool off in the exercise room. I was
there approximately thirty-minutes and when I came back,
Isabella was gone again. She had left a note for that simply
read, "Don't look for us."

THE OTHER SIDE OF A THUG
SHE WAS A THUG'S WEAKNESS 2

by Santana

My heart broke into a million pieces. I had just reunited with her, got her to halfway forgive me, and found out I had a daughter that would be born in a month. I was livid. She just gon' up and leave when she knows how I feel about having a baby. I felt betrayed and helpless. There was no telling where the fuck she'd gone this time and how long it would be until I found her ass again.

KIA

Life had been a constant lying game since Rico
proposed. One minute we were making passionate love then the
next I was sneaking away to be with Dro. Dro was like my side-
nigga and he wasn't happy about it. He didn't even fuck me the
same now. It was always rough and angry, although I can't say I
didn't like it. I just took notice. He was cold toward me but still
stayed posted up in this pussy whenever I offered. I didn't know
how long I could keep up with the dirty game I was playing.

At this point, I didn't care if Rico found out or not
because he lied to me first. Tre told me he knew Dro didn't do
this and he still kept me in the dark. I know it's because he
wanted to be with me but lying to me wasn't the way to go. So
as far as me caring about his feelings, I didn't. At least give me
a choice in the matter. Rico liked to have the control in every
aspect. That worked in the drug game but not in the love game.

I wanted to confront him so badly about the situation,
but it didn't even matter anymore. I knew he would find a way
to flip it on me and make me the bad guy when he was the one
who was been being deceptive from the start of this raggedy-ass
relationship. I didn't know what was to come of either
relationship. Rico took me back before so maybe he wouldn't

call off the engagement if he found out. But if Dro left, Rico might do the same to teach me a lesson. I had to tread lightly because I didn't want to lose them both.

I called Jas for some advice and she immediately answered the phone huffing and puffing.

"Girl, what done happened now?"

"Girllll, so why is my pregnant-ass cousin on her way here to get on my fuckin' nerves for the rest of her pregnancy? She done ran off on her baby daddy twice." We both cackled loudly at her Plies reference.

"Why though?" I perked up for the tea.

"Girl, she said this nigga cheated on her but the crazy part is she wasn't even with him. She was somewhere hiding from him for her whole second trimester."

"Doggg what? Who is her baby daddy?"

"Tre brother. His name is Chase. I don't know him but they both have mentioned him several times so I'm familiar with the name. They done been through so much drama this past year it's ridiculous. If I had time to tell you *this* bitch's heaux stories, you would clutch your damn pearls," Jas exclaimed.

I wanted to hear, needed to hear about someone else's drama for a change. I was so sick of my own.

"Well I'm coming through for a couple days anyway. I need a little vacay from both my baes." I gloated like I had accomplished something.

Well in my mind I had. I had two of the most powerful rival drug dealers fighting over me. Sorry, but this was a huge ego stroke for me. Sure, I've had guys fight over me before but not any of Dro and Rico's caliber. I leaned back on my pillow and smiled widely thinking about how open I had them both. See what these niggas do to you? Turn you into a savage real quick.

"Well bitch, my bag is packed. I'm finna be en route. Either have dinner cooked or delivery ordered. I don't wanna be waiting to eat when I get there," I scolded her playfully.

"I got some dog food for you bitch," she spat and hung up.

I honestly couldn't wait to meet her cousin. She talked about her a lot but I had never met her in person before. She always said she had no reason to come to Detroit and that it "wasn't a place people go to vacation." The bitch was hella bourgeoise but now that I knew she was about that crazy girlfriend, play wit' these niggas feelings type of life, I would be waiting on pins and needles until she got here. I needed that type of energy to make me feel better about my own fucked-up situation.

THE OTHER SIDE OF A THUG
SHE WAS A THUG'S WEAKNESS 2

by Santana

I cranked the radio in my car and turned on Spotify. I rarely smoked but I had a blunt lit and was almost choking to death tryna get high while I took this drive to Jas' house. Once I got there, I rang her loud-ass doorbell and she opened it smiling from ear-to-ear. I thought she was happy to see me until I saw Rico standing in the kitchen with rage in his narrowed eyes.

"Where you been?" he asked as he paced toward me looking like a maniac.

"I went home, to my house, where I live. I know I'm allowed to go there," I snapped.

"Yeah, of course but you barely answer the phone anymore." I could barely focus on him because I was too busy being mad as fuck at Jas for not even warning me that he was here.

Then I looked at my phone and saw that it was on Do Not Disturb. I rarely used DND so I hadn't considered making a favorites list and allowing calls from them. I just turned that shit on and left it. I regretted it now. This interaction with him was about to ruin my whole weekend, unless I lied.

"Sorry. I've been tryna plan stuff for our wedding. I'm still in shock a little, to be honest. It's taking a while for me to process this and Jas and Simone have been helping me. Sometimes a girl needs her girls." I lied my ass off.

by $\mathcal{Santana}$

He clearly believed it the way his mouth curled into a smile. He hugged and kissed me goodbye without any further explanation. I loved that he had a guilty conscience. It made this so much easier.

"So, when yo crazy-ass cousin getting here?" I asked as I sat my bag down.

"She should be here soon. She said she tore up outta Cali like a bat outta hell."

"Was her man abusing her?"

"Not to my knowledge but we gone find out," Jas replied as she answered her door after the doorbell rang.

It was the pizza delivery guy, and her cousin standing behind him.

CHAPTER THIRTEEN

Love on the Run

JASMINE

Isabella had been laid up in my spot for well over three weeks and it was almost time for her to give birth. I had no idea why she wouldn't at least stay in her hometown to have the baby, but she insisted Beaumont was a great hospital and that she'd be fine there. She even had all of her patient information faxed to Dr. Check and he agreed to take her as a patient. I was stuck with her.

It wasn't all bad though. We got to catch up with each other in person finally and I couldn't say it wasn't good to see her. We rarely got a chance to see each other as kids, especially after my mom, Kennedy died when I was ten. After that, the visiting stopped, and we got reacquainted some years later through Facebook. We kept in touch by phone and email and I knew if we lived closer when we were younger, Isabella and I would've been the best of friends. Now we were older, stuck in our ways, and equally crazy on opposite ends of the spectrum.

"I forgot to ask but how's it going with Tre?" She smiled wickedly.

by Santana

"Girl, it ain't goin' nowhere. He got enough on his plate right now for me to be pulling some bullshit like this."

"Bitch, you got feelings for him? Damnnnn!" she exclaimed, laughing like the shit was funny.

"No, but I don't believe in kicking a man while he's down."

"Yes, you do. You just don't believe in kicking a man you love while he's down. I see the way you look when you talk about him. Damn heaux, you had *one job!*" She raised her pointer finger.

"Girl, fuck you and that job."

"You the one that's gon' forfeit all that money." She shrugged.

"If you hadn't noticed, I'm paid around here. Might not be as much as you got but I got more than enough," I snapped back.

"So? Who doesn't want more money? What type of shit is that?"

"Bitch, that nigga is a killer. I'm not finna be playin' with his heart." I rolled my eyes to the back of my head.

"No, his brother Marcus is the killer. Besides, you ain't scared of shit. You big bad Jas, remember?"

THE OTHER SIDE OF A THUG
by *Santana*

"You love danger, Isabella. When you gonna admit that? You love drama and keeping up a bunch of mess. I can't believe you turned into this type of woman."

"We lived two totally different lives, cousin. I can't help the shit I was exposed to even as a child. Maybe I do have issues but it ain't hardly my fault." She started to get emotional.

Her past was certainly traumatic so I couldn't be mad at her for how she turned out, but wanting me to hurt someone I had grown feelings for wasn't gonna happen. I did my share of bullshit, but I couldn't leave Tre alone if I wanted to. I had quickly fallen for him. He was everything I wanted in a man and more. When Isabella first called me with an offer of a half a mill to make Tre fall in love with me and leave him, I jumped at it. I still remember the conversation.

"Hey cousin." She purred into the phone.

"Hey boo. How are you? I've been feelin' lonely not hearing from you."

"Aww, I missed you too. But I have a proposition for you. I'm paying," she added knowing I needed money.

She would send me money and gifts here and there and it helped me to live a comfy lifestyle. The job I had was good too so I lived in a nice condo and drove an expensive car. My wardrobe was fly as hell too and I kept my hair, nails and makeup slayed.

"*What's that? You know I'm wit' a fast flip.*" *I rubbed my hands together.*

"*Okay so there's this guy, his name is Tre. He's fine, I know you'll be attracted to him. I used to deal with him,*" *I cut her off.*

"*Bitch you tryna pass me some leftovers?*" *I asked a little offended.*

"*Girl chill okay? These niggas do it all the time. Plus, he fine, got some good dick and he paid. He was a mistake and I need your help with some revenge. Now I know you're his type plus I've been doing some digging. I know y'all run in the same circle. Your little besties know him cuz they fuck with his friends. I be all up in Chase conversations.*" *She giggled.*

"*So, what exactly do you want me to do? If he runs with my friends he's dangerous. I'm not risking my life for no get-back plan for you.*"

"*Girl I just want you to fuck with him, make him fall for you and then leave him. That's it. That's a matter of the heart, he won't do shit to you just cuz something didn't work out. I just want him to feel pain and embarrassment, like he made me feel. He needs to learn he can't go around fucking with people's feelings.*" *I understood that part.*

From what she had told me, when she got her inheritance he tried to get her to forfeit it. That was bogus and that's the reason I decided to help her. I had no idea I would actually fall for the nigga in the process. I know it doesn't seem like it, I'm very guarded and don't show my feelings a lot but Tre ain't somebody I can just get over.

"Yeah I know, boo. That's why I don't judge you but I can't go through with this." I rubbed her stomach and felt the baby kick. I couldn't wait to see my little cousin.

"Jasmine, you are so fuckin' whack! This nigga ain't shit and you won't even help me get back at him." She sighed and rolled her eyes. I wanted her to calm down. It was too close to her going into labor to be getting herself all worked up.

"Chill out man. The best revenge is yo' paper and you definitely got that. Niggas already after him, tryna set him up. I don't want to add to that. That's not even cool."

"It's not supposed to be cool, *it's supposed to be karma!*" she yelled at me.

Then it happened. Her water broke. I knew something was gonna happen while she sat up here arguing with me and getting herself upset over a nigga she already shitted on. We both started to panic, and I started running around like a chicken with its head cut off trying to gather her things to go to the hospital.

"Oh my God, oh my God!" I panted as I ran to grab her hospital bag and find her something to wear.

by $\mathcal{Santana}$

I knew about childbirth but that still didn't prepare me for someone's water breaking in my living room. Once I grabbed her things, I helped her dry off and change into some leggings, a t-shirt and Ugg boots. It was warm out for September so I skipped a jacket and helped her to the car. I put down a few towels in the seat of my G-wagon cuz leather or not, I didn't want her baby juice in my seat.

I sped all the way to Beaumont, praying silently that we made it and I wouldn't have to pull over on the side of the road and deliver this baby like in some of my favorite sitcoms. Once we made it, I pulled to the emergency door and they put her in a wheelchair. I went to find parking. I sat in my car for a few moments thinking over the situation. She was here, in a foreign city, about to give birth and wasn't even gonna tell her baby daddy. That was so scudded.

I rushed back into the hospital. I sat with her for hours, but I couldn't help but think this was a moment for the father to share with her, not me. After being there all night and morning, she had finally started to dilate and was almost ready for an epidural. I was battling calling Tre and telling him to let his brother know. After a while, I did it. I knew he may not even make it in time to see his daughter come out but he'd get to see her as a newborn. I did the right thing.

THE OTHER SIDE OF A THUG
SHE WAS A THUG'S WEAKNESS 2
by *Santana*

About thirty-minutes later, who I assumed was Chase
came rushing into the delivery room. I sighed a sigh of relief
when he got there. I didn't want him to miss this, especially
after she told me how bad he'd wanted a daughter. I watched his
confusion turn into anger. I suddenly became fearful until I saw
him approach her bed, get on his knees, and kiss her. Then Tre
came in behind him. This had become so awkward.

by Santana

TRE

All I can say is Thank God my bro was already in
Detroit. I know him missing the birth of his daughter would've
killed him. Jas did the right thing by telling me. I guess she
really did have a heart. I was surprised Isabella didn't put us out
of the delivery room but I could tell she wasn't happy. She kept
giving Jas the death stare. I watched the interaction between
them the whole time, and something was definitely up.

The thing that had me in shock was that Jas and Isabella
were related. Another fuckin' plot twist. I knew that Jas knew
everything about everything. I knew she knew what I had done
to and with Isabella. Then everything became that much clearer.
All three of these muhfuckas was in on it. Damn, right under
my nose. The only thing that didn't make sense was the fact that
Chase and Jas didn't seem to know each other at all, but Isabella
was definitely sneaky enough to make the plan work without
them knowing each other.

All this time, my brother and the girl I loved were
conspiring with the enemy against me. I knew from the
beginning she had something to do with this. Now Jas
admittedly talking to Silas that night of the club shooting had
put things in perspective. Damn, I got got. It all made sense
now. Jas was tryna cuddle all close to me in the waiting room

but I wasn't havin' it. I pushed her off me and just left. I hated the fact that I had feelings for her. It would make killing her that much worse on my conscience.

I didn't speak to her for a few days. I was waiting until Isabella's shady ass was out the hospital and feeling a little better before I confronted the three musketeers about their involvement in this shit.

"You home?" I asked Jas when she answered.

"Yeah, but why haven't you been answering my calls?"

"We'll talk about that when I get there. Isabella and Chase there?"

"Yeah, they're still here. She's refusing to go back with him."

"Good, I'll be there soon." I hung up.

Twenty-minutes later, I was pulling up in her driveway.

I approached the door and rang the bell. She let me in and I noticed a weird look on her face. She looked nervous and kinda scared, exactly how a guilty bitch should look.

"Where's the baby?" I asked my snake-ass brother who was at the table eating lunch.

"Sleep right now. What's good witchu bro?" He dapped me up.

"Nothin' much but all four of us need to rap right quick."

"Cool," he responded.

I saw Jas give Isabella another weird look.

"So, I know who's been setting me up this whole time," I started.

"Word bro? Who?" Chase asked like he genuinely had no clue.

"Yep. You three sorry muhfuckas." They all had shocked expressions.

"Hol' up bro, I know you ain't serious." Chase drew back, even laughing a little.

I was serious. Serious as the gun I pulled out of my waist on them. I pointed it at Jas.

"Hell yeah I am. When you couldn't set me up to go to prison, you got this snake- ass bitch involved to get my guard down, ain't that right, Jas?" I gritted my teeth as I spit venom toward her.

"You got it all wrong," Isabella chimed in.

"Nah, it all makes sense now. Y'all hoes are cousins. You had the most motive, the means and the manpower to make this shit happen. I always suspected you, but I doubted your involvement when my brother vouched for you. Now I know he only did that cuz he was in on it too." I paced the floor wondering who to blast first.

I was only hesitating because of the baby in the back. I didn't want to take her parents from her but something had to be done.

"Jas, just tell him," Isabella said.

"Don't do this, okay," Jas said as she became choked up.

"Tell him the truth before you get us killed," she urged.

"Whatever it is you better tell me before I shoot yo ass!" I yelled as she sat there lookin' foolishly at the floor.

"Okay, damn. Isabella offered me money to date you, make you fall for me then leave. But that was it. I have texts to confirm. We weren't in on any plot to put you in jail though, Tre, I promise. It was simply to hurt your feelings like you did hers. But I swear to you that's it. If you kill us I promise this won't stop cuz it's not us. You gotta believe me." She held out her phone and showed me a text thread confirming what she'd said.

I still didn't buy it.

"Bitch, this don't prove shit but it's nice to know that this whole time you've been playin' a nigga. So that's how you got this nice-ass crib, huh? From a payoff from this bitch." I chuckled to hide my pain.

"What? No! I didn't even get the money from her because I told her I couldn't go through with it. The money I used to pay for this came from my lawsuit."

THE OTHER SIDE OF A THUG
SHE WAS A THUG'S WEAKNESS 2
by Santana

"Whatever, bitch," I spat.

I had heard enough. I was ready to shoot something.

"Tre, please listen to me. It's not us. I swear, baby." She tried to come closer to me but I shoved the shit out of her and she landed on the couch.

"She's not lying. She refused the money. She said she didn't want to hurt you." Isabella rolled her eyes as she spoke. Then she continued, "I was mad at you still and yes I did plot to get your heart broken, but she said she couldn't go through with it. That's the truth. Chase and I argued about this very situation. He kept badgering me about being involved in the setup against you to put you in jail, but this was the only plot I had. We argued and he choked me and almost killed me over you. That's why I ran away. That's why I'm even here now. Your brother had nothing to do with this and neither did we."

I cocked my gun ready to shoot. I almost pulled the trigger when my phone finally rang. It was an unknown number.

"Hello?" I answered with the gun still pointed at Jas.
"Drew?!"

I thought he was dead but he was on the other end of my phone with news of who was really behind this shit. I just knew he was about to confirm my suspicions and tell me it was the

350

three rats sitting in front of me, but then he muttered a name that never even crossed my mind.

"It was Marcus. He's behind this."

I was taken all the way aback. "What? Are you sure?" I was so confused at this point.

"Yeah. The day he went to kill Silas, his last words were, "but you the one." Their whole interaction said that Marcus is the one who hired him to set you up at the club and again to try and kill you. Marcus was disappointed that he didn't complete the job. Sorry, brother."

I just stood there in utter disbelief. I couldn't believe what I'd just heard. I couldn't wrap my head around it. I dropped the phone to the floor and was snapped back into reality by faintly hearing Drew say "hello" over and over.

I grabbed my phone and called Marcus but there was no answer. Then I went by my house, and he wasn't there. I thought long and hard about where he could be. Then a thought came to me which would explain exactly why he wanted me dead or in jail. Liyah must have actually told him about Ava and me. She had threatened me plenty, but I guess now she had all the motivation she needed to go through with it. I was so caught up in Jas that I didn't give a fuck about how Liyah was responding to the rejection she'd experienced from me.

THE OTHER SIDE OF A THUG
SHE WAS A THUG'S WEAKNESS 2
by **Santana**

Before this, I was so caught up in Isabella, I didn't
notice how it affected Marcus when I started fuckin' wit' her
behind his back. Damn! This whole time the answer was right
in front of me but I didn't even see it. I was really about to kill
three people that weren't even involved. Thank God, I got that
call in the nick of time. I wouldn't have been able to live with
myself if I had taken three innocent lives. Well, two weren't all
that innocent but they weren't responsible for this shit.

Since Marcus wasn't a resident of Michigan, I knew
there was only a few places he could be, so I went to the casinos
downtown and he wasn't there or checked in at the hotels. Then
it came to me. I sped onto the Lodge Freeway all the way to
Southfield. I hastily made my way to Liyah's house and lo and
behold, Marcus' car was parked behind hers in the driveway of
the house I bought her.

"Ain't this 'bout a bitch!" I exclaimed as I banged the
steering wheel and sped away from the house.

If I didn't leave now and regroup, I was gonna murder
my brother and that bitch and still be in prison. This needed to
be premeditated. Any murder I did had to be. I went straight
home, showered, and popped a couple pain pills cuz my head
was throbbing after all the shit that happened today.

Soon as I got comfy, my doorbell rang. The earlier
discovery had me on edge so I grabbed my burner and went to

the door. It was Liyah. I snatched the door open, my bare chest heaving up and down trying to suppress my need to kill this bitch right here. I peeped around for Marcus since he was known to pop out of nowhere. When he didn't show, I put my gun down and folded my arms waiting for her to speak.

"So, you really choose her over me?" she asked like she didn't have a hand in trying to get me killed.

"You really got some nerve, Aaliyah." I shook my head trying desperately to keep my composure.

"Me? You help to ruin my life and now you just throw me to the wolves over some new ass?"

This bitch was looney as hell.

"You ruined your own life. Let yourself out," I told her, grabbed my gun and returned it to my waist, then walked away.

I heard her run toward me, attacking me from behind with a barrage of punches. I lost it. I quickly turned around and before I knew it, my hands were wrapped around her pencil-ass neck choking the life out her. She clawed at my arms until she drew blood and I finally released her. She collapsed to the floor gasping for air and coughing up spit as her eyes watered.

"Now get the fuck out my house!" I barked as I returned to my room.

I came back out minutes later to make sure she'd left. She was outside by her car being consoled by a couple of my nosy-ass neighbors. I scoffed as I closed the blinds and went back to bed.

*****

The next day, I had been out running errands and plotting my next move in the situation. I had also gotten a letter that my pops would be released from prison in a week. That was the best news I could've gotten. Maybe my dad being out would help Marcus with his fuckin' issues. He always respected my dad if he didn't respect anyone else. In the meantime, I had been watching my back and looking over my shoulder all day anticipating another attempt on my life from Marcus.

I had survived the whole day with no stray bullets coming toward me. As I made my way down my block, I noticed police cars, flashing lights and an ambulance. Maybe one of my old neighbors had fallen in the shower and life alert wasn't fast enough. I chuckled at the thought. But as I got closer, I realized it was my house they were at. Caution tape revealed that it was indeed a dead person being brought out on that stretcher.

I parked and hopped out, running to the scene to find out what was going on at my house. I rushed to the EMT that was rolling a body out and tried to get answers.

"What happened here?" I asked frantically.

"Female victim found strangled in the master bedroom of this home," the female EMT said hesitantly.

by Santana

"Who is it? Please let me see!" Then she unzipped the bag. It was Liyah.

I was approached by three officers. "Are you Tre Carter?" one heavy set male officer asked.

"Yeah but…"

"You're under arrest for the murder of Aaliyah Carter. Put your hands behind your back," he told me as he began reading me my Miranda rights.

How the fuck did this happen? I didn't kill her. She was alive and well when she left. This time, my mind didn't need to even think about who did this. It was Marcus and with his expertise with murder, I knew for sure he could make this look like it was me. I was about to have a hard time getting out of this one. Even if I could gather evidence that it wasn't me, that would mean I would have to snitch on my own blood. God knows I couldn't and wouldn't do that.

"Nicely played, bro," I said to myself as the door to the cop car closed.

The End

99342345R00203